THE DETECTIVE AND THE DON'S DAUGHTER

The Detective and the Don's Daughter

Thom Bennett

DARK PORCH
Dark Porch Publishing

ISBN: 978-1-990564-06-2 (Book)
ISBN: 978-1-990564-07-9 (eBook)

DEDICATIONS

This book is dedicated to DREW BENNETT, my beloved son and tech-savvy guru; ED PIWOWARCZYK, my editor and a first-class professional; MELODIE CAMPBELL, colleague, friend, and valued inspiration; and DONNA KOWALCHUK-STEWARD, my Number One fan.

ALSO BY THOM BENNETT

Novels

The Death Merchants

The Man With Hemingway's Face

Collections

Dark Porch Mysteries

Promises

The Christmas House

13 Tales from the Dark

The Detective & the Don's Daughter

For Young Readers

The Halloween Fog

There's Something Out There

FOREWORD

For the benefit of readers who are *not* familiar with the Cass Gentry novels and short stories, Cass was born in the Southern Ontario town of Riverton, near the shores of the Blyth River. His father was the owner of an industrial factory, and his mother was a refined gentlewoman who doted on their only child. When he finished his junior year at high school, his father arranged for him to finish his secondary schooling at Eagle Ridge military school, located near West Point, the prestigious United States Military Academy on the banks of the Hudson River in New York State. He wanted to have his boy toughened up and ready for manhood.

Upon graduation, young Cass was so toughened up and independent that he decided to stay in the States and continue his education at New York University. When the Korean War began in 1950, Cass enlisted, distinguished himself in battle, got his green card, and spent a few years working in a special ops department in Washington. When this assignment was completed, Cass was granted an American green card and dual citizenship papers.

Shortly thereafter, Cass decided to acquire the necessary credentials to open his own private detective agency, and he moved into a double apartment in Manhattan's Greenwich Village. By this time, his tyrannical father had disappeared from home in Canada, while at the same time providing generous financial support for the family. Meanwhile, Cass developed a successful agency and proceeded to visit his mother in Ontario as often as his business allowed.

Readers first met Cass Gentry in the novel entitled *The Death Merchants*. In it, he collides with a corrupt university professor, and forms a cautious alliance with a mafia *Don,* the notorious, but charismatic, Frank Palladino. This will have lasting consequences for both of them, as Cass assists the *Don* in a delicate, personal matter, and settles scores with the evil educator, as well.

Cass Gentry's next adventure, *The Man With Hemingway's Face,* is one in which he legally assists *Don* Palladino. This caper/adventure rapidly moves from the streets of New York to Bigwin Inn in Ontario's playland, where Ernest Hemingway is hiding out for private reasons of his own. The action swiftly moves from there to Miami, and on through various stops in the Bahamas, before the exciting conclusion. Along the way, Cass meets Frank's equally talented daughter, Eleanor Palladino, a relationship that is explored in the collection of mysteries that you are presently holding—*The Detective & the Don's Daughter*

With regard to the name of my detective, he was affectionately named after my department chairman and the head of my dissertation committee at Michigan State University, where I received my doctorate degree. Castelle G. Gentry was a brilliant educator and an inspiring leader in the field. Unfortunately, he passed away before I began writing mystery novels. Thus, when it came time, I honored his memory by giving my hero his name.

ACKNOWLEDGEMENTS

In conclusion, I would like to offer sincere thanks to ED PI-WOWARCZYK, my editor, who, once again, has performed his usual magic, for which I am extremely grateful. Ed is an excellent professional, and I am very fortunate to have him on my team.

Next, I would like to thank mystery writer MELODIE CAMPBELL, author of the *Merry Widow* series. Truly, she has been an inspiration. Her corresponding friendship, creativity, and advice are always greatly appreciated.

I would also like to thank DONNA KOWALCHUK-STEWARD, a long-time friend and my Number One Fan.

Finally, I wish to thank my beloved son, DREW BENNETT, whose creative skills and technical wizardry helped make this book a reality. Not only is he my tech-savvy guru and cover designer, but he continually acts as a sounding board for discussions on character and plot development. My gratitude for Drew's help and guidance continues to be boundless with every book that I write.

~Thom Bennett

1

THE EMPTY GRAVE

(A Cass Gentry Mystery)

Suddenly, I was standing in the middle of a clearing, staring down at a hole in the ground. Only it wasn't a hole, but the discovery was worth it.

To be honest with you, the search unfolded just as the guy had suggested. If I stood in the doorway of the old concrete building, faced west and walked directly for the tree line, I'd find a barely visible pathway. Follow the pathway for about five to ten minutes, and the woods would open up. I'd find it there.

And indeed, I had. Only it wasn't a hole. It was too smooth, too evenly dug, too uniformly rectangular. I had seen far too many such holes in my lifetime not to recognize this one for what it was---a freshly dug grave.

One day earlier

Wednesday, July 20, 1960

After sleeping in following my weekly poker game with friends, I was rummaging around my double apartment office on Jones Street in the Village. I'd already changed the calendar and was now at my desk, unwrapping a framed picture my art dealer and friend had delivered to me last night.

My name is Cass Gentry and I'm a licensed, New York City private eye. I'm also a serious art collector who specializes in original pieces that were used to illustrate old novels by writers like Dickens, Stevenson and Conan Doyle. Last year, when I was working *The Death Merchants* case, I'd purchased a signed copy of an original picture from Anthony Hope's 1894 classic *The Prisoner of Zenda*. The illustration was by Charles Dana Gibson, creator of the Gibson Girl.

Frankly, my emerald green eyes lit up as I unwrapped my latest acquisition, which I must admit is a slight departure from my usual tastes. I'd just purchased an original piece of comic book art—-the cover illustration for the Classics Illustrated version of Hope's swashbuckling adventure.

This work was by an artist named Henry Kiefer, and it was a fine rendering of the sword-wielding hero breaking into a dungeon to save his look-alike cousin, the prisoner of Zenda Castle. My plan was to hang the Kiefer drawing right beside the Gibson print in my gallery of treasures.

"Sorry to interrupt, Mr. Gentry." A darkly handsome man stood in the doorway.

"Come in, Mr. Smith," I said. "Take a seat. You're not interrupting me."

The man crossed the carpeted floor and sat in a wingback chair near the desk. His movements were economical, liquid, almost feline. His age was difficult to gauge—anywhere between 40 and 70—but his voice was youthful, strong, assured.

"What can I do for you, Mr. Smith?" I inquired, setting aside the piece of art.

"Two things, Mr. Gentry. First, I'm going to need time off, the week after next."

"No problem, my friend. Anything I should be concerned about?"

"Nothing. It's my annual powwow. This year it's near Billings, Montana."

"Down the road from the Battle of the Little Bighorn, I presume."

"Affirmative."

"Ah, Custer's Last Stand! Give the ol' Colonel hell for me."

Willard "Zuni" Smith smiled, knowing that I sympathized with native Americans. We had known each other for almost ten years. First, Smith had been one of my special-ops instructors following my service in Korea. Then he signed on as my man Friday when I retired from the military to set up my private practice.

But Smith, a full-blooded Zuni from New Mexico, was more than an employee; he was my mentor, business associate, live-in father figure and close friend. Honorable to a fault, he had never asked me how I could afford to live as a gentleman detective, or where my extra money came from.

"What's the second thing?" I asked.

"This note came by courier last night," Smith said. "While you were out."

"Give me the short-and-sweet version."

Smith stretched his long legs and crossed them, then settled into his plush, leather chair. "Well, it seems that a fellow named Ryan Brady wishes to engage your services. He's suggested a sizable retainer and a very lucrative payoff if you solve the case."

"Not meaning to sound avaricious," I said, "but did he provide actual figures?"

Smith consulted the note and quoted the two numbers.

I nodded for Smith to continue.

"The note also states that the situation may be a matter of life and death. Therefore, he wishes to meet with you as soon as possible. He suggests a face-to-face this evening."

Leaning forward in my chair, I rested my elbows on the desk and steepled my fingers. "Please go on, Mr. Smith."

Smith consulted the note once more, and continued. "If you are interested in hearing the entire proposition, you are to meet Mr. Brady in his room at the Algonquin Hotel this evening at 7 p.m., Room 309. He'll have dinner and beverages sent up."

Straightening the wrapping paper around my new picture, I considered the information. Finally, leaning back in the desk chair, I prompted, "What do you think, Mr. Smith?"

My mentor took a deep breath and exhaled slowly as he rearranged his legs. "Rather bizarre, Mr. Gentry. On the one hand, he provides very enticing information—the matter of the life-and-death plea, and the generous fee."

"Indeed. On the other hand, no personal information is offered. Just a name, which could be bogus, and a time to meet. Anyone can rent a room at the Algonquin if they have enough money, then disappear the very next day."

"Yet, you would be left with the retainer, Mr. Gentry, instead of an empty wallet."

"I assure you, Mr. Smith, my wallet will never be empty," I said with a sly wink. "Nevertheless, the whole affair seems a little hinky to me."

"So, what are you going to do?"

"Keep the appointment, of course. Although the business appears slightly suspicious, it's definitely intriguing."

"You mean the financial aspects of the case?"

"No, my friend. The business of life and death."

"But whose life? Whose death?"?

"That, Mr. Smith, is the intriguing part of the business."

At 6:55 p.m., I entered through the brass-and-glass doors of the Algonquin Hotel at 59 West 44th Street. Walking directly into the oak-paneled lobby, I carefully skirted the lobby cat napping in the middle of my path. I was about to approach the desk clerk, when a short, middle-aged man with a weather-beaten face came up to me.

"Welcome back to the Algonquin, Mr. Gentry," the man said in a chipper voice.

"Thank you, Boyd. How've you been?"

"Fabulous, sir. The missus and I just had another baby."

"How many is that, Boyd?"

"This one's number seven. Only need two more to get our baseball team."

"Wow," I joked, having known Boyd long enough to remember his desire for a large family. "I bet your wife can't wait. Maybe she'll get lucky and have twins next time."

Boyd laughed and said, "We're calling him Andy."

"After Andy Carey of the Yankees?"

"You got it! Andy goes along with the other Yankees' names we've called our kids."

"It takes all kinds, Boyd. It takes all kinds."

"Can I help you, Mr. Gentry?" the little man said. "Going to the Oak Room for dinner?"

"No, thank you, Boyd. I've got an appointment with someone on the third floor."

"Not to worry, Mr. Gentry. I'll take you right up myself."

As we headed for the elevator, I glanced over at the Oak Room and had a little stab of *deja-vu*. Not so long ago, I'd had a dinner date there with a charming, young woman named Eleanor Palladino. She was in town for a matinee performance of *West Side Story* on Broadway, and called me up. She and I'd met during the wrap-up of my mystery case *The Man With Hemingway's Face.* Frankly, I'd really like to see more of her, I pondered, as Boyd and I rode up in the elevator.

Moments later, I was knocking on the door to Room 309. It opened almost immediately, as if the man inside had been waiting with his hand on the doorknob. At a shade over six feet, he was as tall as me, sturdily built and distinguished by close-cropped, ginger hair and a neatly trimmed mustache. I figured he was slightly older than me, but he could have been any age from mid-thirties to mid-forties.

After shaking hands and introducing ourselves, we settled into comfortable chairs around an occasional table. Ryan Brady suggested we order dinner and drinks, but I declined.

"I'd rather get down to the business at hand, if you don't mind," I said.

"Quite right," Brady said in a clipped, military manner. "I'm not hungry at the moment, either. Perhaps later."

"Perhaps," I nodded.

"Á drink, then?" he offered. I can order up soda water if you're not into alcohol."

I agreed to soda water, he dialed up room service and ordered the soda, along with a Chivas neat and a bowl of Spanish peanuts for himself.

"Your note mentioned a matter of life and death," I began, once Brady had placed the order. "Would you please elaborate."

Brady took a deep breath, looked down at his folded hands, then back up. "It's about my wife, Mr. Gentry. She's been kidnapped and being held for ransom. The kidnappers say that if I don't follow their instructions precisely, they will kill her. In fact, they suggest they will bury her alive."

Brady paused; I remained silent. The only sound in the room was a clock quietly ticking.

Finally, Brady continued. "She had gone out to the theater last Saturday night. Saw *Gypsy* at the Broadway Theater. Seen it before, in June. Loves the show; loves Ethel Merman."

"What's not to love? It's a great show," I said. Then, "Is that the night she disappeared?"

"No. She came home after the curtain. We're on Riverside Drive, so she took a cab. Doesn't like driving in the city at night."

Settling back into his chair, Brady continued with the story. "When she arrived home, she told me all about the show, and that Merman had three extra curtain calls. Everything was perfectly normal."

I nodded, while Brady continued speaking in a terse, unemotional manner.

"Next morning, she went off to church, while I worked in my home office. I'm an insurance lawyer, and this year's been very busy." He paused for a few seconds. Then, looking down at his hands, he said, "She never came home."

As if on some ill-timed cue, there was a knock on the hotel room door. Brady admitted a pleasant-faced young man carrying our drinks on a silver platter. The waiter, freshly scrubbed and exuding the unmistakable odor of Old Spice aftershave, set down the drinks and peanuts on the occasional table, accepted a tip from Brady, and promptly left.

Brady took a small sip from his whiskey, followed by a sip of water. Then he sat fiddling with his ring, while I took a long pull from my soda water and gently set it down.

"Did you check with the church to see if she'd arrived there?" I asked when Brady appeared ready to resume his story.

"I did, but we're not regulars, and the church is so big. The priest had no recollection of seeing anyone that matched her description."

"If you give me a picture of her, I could try asking around myself."

"No need," Brady said. "I have something better." He opened a file folder that lay on top of the table, pulled out two pieces of paper and set them on the manila folder. "The top sheet is the ransom note, while the second is a set of instructions I had to follow in order to get my wife back alive. I received both of them by courier on Monday afternoon. You can follow the instructions as I explain what I was doing all day yesterday."

Taking the proffered papers from Brady, I started to scan them, as he leaned back in his chair and crossed his legs.

"As you can see," Brady began, "the top paper says that unless I follow the instructions precisely, my wife will be killed within the week. In fact, she will be tortured...then buried alive."

Brady paused, twisted the ring on his wedding finger again, and appeared to be gathering his thoughts. This is the story he told me in Room 309 of Times Square's Algonquin Hotel.

The journey to save my wife began shortly after ten o'clock yesterday morning. Upon crossing the George Washington Bridge into Jersey, I followed the instructions back into New York state and proceeded north along the Hudson valley. Passing West Point Military Academy, I traveled for another hour and a half, slowing down after passing the village of Millerton. Between Millerton and the city of Kingston, I turned onto a county road with the dog tag of Cheese Factory Road.

At this point, I had to carefully consult the odometer reading, so that I didn't miss the final turnoff. At exactly 1.7 miles, I went down a long-forgotten farmer's lane that dead-ended in less than a minute. When I could go no farther, I stopped, parked my car and crossed through the trees on the driver's side, where I very soon came out onto a seemingly unending expanse of farmland. Once again, the instructions proved to be accurate.

Within minutes, I was standing on top of a knoll, surveying freshly plowed meadows and feeling a light breeze temper the noonday heat. On all sides of the knoll, the pastures extended in undulating greens, browns and yellows.

A half mile to the east, I could see a well-kept barn, noteworthy for having a glaring red door. The sun, which was high-noon bright, seemed to highlight the door's brilliance. However, the longer I stared at the barn, the less vivid the door's color seemed. A trick of the light, I told myself as I resumed my journey toward the southwest in accordance with my written instructions.

Within 10 minutes, traveling slightly downhill toward an old, wooden fence, I soon saw a deserted concrete building that the kidnappers had written about. Inside, I was supposed to find another message that would lead me to the next set of instructions.

By the time I approached the fence, I was starting to sweat and hoped that the breeze would pick up or that the old building would present some cool shelter. I gingerly crossed over the ancient wooden barrier, and prepared to continue my march. At this point, the building was only several hundred yards away; all that stood between me and my goal was an area of tall grassland. I moved forward slowly.

Then the sound began.

It was faint at first. Then slowly, ever so slowly as I marched along, it gained in volume. It could have been my legs sweeping against the weeds and grasses, for when I stopped, the noise also stopped. When I moved forward, the whispering began once more, slightly louder this time, like thousands of insects buzzing indignantly at my intrusion.

I stopped again. This time, the sound continued for a second or so longer. I moved faster through the tangled growth, beginning to fear the noise that seemed to surround me. I moved faster still, acutely aware that I was starting to sweat profusely and that my heart was beating dangerously fast.

Suddenly, I was through the tall growth, and immediately started walking on close-cropped grass. Thankfully, at last, there was...silence. Only the sound of a gentle wind was audible. I stood still for a few moments, shook my head and dismissed the whole affair as the product of an overwrought imagination, brought on by the sudden disappearance of my wife. I figured the sounds were nothing more than my legs brushing against the long grass.

There before me stood the old concrete building, abandoned and desolate. It was a small structure from the last century, made of mortar and stone. As I peered through a large opening that had no door, I could see that the interior contained a single room, measuring about 12 feet by 24 feet.

The stairs were missing in action, but it was easy to climb up inside. Once there, I looked around, but there wasn't very much to see. Directly opposite the entranceway, on the east wall, was a single window minus any framework. On the far south wall, there appeared a curious-looking groove that ran the width of the building, from one wall to the opposite one. I went over to investigate.

The groove was smooth, originating when the concrete flooring was first poured. It was approximately six inches wide, and as it ended at the two walls, there appeared round openings that would have dispersed any liquid in the groove out of the building and onto the ground below. Perhaps the most startling thing that caught my attention was an ancient frayed rope that hung down directly over the groove from a rusted ceiling device. I had a disconcerting thought that this place might have been a slaughterhouse, where an animal's corpse would be hung over the groove and its blood carried away to the ground outside.

As if that thought wasn't bad enough, my mind leapfrogged to the conclusion that this might be where the kidnappers would torture my wife! The thought chilled my blood, and I spun around, half expecting to see them quietly standing behind me, one with a gun, the other with a large butcher knife.

The building was empty, of course. I was alone, and as I glanced around the quiet interior, I could see nothing that would provide me with a clue as to my next set of instructions. Dejected, I headed back to the entrance, prepared to hop down to the ground and investigate the exterior of the building. However, just before I jumped, I noticed there was some fresh writing scrawled on the wall to the right of the opening.

Look out the doorway facing west. Walk to the tree line. Find the barely visible path. Follow the path to the clearing.

After a few seconds of silence from Brady, I piped up and asked, "Did you follow the instructions?"

"Naturally! It was the only way I could find my wife."

"And what did you discover, Mr. Brady?"

"A lot of bloody annoying trees," he said, as he finished his drink in one long swallow. "Then, after struggling through the pathway for about five or 10 minutes, there was a clearing, and in the middle of the clearing was a hole."

"What kind of a hole? Round, square, smooth, jagged, how deep?"

Brady paused to think, while at the same time sliding his ring off and on his finger. Finally, he said, "About four or five feet in diameter. Not very smooth, deep enough to stick in someone's body, if he wasn't too tall."

"Is your wife tall?"

"I'd say she's medium—about five-four."

"Was there anything else?"

Brady paused, slowly nodded his head and cleared his throat. "Yes. There was a stake inside the hole. Attached to it was my wife's blouse."

"Anything else?" I prompted in a flat, unemotional voice.

"There was blood on the blouse and a note, pinned to it. The note said: *Return here. Thursday. 2:00 p.m.*"

Early the next morning, I ate breakfast with Zuni Smith, gave him instructions for the day and headed north to start my assignment for Ryan Brady. By 10:45, I was driving north through New York State, alongside the Hudson River. I was attired in my customary summer black outfit: a Brooks Brothers tropical-weight suit, a Rene Lacoste polo shirt and imported Dolcis Vincenza leather slip-ons. Frankly, I have numerous sets of the same black clothing, reasoning that black is always in style, and it saves me time and worry about what the hell I'm going to wear for the day.

It was a beautiful summer morning, and I had the top down on my Jaguar XK-140. The car radio was playing the Everly Brothers' hit "Cathy's Clown," and I was just passing West Point, the American military academy Brady had mentioned last night.

I was pretty familiar with the area, as I'd spent several years nearby at the Eagle Ridge military prep school, finishing my secondary education. Although I was a Canadian by birth, my father had some kind of pull and enough money to send me there, considering it to be a finishing school that would toughen me up. Indeed, it did, and I liked the States so much I decided to stay on in New York City to complete a degree at NYU. Upon graduation, I fought in the Korean War, and my stint was followed by special-ops training and service in Washington. My mother's been trying to get me to return to Canada ever since.

Elvis was whipping up a storm with "It's Now or Never" on the radio, while I was in the middle of reviewing last night's appointment with Brady at the Algonquin Hotel. As soon as I'd returned to my Jones Street residence, I'd made notes about the meeting, and tried to put my thoughts in order.

To be honest, my cautionary antennae had gone up when Brady asked me to take his place for the return trip to the gravesite to receive the final set of instructions. Because of my profession and the fact I had contacts in the police force, Brady argued that I could do what was necessary to save his wife, and perhaps apprehend the villains in the bargain. To sweeten the deal, he immediately handed over the original retainer, along with a very generous bonus. The case was an intriguing challenge, all right, and the money was definitely good, but I still felt uneasy.

As a result, my wariness prompted me to phone my gangland contact, Frank Palladino. After supplying him with some basic details, the mobster put me in touch with one of his oldest friends, a well-known Broadway producer named Charlie Silverman. Silverman, after a quick search, provided me with information confirming my growing suspicions. It didn't take me long to make a few more calls, and when I finally got what I'd been looking for, I woke up Zuni Smith and got him into the office to thrash out our strategy.

As Bobby Darin sang "Mack the Knife," I parked my Jag down the old farmer's lane and headed up the hill to the top of the knoll. I looked east and about a half mile away was able to see the barn with the brilliant red door. Only the door wasn't brilliant red, as Brady had described it, but a washed-out, dirty pink. It hadn't seen a lick of paint in more than half a century.

I checked my watch. I was a little early, but my plans with Zuni Smith were already in motion. The only thing that was missing was Frank Palladino's daughter, Eleanor. With her *special* skills, she would have been a major asset on this assignment. However, wishful thinking would not make her part of this particular mystery.

I started downhill, bearing slightly to the southwest, until I'd reached the wooden fence. Crossing over, but being careful not to snag my lightweight summer blacks, I headed to the long grass which swished and swayed, but made no threatening sounds. Again, Brady had misrepresented some detail in his story. Deliberate, to get my attention, or just careless?

Upon entering the concrete building, I found everything the way Brady had described it, right down to the groove, the frayed rope and the note on the wall.

Eight minutes later, I entered the woods and started to fight my way along the path. I had to agree with my client—the trees were bloody annoying.

Almost 10 minutes passed before I was there, standing over the hole. Only it wasn't a simple hole about four or five feet in diameter, just deep enough to stick in a short body. It was too smooth, too evenly dug, too uniformly rectangular. I recognized it as a freshly dug grave.

"What do you think?" came a voice from above me. "Do you know what it is?"

"Seen a few in my time," I said without turning around. I recognized Brady's voice and figured that he was up in a tree somewhere behind me. And most likely armed.

"Know who's going to die in it?" Brady said.

I paused for a moment, then responded, "What would you say if I suggested it would be *you?*"

"I'd say you'd died with a lie on your lips."

Then the silence of the woods was broken by the sound of a rifle bolt sliding into place.

"Son of a bitch!" Brady cried in surprise. It was not him who had armed a weapon.

"Actually, he's not a son of a bitch." I slowly turned around to look up to face my adversary. He was sitting in a tree and aiming a rifle of his own at my head. "He's my friend and colleague, Mr. Zuni Smith."

Hours later, Mr. Smith and I were sitting in the Jones Street apartment, reviewing the events of the past two days. "Twilight Time" by the Platters was playing on the living room stereo, and we were enjoying ice cold bottles of Schlitz beer.

"What was the first thing that got you on to him?" Smith asked. "You only gave me a bare-bones outline last night."

"It was a slip he made," I began. "He told me his wife had gone to see Ethel Merman in Gypsy last Saturday night."

"What was wrong with that?"

"He said she'd gone to the Broadway Theater to see it. Last Saturday night, the show was dark. It had finished its run at the Broadway on the Saturday before. It's supposed to reopen in August at the Imperial Theater. I'd heard about the closing, but when I got home last night, I confirmed everything with Charlie Silverman, the Broadway producer. Gypsy reopens on Monday, August 15. My client said that his wife had seen the show before, in June, and loved it. Logically speaking, he was plotting this little caper last June, when the show was still at the Broadway Theater."

"That was just a small slip, Mr. Gentry," Zuni Smith said. "But there must have been lots more to trigger your skepticism."

"Indeed, there was. Specifically, the ring. He kept fiddling with his wedding ring. At first, I thought he was perhaps a little nervous. Then I became convinced he was uncomfortable wearing it. Finally, he slipped it off and on entirely. It was then that I noticed his ring finger was as tanned as the rest of his left hand."

"If he had been married for some time," Smith interjected, "there would have been a white patch of skin where the ring prevented any tanning!"

"Precisely. Either he was not married at all and put on the ring to make his story more plausible, or else he had just gotten married recently. If the latter was the case, you'd think he'd have mentioned it and referred to her as his bride of so many weeks or months. Regardless, it opened up the possibility that he wasn't married, and that his entire kidnapping story was bogus."

We sat in mutual comfort and satisfaction, sipping away at our drinks. After a moment, I continued with my explanation, "So, last night when I got home from my meeting with him, I proceeded to follow that line of reasoning. If it was all a lie, then why the elaborate goose chase over hill and dale? Why the hole in the woods and the suggestion of a burial site?"

"Obviously someone was going to die," Smith offered, "and someone was going to be buried there."

"And who else would that be?" I said. "There was only one other person in play at the time, and that person was *me*—the guy he'd asked to take his place at the empty hole the very next day after our meeting. If I was the target, that would answer a number of other questions."

"Like why would he check into the Algonquin," Smith suggested, "when he supposedly lived only five or so miles away on Riverside Drive?"

"Correct, and why would he say that he was a lawyer when clearly he was ex-military?"

"What gave that away?"

"Numerous things. His very short hair, neatly trimmed mustache and his clipped speech when he wasn't reciting his overly dramatic tale of his travels to the empty grave site. His bearing was also fairly rigid. Clearly, he's an officer, especially when he noted passing West Point Military Academy in his story to me. Normally, people might mention the town, but not so much the military academy unless there was a personal connection to it."

"Or he was a travel guide," Smith smiled and drank some of his beer.

"Further, he referred to the name of the Cheese Factory Road as its dog tag; said that the building's stairs were missing in action; and used the term march instead of walk several times."

"Well done, Mr. Gentry. Please continue."

"When I reached the possibility that I was the actual victim, I made several more phone calls," Gentry said. "One of them was to the un-listed number in Washington we've used before in such investigations as The Death Merchants, and last autumn's case about The Man With Hemingway's Face. After a few transfers, I explained my problem to the duty officer and suggested where he might look in military records. I gave him my client's initials, his probable range of ranks, his approximate age and physical description, and the possibility he served in Korea."

"You thought there was a connection to the Korean conflict?"

"Strong probability. Based on our relative ages, it was a definite field we would have shared if he was ex-military."

"And indeed, it was, as it turned out," Smith said.

"So, a little after midnight this morning, the phone rang, I had my answer from our contacts in Washington, and I woke you up. Where-upon, as you know, we plotted our strategy for closing the case of the empty grave."

"Actually, he's not a son of a bitch," I said, slowly turning around and looking up to face my adversary. He was sitting in a tree and aiming a rifle of his own at me. "He's my friend and colleague, Mr. Zuni Smith. As well as being awarded the army's Expert Marksmanship Badge with three Clasps, he's a very fine fellow, with impeccable parentage. Conclusion: no son of a bitch, but an excellent shot.

"Brady scanned the trees around him before spotting Smith 20 feet down the pathway. "How the hell did you get there?" he asked.

Smith responded from his place on the trail, "I followed Mr. Gentry at a discrete distance in my own car. I parked in the farmer's lane, and then headed to this rendezvous spot."

"Therefore, Colonel Robert Brennan," I continued, "I suggest you throw down your weapon, then climb out of the tree very slowly. Please note that Mr. Smith will shoot to kill."

"And I have a clean shot from here," Smith added.

"It really doesn't matter," responded Brennan, as he lowered his rifle. "I'm going to die soon, anyway. But first, tell me how you figured out my little plot."

"I'll be happy to, Colonel, but if your rifle moves even an inch, my friend will shoot you out of the tree. Understood?"

"Of course."

"To begin, after our meeting last night at the Algonquin, it soon became apparent that you were not telling the truth about your kidnapped wife. You are neither married, as far as I can tell, nor has your fictitious spouse been kidnapped. It was also apparent that you are not a lawyer, but either ex-military or still in the service."

"How did you make those conclusions, if I may ask?"

"Powers of observation and a great many slips on your part. I'd be pleased to outline all of them later. However, right now, let's concentrate on the real reason why you hired me."

"Which is?"

"To kill me and dispose of my body, of course. Now, the disposal part is obvious, but the real puzzle was why me? I'd never met you before our meeting at the Algonquin. What had I done to offend you to the extent you wanted me dead?"

"Good question." Brennan slowly rearranged his position in the tree, careful to make no threatening moves with his rifle. "But I assume you already have the answer."

"I do. But I needed some help. You were correct in assuming I had good contacts with the police. In this case, however, I used my contacts with the Army Security Agency. I gave them a list of research descriptors to see if they could ferret you out for me."

"What kind of descriptors?"

"Your physical description, age range, active service or recent retirement, possible rank ranging from major to major general, service in Korea and your initials."

"My initials?"

"Just a shot in the dark, Colonel. Many people who use aliases pick names that have the same initials ... because of monogrammed clothes, jewelry, luggage and so forth. The fact that you changed your real name from Robert Brennan to Ryan Brady was a great help. As a consequence, your initials and a number of other matching descriptors really helped the agency to hit pay dirt. They were able to respond to me within a few hours."

"And they came up with me!"

"Not only you, Colonel Brennan, but the fact you had come from a rather large Irish family, another one of whom also fought in Korea."

"Sean," Brennan said in a quiet voice.

"Indeed, Sean. Corporal Sean Brennan of the Second Infantry Division, Charlie Company. Under the command of ... Captain Cass Gentry."

"Yes, you! The man who left him to die on Bloody Ridge, in the fall of '51. My baby brother!"

"I did not leave him to die, Colonel. We were under heavy fire and cut off from the rest of our unit. Sean was badly wounded, and I left him to find a medic. By the time the medic and I returned, Sean was dead. I was wounded by a KPA grenade and barely able to carry his body back down the hill."

After a moment, Brennan asked, "And you expect me to believe that?"

"Believe what you wish, Brennan. But I'm telling the truth. However, I'd like to ask you something, if you don't mind."

"Go ahead."

"Why did you decide to come after me?"

"I promised him. I stood at Sean's grave and vowed I would hunt you down and kill you."

"But why now?" I said. "Sean was killed almost nine years ago."

"I thought I might get over it, but his death and the vow kept haunting me." Brennan shifted his position slightly, but made no move with his rifle. "I thought about it, obsessed over it for a long while. I was transferred around the world, moved back home, then something happened that sealed the deal."

"What was that, Colonel?"

"Last month, I found out I had inoperable cancer. If I was going to keep my vow to Sean, I had to do it now."

"Sean was a good soldier," I said, "and I'm very sorry for your loss and your illness, Colonel. However, as trite as it sounds, you must know that killing me won't bring him back."

"Time to come down, Brennan," Zuni Smith interrupted. "But drop the weapon first, if you don't mind."

After a long silence, Brennan looked down at me, and seemed to make up his mind.

"A promise is a promise," was all he said. Then he lifted his rifle in my direction. Zuni Smith immediately fired, hitting Brennan high in the shoulder. Crying out in pain and frustration, Brennan fumbled to hold his weapon steady as he tried to aim at me. Another shot from Zuni Smith hit him in the back of the neck, and he pitched forward out of the tree.

I rushed over to Brennan, who looked up at me with wide, unseeing eyes. I didn't need a medic to tell he was dead already.

"What do we do now?" Smith said as he joined me beside the body.

"I'll get in touch with our friends in Washington. The Agency's boys will be here in no time and clean things up. Then they'll notify the family and make sure Brennan gets a proper burial. He was misguided in coming after me, but he shouldn't be remembered for that."

"What do you intend to do with his retainer?"

I thought for a moment, then said, "How about a generous contribution to the Veterans of Foreign Wars? Perhaps in Brennan's name."

"Most appropriate, Mr. Gentry." My mentor smiled at me. "I'd expect nothing less."

2

TOO MANY LOVE LETTERS

(A Cass and Eleanor Mystery)

Thursday, August 4, 1960

Two weeks after we completed the case of *The Empty Grave*, my mentor and friend, Zuni Smith, traveled to Billings, Montana, for his annual powwow. That was good news for him and bad news for me, as I'm now on the hook for my own meals.

Since I'm not a great cook, nor am I anywhere near as good as Mr. Smith, I had happily given up on cooking for myself, and that's why I was having breakfast around the corner from my Greenwich Village apartments. Best in the Village is not a ritzy restaurant, but the food is every bit as good as its name implies.

Breakfast is a beautiful thing when your plate is piled high with bacon, eggs over easy, smoky baked hash browns with paprika, and a pair of pancakes smothered in Canadian maple syrup. That's the delicious sight I was staring at when a stranger with a briefcase suddenly popped up beside my booth. One second, I was slicing into a golden pancake; the next, I was listening to someone clear his throat to get my attention.

The throat-clearing worked; I said, "Can I help you?"

"If you're Cass Gentry, I think you can," he said, "but if you want to finish your meal first, I'll wait over at the bar."

The man looked dapper in a made-to-measure suit from the Garment District, and his rakish beard and mustache were neatly trimmed.

I gestured for him to sit, and went on applying my knife and fork to the pancake.

When he'd settled in, he thanked me and quietly waited for me to finish my meal. Figuring I wouldn't be able to enjoy my breakfast with him politely watching me, I asked if I could order anything for him. He declined, so I called over my waiter and asked him to keep my breakfast warm. The waiter removed the food, and I grumpily asked the man to get on with his business.

He said, "My name is Charlie Silverman, and I need a professional private eye."

I didn't respond, even though I'm a licensed New York City PI. and his name rang more than a faint bell.

"We've met before," he continued, then corrected himself. "Actually, we haven't met in person, but we've spoken on the phone. Frank gave you my phone number."

Crap, I thought. That was only two weeks ago and Charlie Silverman had provided the first big clue to help solve *The Empty Grave* case. I apologized and reached across the booth to shake his hand.

"Not to worry, Mr. Gentry. I'm sorry to interrupt your meal. But I need your help, and Frank suggested you're alone this week. He also told me I might find you at this restaurant in the mornings, if you're not at home. You weren't at home."

Now, if you haven't read any of my other cases, let me explain that *Frank* is really a fellow named Frank Palladino, the head of a major crime family that controls a number of unsavory activities along the Eastern Seaboard. We have a rather bizarre relationship which started in *The Death Merchants* case and reached a most interesting high point last fall in the case of *The Man With Hemingway's Face.*

I might also add that I'm presently dating his daughter, Eleanor Palladino.

"How may I help you, Mr. Silverman?" I hoped it had nothing to do with Frank's business. My relationship with the Palladino family is complicated enough, as it is.

"As you know, I'm a Broadway producer," Silverman began. "I have offices on Shubert Alley, and I produce shows that appear on Broadway, as well as Off Broadway. Presently, I have a show running Off Broadway, and it's doing respectable business. If it catches on, I may be able to transfer it to one of the bigger Broadway houses."

"Sounds encouraging," I offered, wondering where this was going. The only thing I know about the theater scene in New York is going to shows, and I've heard of no scandals involving any of the present productions. "Is there something I can help you with, Mr. Silverman?"

"Call me *Charlie*, if you don't mind. Or *Uncle Charlie*, if you'd like. Frank and I grew up together as kids, and he thinks a lot of you. We can be less formal, what with you sort of being in the family."

"*Charlie* is fine," I agreed, not knowing in what context he was using the word *family*. Was it because I had helped Frank with the recent Hemingway case, or because I was dating his daughter. "Tell me how I can help."

And so he did.

Charlie Silverman was producing a mystery/thriller entitled *Ravens Cliff, Island of Games*. It was one of those whodunits with lots of twists, where everyone is a suspect when one of the characters disappears and is presumed murdered.

His problem, he told me, was that a company member, a woman who is the props mistress, had been receiving romantic letters from various members of the cast and crew.

"What's wrong with that?" I interrupted. "Some women would love such attention."

"You'd have to meet this person in order to understand why the circumstances are a little bizarre."

"Tell me about her."

"She's quite awkward, a bit of a *klutz*, to put it mildly," the producer began. "She's also slightly googly-eyed, and has hair that sticks out all over the place. It's not that she's unattractive, Cass. It's just that her weird mannerisms accentuate her...shall we say *peculiarities.* If she combed her hair a bit, spruced up a little and stopped being so twitchy, it would go a long way to normalize her personality."

"*Twitchy?*"

"Yes. You know, mumbling to herself, waving her hands about when she talks, that sorta thing."

I paused for a moment, and tried to visualize this woman who had drawn such amorous attention from other members of her company. Then I told Charlie, "I'm a little surprised that you hired such a person, if she's as *twitchy* as you say."

Charlie thought for a few seconds, and then explained that she had impeccable credentials. "Her name is Betsy Blake, and I hired her right out of college. Actually, she graduated at the top of her technical program. In fact, she's qualified to work in both our properties and wardrobe departments. Her hire was like acquiring a young talent on a two-for-one sale."

"Lucky you," I responded. "Sort of!"

"Actually, I'm quite pleased with her work, in spite of her kooky nature. She's worked out well, except for these surprising letters. Apparently, they have caused her a lot of distress."

"Why is that?"

"Well, she finds them really upsetting. Although a few of the men have been friendly to her, in a kinda *fatherly* way, the rest have ignored her completely. It appears to her they could be making fun of her."

"Tell me about the *Ravens Cliff* company," I suggested. "Just to give me a feel for the situation."

"I'd be pleased to," he said, and told me how he'd based the company on his days as a summer stock producer and director.

While he was talking, part of me was listening, but at the same time I was starting to formulate a plan. First, however, I had to learn a lot more about the issue of the love letters, and why that had prompted Charlie to search me out.

When he had finished, I thanked him for the company information, and repeated my puzzlement concerning the love letters.

"Normally, I'd agree with you, Cass," he said. "Most young women would be delighted to receive such amorous attention. But Betsy Blake is not your ordinary young woman. She was immediately suspicious of the letters. In fact, she was *extremely upset* by them. She wanted to quit."

"You're kidding!"

"Negative. She felt the guys were making fun of her—trying to humiliate her. Gave me a week to sort things out, or she was out the door! Frankly, Cass, I really don't want to lose her."

"How many letters were there?"

"Seven, all written by men. But I'd categorize only five of them as seriously *romantic.* Two of them were more brotherly in nature, offering fealty and support. Although all the letter writers promised support, the other five added their amorous affections, their undying love."

"Why were the two men different?"

"Both of them are homophiles. They're not attracted to females."

"Do you have the letters from the two groups of men separated?" I asked. "And were the letters signed?"

"Yes, to both of your questions," Charlie replied. "In fact, I've brought the letters with me, along with the contracts, résumés and head shots of all members of the company."

Before Charlie could open his briefcase, I suggested he wait until later, and asked if he had the rest of the morning and afternoon free. He hemmed and hawed a bit, but eventually agreed with my suggestion of working out a plan with me and an associate. He agreed, but added that he'd have to be back to the Village in time to get his subway connections to the theater for the evening performance.

"No problem," I assured him. "When we get back from our meeting, I'll drop you off at the theater myself."

"That's wonderful," he enthused. "I'm very pleased!"

"You won't be when you get my bill."

"*Oy vey!*" he muttered. "I shoulda asked first."

An hour and a half later, we were crossing the George Washington Bridge into New Jersey, heading for my favorite Italian restaurant in Teaneck Township.

I had tried to pay for my uneaten breakfast, but the manager said to *forgetaboutit.* Instead, he sent me along with a muffin and an orange juice to tide me over. I gave him a generous tip and told him I'd be back tomorrow, same time, same order!

After leaving the restaurant, we walked over to my apartment, and I got changed into my traditional summer outfit of a Brooks Brothers tropical-weight suit, a René Lacoste polo shirt and imported Dolcis Vincenza leather slip-ons—all in black. Frankly, I have numerous sets of the same clothing, reasoning that black is always in style, and it saves me time and worry about what I'm going to wear for the day.

My dark hair complements the color scheme, but not my eyes. Mother Nature had given me emerald-green peepers, which were more than slightly unique. In fact, one old flame had referred to them as being *pretty freaky*.

While I got dressed, Charlie Silverman sat in the living room with a Scotch and soda. Then I phoned up my lady friend, Eleanor Palladino, and asked if she was ready to become an unlicensed, underpaid assistant in the Cass Gentry Detective Agency.

"How underpaid?" she shot back.

"How about settling for a lunch at Casa Romano?"

"When?"

"1:30."

"*What day?*"

"Today."

"Sorry, I've got a date."

"Can you break it?"

"Nope."

"Who's the lucky guy?"

"My boyfriend, Cass Gentry, you goof."

A few miles outside of West Englewood, I was slowing down my Jaguar XK-140, enjoying the sunny day and warm breezes. Charlie and I sat with the ragtop down and the car radio up.

Canada's young export, Paul Anka, was singing "Lonely Boy" on WNBC, and I had to smile. Paul was more than a dozen years younger than me, and a lot richer, although I'm not hurting for cash. However, the point I'm trying to make is that I, too, had come from Canada a number of years ago.

My dad had enough bread and political clout to send me to Eagle Ridge military academy in upstate New York to finish my high school education and to toughen me up. It toughened me up, all right, and after staying on in New York to get a degree at NYU, I fought in the Korean conflict. That was followed by some special ops training and more combat.

When I'd finished with my active service and a few years in Washington, which I can't discuss, I returned to the Village, got my private dick's license, and have continued to fight a different kind of bad guy ever since.

Ten minutes later, as Johnny Horton was refighting "The Battle of New Orleans," we pulled into the parking lot of Casa Romano. Sliding in beside a freshly washed, green MGA, I cut the radio on Mr. Horton, walked over to join the beautiful blonde standing beside the sports car, and exchanged a warm embrace. Charlie Silverman joined us, and Eleanor Palladino gave him a big hug, as well.

"Hi, Uncle Charlie," Eleanor said.

"Hi, kiddo," Uncle Charlie said.

"Uncle Charlie?" I said. "You know Charlie Silverman?"

"Doesn't everyone?" Eleanor said.

Then the three of us walked into the out-of-the-way Italian restaurant where Eleanor and I had had our first date last fall. We were immediately greeted by the owner's son, Alessandro, and I told him the reason for our meeting—a little talk first, then a light lunch, followed by some more talk.

"Would you like a private room?" Alessandro asked.

"Am I my father's daughter?" Eleanor said.

"Follow me," Alessandro said, and led the way into a smaller room off to the side.

Within a minute, we were sitting in a comfortably appointed room with warm brown wainscoting, topped by dark red wallpaper. The furniture was sturdy oak, in the Italian Provincial style, and consisted mostly of a circular dining table with matching chairs. The room was meant for private guests, enjoying either special occasions or business meetings of a more serious nature. The table was already cleared for the latter. When we were seated, Alessandro discreetly vanished.

"So, you and Charlie are related," I said to Eleanor, as we settled in.

"Not by blood," she replied, "but we've become good family in recent years. Father and he were childhood buddies, and I've been extended the pleasure of being his honorary goddaughter."

"The honor's been all mine," Charlie added, as he opened his brief-case, extracted numerous papers, and started to set them down in neatly ordered piles.

When he was finished, Charlie briefly filled Eleanor in on what he'd told me earlier. I could tell that Eleanor was already brimming with a myriad of questions, and it didn't take her long to sound off.

"What puzzles me, Uncle Charlie, is why the young woman was so disturbed by the letters."

"Frankly, Betsy Blake's no fool. She freely admitted to me she knows she's a bit of a *schlemiel*. She's awkward and *klutzy*, and has these twitchy habits I just told you about. Furthermore, she does very little to spruce herself up. Call it low self-esteem, if you will, but I think she's really finding it hard to believe she deserves such attention."

"Point well taken," Eleanor admitted. "What is even more telling is the fact she's got smarts—graduated at the top of her class, and qualified for both of those technical departments of yours. Which suggests she's likely sharp enough to suspect that the sheer number of similar letters could indicate a company plot—all of her colleagues laughing up their sleeves at her."

"Excellent, Eleanor. That's been nagging at me, too. What do you think, Cass?

"I think I've got myself a new partner."

Eleanor sat there with a smug little smile on her face, and I winked at Charlie. He started to pass out the infamous letters, as well as the head shots, résumés and contracts of his people.

"The first member of the acting company," Charlie began, "is the woman who plays the matriarch of the family in the play." Eleanor and I shared the picture and résumé as Charlie continued. "Although not necessarily a suspect, she's a fine character actress and acts like Old Mother Goose around the younger members of the company. Her name is Donna Lawrence, and she's appeared in a lot of television shows like *Dragnet, Perry Mason* and *Leave It To Beaver*. She also been a guest star on *Have Gun, Will Travel* and *Gunsmoke*, to name a few westerns. I suggest you talk with her, as she's been around the block a few times and may be able to fill you in on the company gossip."

Eleanor and I put down Donna's paperwork and picked up the second set in order.

"Next of interest, I've selected these male members of the cast," Charlie continued. "They're a suitable age for Betsy. The first one is Jack Kelly, who plays Donna's son in the show. Jack's young, virile and has such a chip on his shoulder that you'd think he was a movie star like Tony Curtis or Rock Hudson!"

"You should be so lucky to have one of those two guys in your company," I said. "But has Betsy indicated any fondness for Jack?"

"Not in the slightest. In fact, she admits she has no amorous feelings for anybody in the company."

Charlie scanned his notes and continued with the next young performer. "Lance Beaumont is the guy who plays the detective in the show. He's about the same age as Jack, but has a much nicer personality. Lance is very popular with everyone."

"Are you saying Jack Kelly isn't popular?" Eleanor asked.

"What would you think if you were the cleaning lady, went into his dressing room and found him kissing his own reflection in the mirror?"

"I'd say you just made that up!"

"Yes, I did," Charlie laughed, "but that shows you what folks think about Jack."

"I'm sure we'll find out for sure when we interview them," I interjected.

"Oh, really?" Charlie said in surprise. "Do you actually think it'll be necessary to speak with each person?"

"Perhaps, Charlie, perhaps not," I replied. "But let's wait 'till we go over all this paperwork first. I already know I wish to speak with Donna and Betsy, for sure."

"Fair enough," Charlie responded, just as Alessandro entered the room and asked if we were ready for lunch.

Eleanor and I exchanged glances, and gave Alessandro the high sign. He made some suggestions that had me salivating.

After our host had exited to the kitchen with our order, Charlie continued. "Although the next cast member has a very small part, I'll include him in the lineup. His name is Max Lucian, and he plays Donna's husband in the show. Actually, he only appears in the first scene of Act One, but we make good use of his talents.

"Max is an old pro, and is wonderful with voices. He does all the offstage voice work for us, including some ghostly sounds from what's supposed to be the Spirit World. We're lucky to have him, as he's in great demand for voice-over work in radio and television."

The producer continued down his list. "The next two men we can eliminate. They're members of our tech crew and are about the same age. Douglas Richmond is our stage manager, and Jamie Drake is our lighting technician. Both of them are excellent professionals, and I wouldn't hesitate to use them in any of my future Broadway shows. Obviously, I've eliminated them because they are the two homophiles I mentioned earlier. Further, Doug and Jamie are a couple."

At that moment, Alessandro and a member of his kitchen staff entered the room with plates of food. Following close behind was an older gentleman, smiling and carrying a large carafe of red wine. I recognized him as Alessandro's father, the *padrone* of Casa Romano.

With a bow, the father presented the wine and said, "For the daughter of Don Palladino, and her friends." Eleanor stood up, kissed him on both cheeks and told him she would pass along his respects to her father. The older man gave a deep bow to Eleanor, turned about and left the room, his head erect, his back very straight.

Alessandro then brought in what he described as a *little sampler* of Italian delights, enough to feed three sumo wrestlers for a week. The dishes consisted of cold meats and cheese antipasti, sliced oranges in olive oil and fresh ground pepper, and *capellini pomodoro.* Delicious, especially the subtle sauce on the angel hair pasta!

Just as we started to feel slightly comfortable, Alessandro returned with the second course, *pollo d'nonni—* boneless chicken breast marinated in soy, sherry, garlic and herbs. The chef threw in a few mushrooms in the sauce, as well.

Eleanor reminded us we still had dessert and an aperitif to look forward to. I looked over at Charlie, who appeared slightly green around the gills; he shook his head, but he had enough stamina to try the chicken and finish his glass of wine.

After we sampled the chicken—which was excellent, I might add—I asked Eleanor to beg Alessandro to cease and desist from bringing anything more. When he came back into the room to clear away the second course plates, she quickly spoke to him in Italian. I picked up enough to understand she was being most apologetic. He shrugged, and asked, in English, if we'd enjoyed the meal. Charlie and I pretended to collapse from exhaustion, and Alessandro cleared away the dishes with a hearty laugh.

When we were alone once more, Charlie said that he had two more members of the company to mention.

"Both of these men are older than Betsy, but I feel they're worth noting," he said. "First, is the director of the show, Sandy Alexander. He's actually closer in age to Donna and Max, but he has a reputation for being a bit of a Don Juan, which might be relevant to our investigation. Sandy is suave, debonair, has been married twice before and remains a certified *roué.*"

Charlie added, "Nevertheless, he's a great director, specializing in thrillers and English comedies. He's also directed television specials including a major *Playhouse 90* production, and some of the more recent TV series, such as episodes of *Peter Gunn* and *The Naked City.*"

"I'll look forward to meeting him," I said. "*Peter Gunn* is one of my mother's favorite shows."

"I'm sure," Charlie said. "Craig Stevens, who plays detective Gunn, is the epitome of *cool.* I think they modeled the character after Cary Grant."

"And the last potential *suspect* is… ?" Eleanor interjected, trying to get the discussion back on track.

"Right. That would be our head of wardrobe, Mike Asher. Mike is a little older than Betsy, an excellent worker and very supportive of the cast. He's very flamboyant, and I can say that he's quite friendly with Betsy."

Charlie paused. "As for the other women in the cast, I think I'll leave them up to your own researches. None, in my estimation, would qualify for serious scrutiny in this matter. However, I'll bow to your discretion."

With that, Charlie started to pack up his notes. "I'll leave the résumés, photos, contracts and letters. The two of you can decide how to proceed from here."

"We'll get right at it," I suggested. "Perhaps to save time, one of us can research the letters, while the other concentrates on the company members' information."

"I'll do the letters," Eleanor said, and we started to separate the documents.

Within minutes, we were packed up, bid Alessandro farewell after leaving a substantial tip, and rolled out of the building to the parking lot. I kissed Eleanor goodbye; told her I'd call her that evening and pulled away from Casa Romano.

On the way back through Jersey, Charlie and I agreed to rendezvous at the theater on Saturday, between the matinee and evening performances. We would speak with the company members if we found it necessary. I definitely wanted to talk with Donna, the company matron, and Betsy Blake herself.

After that, the return trip was very quiet. Charlie was fast asleep before we reached the George Washington Bridge.

Friday, August 5, 1960

Shortly after nine o'clock the next morning, I was sitting in my usual booth in Best in the Village. A full complement of breakfast food rallied 'round my table, and I was happily munching away on syrup-soaked pancakes. Today, I had substituted Iowa sausages for the bacon; otherwise, everything was the same.

Thankfully, this time my waiter was the only person who interrupted, so I had plenty of solitude to review my notes from last night's research. Everything seemed pretty much in order, although the documents raised a few questions, which I would discuss with Eleanor when we met later today.

Last night, our phone conversation was fairly short, as Eleanor was right in the middle of some serious *detection,* as she playfully phrased it. The letters revealed some interesting points, which she was not willing to discuss over the phone.

When I mentioned my meeting with Charlie tomorrow afternoon at the theater, she suggested that I drive over to her house in Teaneck Township, compare notes, stay over and head to the theater. My heart skipped a beat at the thought of an overnight visit with her, but recent history suggested I'd be staying in one of the guest bedrooms.

By the middle of the afternoon, I was heading up a long, tree-lined driveway, which wound lazily through a stand of maples, and approaching an iron, spiked-topped gate with a small guardhouse on the other side.

There were two serious-looking hoods hanging around the guardhouse. A large, broad-shouldered gunsel checked out my Jaguar from his side of the barrier, recognized me and gave a thumbs-up to the other guard who was standing outside the little building. That one was carrying one of the new Winchester autoload shotguns—a nasty little number that could shred the Jaguar's grill, windshield and my head to bits in an instant.

The guardhouse gate opened, and I drove through with a chipper salute to the two torpedoes. I followed the drive until I arrived at the front of Frank Palladino's impressive two-and-a-half-storey, neo-Tudor mansion. It had lots of parapet gables, large leaded windows, steeply pitched roofs and plenty of chimney stacks. An oriel bay window projected out over the Tudor arch of the front door.

Two thugs with undisguised bulges under their sports jackets nodded to me, and I immediately surrendered my car keys to one of them.

Almost instantly, Eleanor appeared at the front door, so I picked up the manila envelope beside me, joined her and was ushered into a large hall whose walls sported the mounted heads of numerous wild animals. I'm sure they would rather have been back home in Africa.

A door on the right-hand wall was open, and we walked through into the den, which took up a quarter of the back of the mansion. It's a beautiful room—expansive, oak-paneled and very plush in a masculine kind of way. One wall was lined with books, while two others held more mounted animal heads. If I'd owned the home, I'd have put up framed pieces of art.

The room's centerpiece is an immense desk that looks like it belongs in some billion-dollar company's boardroom. The desk is framed by blood-red leather couches and armchairs, and accompanied by solid-looking coffee and end tables.

I paused to look around, remembering the first time I'd set foot in the room. Frank Palladino and I had met once before that event, and he had sent for me to help him in what became the Hemingway case. It was also the day I learned that my deadliest enemy was still alive. Eleanor immediately guessed what I was thinking.

"Don't worry," she said. "You don't have to see him. He's still in Sicily under *house arrest,* and going through what father calls a serious rehabilitation."

"I hope he takes the cure. Next time, I might have to kill him."

"I understand how you feel, darling. Even if he's my brother, I dislike him as much as you do. Perhaps more."

Nodding my head, I couldn't blame her, because she had known him longer, and he hadn't been the sweet, overprotective big brother you read about in teen novels. As for me, my problems with Joey Palladino had started with *The Death Merchants* case and continued on through last fall with the Hemingway business.

However, it was time to put those thoughts aside. Time to move on, for we had a new case that was demanding our attention.

But first, I embraced Eleanor, which quickly turned into a passionate round of kissing. I don't remember who broke the magic of the moment first, but eventually we were sitting around the coffee table, addressing our research notes from last night instead of our romantic needs from a few minutes ago.

"By the way, how's your father?" I started.

"Good, He and his *capo*, Rocco, are down in Florida, looking after some business at our hotel. Rocco's interviewing applicants for jobs at the Esprit Royale, while Father continues to negotiate with the other members of the gambling consortium down there."

She paused to organize the love letters that allegedly were sent by members of the theater company to Betsy Blake. "Now, are you ready for some interesting thoughts on these letters?"

"Affirmative, my dear. Dazzle me with your brilliance."

Eleanor laid down the seven letters on the table. Each was spread out and facing me. "I want you to read the second paragraph of each one. Take your time, read slowly. Then let me know what you've noticed, if anything."

"Yes, ma'am," I said, unable to suppress a grin. After a few minutes of reading, I looked up and gave her another grin. Only this time, it was laced with a *soupçon* of respect. "There are striking similarities."

"Not just vague similarities," Eleanor added, "but whole word-for-word sentences."

"I agree."

"Turn over the letters and read their top paragraphs and their last ones."

It didn't take me long, this time. I knew what I was looking for. When I finished, I sat back in the enveloping, soft leather of the couch and shook my head in admiration. "Good work, Eleanor. It appears that all these letters could have been written by the same person."

"Precisely. What else did you notice that was even more obvious?"

"They were written in different formats. Two of the seven were handcrafted—one printed, the other created in a rather wobbly, cursive writing."

"What about the other five?" Eleanor asked.

"Those five were typed, but I would bet they were created on different typewriters."

It was Eleanor's turn to grin. "You'd definitely win your bet. I spent hours last night checking and rechecking all of them with a magnifying glass. I'm almost positive they were typed on five different machines."

"Conclusions? The letters were typed by *five different people* on five different machines. *Or* they may have been written by only *one* person, who went to an awful lot of trouble to disguise the fact."

We sat back quite pleased with the discoveries, but let our minds race ahead to our next move. After a minute, I suggested we contemplate the first conclusion, and consider Betsy's original theory—the letters were a united conspiracy against her.

"It may seem a bit paranoid," Eleanor suggested, "but it's a definite possibility. Perhaps a group—or even all—of the letter writers disliked her to the extent they wanted to humiliate her. It would also explain why the typewritten letters were done on five different machines."

"Seems reasonable," I agreed. "One person, or a few of them, could have collaborated on composing the missive, and five different members of the gang could have gone off, found machines and typed up their own letters. That leaves two more."

"One of them printed the letter by hand, while the other wrote his in cursive script—perhaps writing with his left hand if he's right-handed. That would account for the shaky scrawl."

Rummaging through the papers, I located the letter in question and glanced at it. "That appears to be the case. The writing's not only shaky, but the script slants to the left—a sure indication that someone deliberately tried to use his other hand if he's normally right-handed."

I passed the letter over to Eleanor. She perused it briefly, and then said, "It would also explain why all of the signatures appear different. But let's check them out, just in case."

"In case what?"

"In case they're forgeries. If they're authentic, or at least appear to be so, then we'll be one step closer to the truth. Did you bring along the contracts? Everyone will have their signatures on them."

Opening up my manila envelope, I withdrew the contracts, and passed them over to Eleanor. She immediately found the relevant seven, walked over to her father's desk and spread them out in a straight line. I followed her with the seven letters and placed them under the appropriate contracts.

Less than 15 minutes later, we were sure. As the carny folks say on the fairground, "Nice try, but no cigar!"

The forgeries were pretty good, but there were enough anomalies to suggest the signatures were not authentic. We circled Frank's desk and sat down in two leather chairs facing each other.

Eleanor started the analysis. "Let's go back to our two, basic conclusions," she began. "Either they were written by a consortium of people, or by only one person, who went to a lot of trouble to write all the letters and tried to make it appear that they'd been written by a group."

"Okay," I agreed, "Let's consider the first option. What's obviously wrong with that one?"

"Simple," Eleanor fired back. "If that was the case, why didn't each member of the group write his own letter? All of them would have been different, but would have had the same romantic message. Much more natural."

"Natch. Just as important, why didn't they sign their own names—rather than try to forge them, or get someone else in the group to forge them?"

The two of us sat there for a few moments, thinking that over, until Eleanor broke the silence. "Would you like something to drink? This is thirsty work."

"What did you have in mind?"

"You know the old saying, *coffee, tea or something stronger?*"

"What happened to *me?*"

"Pardon?"

"I thought the old saying was, *coffee, tea or me.*"

"Nice try," she murmured. "Maybe later."

"Promises, promises. That's all I ever get is promises."

"What about last weekend? At least, that was a half-kept promise."

"Hmm," I said. "Let's get back to work."

Early that evening, we tooled into Hackensack to catch a movie. Eleanor was driving her MGA convertible, the night was mild with no clouds in sight, and I was reminded of our first date early last October. That night, we were heading to Casa Romano, and I was already involved in the Hemingway case.

Tonight, our decision was simple. Both of us wanted to see Alfred Hitchcock's new film, *Psycho,* but it was only playing at the DeMille Theater in Manhattan. So, we chose *From the Terrace,* a romantic potboiler starring Paul Newman and his wife Joanne Woodward. Both of us were fans of the Newmans, and...well, Eleanor and I were in an amorous mood ourselves.

On the whole, it was a very fine film, with excellent performances and music by Elmer Bernstein, that helped massage the intimate undercurrents of what was happening on the screen, as well as between Eleanor and me. The musical score also lulled me into reviewing some of the thoughts we'd developed this afternoon.

If the letters had been written by a consortium of Betsy-haters, it was also possible that they'd deliberately made a hacked-up job of them, which, in turn, leads us to a more devious thought—maybe they were attempting to make it look as if *Betsy had prepared the letters herself.* That would explain a lot of things, including the forged signatures and the similarities of those three paragraphs.

However, the reverse was also plausible. What if Betsy actually wrote them herself, but deliberately endeavored to make it look as if they were crafted by some Looney Tune with less smarts than her. She might be a little kooky, but everyone knew she was no slouch in the brains department.

The $64,000 question was: *Why* would she do it? Eleanor and I had come up with a few suggestions:

1. She writes the letters. Gives them to Charlie. People find out through the rumor mill, and believe the letter writers are jerks. They feel sorry for Betsy. Betsy gets friends.
2. Actually, she was fooling around with one of the guys and he told her to "get lost." So, she figures that word will get out about the letters, and maybe someone might get interested in her.
3. She was having an affair with *more than one* of them. She'll settle for anyone!
4. Revenge on everyone. Throw the poop up in the air and see where it lands!

At that point, I got an elbow in the ribs!

"What?" I whispered to Eleanor.

"You were starting to snore," she replied softly.

"No, I wasn't," I responded in a stage whisper. "I was going over Betsy's letters."

"You were starting to snore," she repeated, a little more forcefully. "In the movie, I think Paul Newman's wife is going to have an affair."

"Let's just cool it," a voice from behind us rasped. "There's no Betsy in this movie. So let's keep quiet, and we'll see if Paul finds out about his wife's affair with the doctor."

"You've seen the movie before?" I asked out loud.

"Yes, but it was a lot quieter that night!"

"Shhh!" came a chorus from our section of the theater.

Saturday, August 6, 1960

Next day, after a hearty brunch, compliments of the Palladino cook, Eleanor and I took off for the city. I worried that we wouldn't find parking, and would end way up in Queens and have to take a cab back to 43rd Street and 7th Avenue. Luckily, there was a parking lot with a few spaces within walking distance of the theater.

By the time we arrived backstage, we'd only missed the opening 20 minutes of *Ravens Cliff*, and were able to speak with two of the male members of the company.

Eleanor found Mike Asher in the wardrobe department, and I was able to run down Max Lucian in one of the dressing rooms.

As his acting stint for the day was done, Max was just taking off his makeup. I introduced myself and told him the reason for my visit. Max said he had about 15 minutes to spare before he had to leave for some voice-over work downtown.

I handed him his letter to Betsy. "Do you recognize this?"

He took the document from me, gave it a long, slow read and then handed it back. "Is this some kind of joke?" He wasn't laughing.

"It could be," I said. "What do you think?"

"If it's a joke, it's in damned poor taste. That's not even my signature."

"I know. We've matched it with your contract signature."

"What were you doing looking at my contract?" Lucian barked. "That's an invasion of privacy."

"That's a legal document, belonging to Charlie Silverman's company. He shared it with me, because he has *six more letters just like yours, from other employees. All of them men.*"

Max Lucian opened his mouth to speak, but thought better of what was about to spill out.

I pressed on. "Do you know anything about that? Seven letters from seven different guys from the cast and crew of *Ravens Cliff*? Everyone professing their love for Betsy Blake."

"Were they forgeries, too?"

"Looks that way," I replied. "And you're not in on some little game to upset the young woman?"

"Absolutely not!" Lucian spat out heatedly. "Why the hell would I do that? I like the kid. She's a little weird, but I kinda feel sorry for her, and she's a damned good prop mistress." He left the makeup table and started to climb into his street clothes.

I had a few more questions for him, mostly about the possibility of a group plot to upset Miss Blake. It was like throwing undercooked spaghetti at a wall—nothing stuck. He'd only known her for a short period of time, he liked her, felt sorry for her, even took her out for lunch one day. But no dice. He knew nothin' from nothin' about nothin'!

After Lucian split for his appointment, I mooched around and eventually found Mike Asher's wardrobe office. It turned out to be a little stall, off the side of the costume room, and about half as big as my mother's wardrobe closet back home. There was just enough room for a small desk and two chairs, occupied by Eleanor and Asher, the man who dressed the cast members.

After introductions, Eleanor did a recap of their discussion to bring me up to speed. While I listened to her rundown, I scanned the room and Mr. Asher himself.

Mike Asher was a tall man, with straw-blond hair that kept falling over his left eye; he'd shake the errant lock back and finger-rake it into place. He had bright blue eyes that kept darting restlessly about the room as Eleanor spoke; once, he caught me looking at him. I was trying to size him up, but I think he must have misunderstood me, as he slipped me a dazzling, wide-eyed smile and a naughty wink.

I turned my head and checked out a wall with numerous photos of glamorous women, each in strikingly beautiful costumes. I concluded they were creations of his from some of his more noteworthy productions.

I also figured he was either a member of the same fraternity as the stage manager and lighting technician, or he was one of those rascals who had a deceptive, fey personality that held a magnetic attraction for women of all ages. If the latter was the case, he was likely getting more action than the entire Yankees baseball team.

When Eleanor was finished, it appeared we'd hit a dead end with Mike Asher. No matter how you cut it, he insisted that he hadn't written any letters to Betsy Blake, hadn't been involved in a conspiracy to humiliate her, and hadn't heard any rumors about anyone who knew anything about such a nasty plot. He thought that Betsy was a tad strange, but harmless. She had a good work ethic, did her job well and minded her own business. With that, he flashed us what I assumed to be his trademark smile, and gave me another naughty wink. This time, I winked back, just for the hell of it.

After we left, I said, "What do you think?"

"About what?" Eleanor said, with a cheeky grin.

"Mike Asher. Is he a lady-killer or a *man*-killer?"

"Why would you think Mike's a lady-killer?"

"Those pictures on the wall. All those beautiful women."

Eleanor started to laugh like mad. Two minutes later, when she finally got herself under control, Eleanor said, "Those aren't beautiful women, sweetie. They're pictures of Mike. He's a drag queen!"

Moments later, we were standing outside the properties room of the theater and trying to decide which one of us was going to interview Betsy Blake. Both of us had come to the conclusion that Betsy was in the lead when it came to grabbing the brass ring on this particular merry-go-round. Eleanor was even going to give me 5:1 odds on it. I refused to take her on.

But who was going to interview her? Eleanor thought that Betsy would respond better to a woman, while I reasoned that I had more experience questioning suspects. To be honest, I really believed that

Eleanor had a solid argument, but I was so intrigued by the case that I tried to pull rank on her. That didn't work out too well.

Eventually, we flipped a coin, and I won. Eleanor fired off a withering look, that would have frozen all the pigeons in Washington Square park, and then marched to the dressing rooms to interview Donna Lawrence, the play's matriarch. It was almost time for the intermission.

I wrapped on the door of the props room, while considering where to take Eleanor to dinner this evening. She didn't usually hold a grudge, but my friend, Zuni Smith, always told me, "If you carry an umbrella on a cloudy day, it won't rain."

The door slowly cracked open a smidgen, and an eye peeked out.

"Yes?" a barely audible voice muttered.

I told the eye that I was a private detective, and had been hired by Mr. Silverman to help Miss Betsy Blake with a problem she was having.

The door opened cautiously, and the little voice asked to see some ID; I showed her my license. She told me to come in, but not to talk too loudly—she was having a bad headache day.

Within minutes, we were sitting around a highly polished table, and I was tempted to say, "There, that wasn't so bad, was it?" However, I resisted, and launched into my questioning.

"Miss Blake," I began, "would you please tell me, in your own words, what appears to be the problem."

At first, she took out a hankie from her smock, and proceeded, ever so slowly, to eliminate invisible specks of dust from the highly polished table. After half a minute, she launched into her story, which turned out to be very much the way Charlie had related it to Eleanor and me.

She spoke in a quiet, rather mousy way, never looking at me, always dusting the table. When she was finished, she looked up and fixed her eyes on something that was behind me and at least a yard or so to the left of my head.

After a lengthy pause, I said, "Why did you report these letters to Mr. Silverman?"

She slowly looked around the room, as if following the trajectory of a tired moth. She sucked in a slow breath, and proceeded to fold up her handkerchief into a very small square.

When it became obvious she wasn't going to answer, I leaned across the table toward her and repeated my question.

Backing away as if I were going to attack her, Betsy started to wring her hands and scan the ceiling of the room, as if the answer would suddenly appear up there.

I leaned back in my chair, gently set my envelope of papers on the table and said in a very subdued voice, "Betsy, I'm here to help you, not scare you. Please tell me why you gave the letters to Mr. Silverman."

Returning her eyes to the spot to the left of my head, she drew in another breath. As she started to unfold the hankie, she said, "They were making fun of me."

"Who, Betsy? Who was making fun of you?"

"The men. All the men that wrote those letters."

"Why would they do that, Betsy? Why would those guys want to make fun of you?"

"Because they're men," she said, as she began smoothing out the now-unfolded piece of cloth. "Men do stuff like that."

"I don't understand, Betsy. Why would they pick on you? You help them at work. You look after their props. In fact, everyone we've talked to so far says you're really good at your job."

"Doesn't matter!" she snapped, shooting a quick look at me. She glared for a few seconds, but then the anger was gone, and she was once more staring at the invisible spot beside my head.

"Don't you believe what they say in the letters?" I asked.

"Look at me," she whispered. "Just look at me, and answer your own question."

"There's nothing wrong with you," I responded. "Some people say you should comb your hair a bit, dress up more, wear some makeup. Big deal! Makeup is overrated. One of the most beautiful girls I know wears hardly any makeup at all, and she sure as hell doesn't dress up when she goes to work!"

Betsy Blake risked a quick, shy peek at me, and squeezed out a tiny smile. "Really?"

"Really." I hoped I was starting to get somewhere with her. "Why don't we have a look at these letters, and try to figure them out?" I began to haul them out of the envelope.

"NO!" she shouted. "I don't want to see them!" She got up so fast that she almost knocked over her chair.

"It's okay, Betsy. You don't have to see them, if you don't want to."

"I hate them! I never want to see them again!" She started to flail her hands around in erratic, grasping circles.

"Please, Betsy. I'll put them away, if you want." I started to put them back into the envelope, while she began walking around the room, clenching and unclenching her hands as she went. "We can forget all about them if it makes you feel better."

"You're just saying that, aren't you?" she said slyly. "You're just trying to calm me down."

"Why would I act like that, Betsy. I'm here to help you. You know that."

"No, I don't, Mr. Detective." Her voice started to get lower, more guttural; it was almost a feral growl. "The only thing I know is you're here to *trick me*. Isn't that right, Mr. Detective Man? You want to trick me!"

"There, Betsy, the letters are gone. All put away. Sit down, and we'll just talk, talk about the new show. I hear *Ravens Cliff* is a big success."

"Shut up!" she snarled. "You want to trick me, don't you? You want to get me to say *I wrote those damned letters!*"

By now, she was looking straight at me, her eyes blazing with malice and undisguised hatred. I was about to respond to her accusation, but she started to walk toward me, launching into a maniacal barrage of curses and vulgar phrases.

Standing up and facing her, I quietly said, "Perhaps we should leave it for now, Betsy. Mr. Silverman and I can come back when you're...feeling better."

She stopped. Time froze for a moment; there was dead silence. Finally, she said, "Please don't patronize me, Cass."

She was smiling, and her voice had changed; now it was soft, throaty, almost seductive. "Sit down, Cass, and we'll discuss the letters like two adults."

Professionally, I wanted to take her up on the offer. However, the tap-dance being performed by the little hairs on the back of my neck told me to get the hell out of the room. This behavior was definitely beyond the realm of normal, and I briefly thought that scenes from *Psycho* were starting to play out in this room.

"Be cool, Cass. Loosen up. Sit down. Relax." Her husky voice was that of every *femme fatale* I'd ever seen at the movies. Even her face seemed to be taking on a new mien, as she moved toward me once again.

I remained standing, wanting to grin at the madness of the situation, but my mind kept telling me: *Don't turn your back on her!*

Now she was standing in front of me. "Come on, Cass, what's it to be? Do you want to talk, or what? Maybe lie down and relax?" Her smile had become a provocative leer. "I've got a couch over in the corner. I could lock the door."

Before I could answer, she had her arms around me, and was attempting to kiss me on the mouth. I moved my head out of the way, but she started nibbling on my ear instead.

Then three things happened in quick succession.

First, there was a knock on the door. Next, I heard a *snick*—the sound of a switchblade being opened behind my back. Then, I grabbed the front of Betsy's smock with both hands, wheeled her around and slammed her on top of the highly polished table.

Betsy Blake tried to lash out with the blade, but she was at a disadvantage because of her position on the table and my arms keeping her at bay. She managed a near miss; the blade sliced the arm of my suit jacket, but didn't cut me.

I let go of her smock, grabbed her knife hand and followed through with a solid twist that must have dislocated her wrist. Through her scream, I could hear the switchblade land harmlessly on the floor beside the table.

"Betsy!" cried an older woman's voice from just inside the room. Eleanor was standing beside the woman, and the door to the properties room stood wide-open. "Betsy!" the older woman repeated. I assumed she was Donna Lawrence, the company matriarch. "What have you done, darling?"

Betsy was curled up in a fetal position on the table. She was holding her wrist and whimpering softly. Donna Lawrence crossed the room, swept Betsy into her arms as best she could, and started to speak to her as if she were a small child. "It's all right, dear. Everything will be all right."

Then Eleanor came to me. "Are *you* all right?"

"Pretty good," I said. "Pretty good, considering. But I'll tell you one thing."

"What's that, sweetie?"

"I think I'll take a rain check on seeing Hitchcock's *Psycho*."

Nodding her head, Eleanor flashed me a dimpled smile, as if to say she already knew what I was talking about.

A few hours later, we were sitting at a window table in Lindy's on Broadway. I'd given Eleanor her choice of restaurants, and she'd told me she'd been hankering for a slice of cherry cheesecake all day. Lindy's was the best, if not the easiest, choice to satisfy that particular need.

In the interval between Lindy's and the struggle in the props room, the *femme fatale* had disappeared from the scene, Betsy Blake had returned as her normal, mousy self, and her abused wrist had been attended to by the company's on-call physician.

Then Charlie Silverstein, Donna Lawrence, Eleanor and I had ensconced ourselves in Charlie's office and played a game of *Truth or Consequences*.

Donna had provided the *truth*. As *mother* of the company, she had already befriended Betsy, and discovered that the young woman was under the care of a psychiatrist. It seemed that poor Betsy had a split personality, or what the medical profession was calling *multiple personality disorder*. Betsy Blake was her normal personality, but under stress, it appeared that Betsy's other persona, the evil film noir dame, would emerge.

During our discussion, Donna argued that some of the company members were razzing Betsy, prompting the darker personality to emerge and write the letters. But to what end? That was still unclear. For pity? For an enhanced reputation? For plain old revenge? Maybe all of the above.

Unfortunately, Betsy couldn't tell, because she was not aware of her other personality. She firmly believed that the letters had come from all of those nasty men! Any deeper explanation would have to be left to her treating psychiatrist.

As for *consequences*, it was decided, and Betsy later agreed, that she would take a paid leave of absence from the company and go through more intensive therapy with her psychiatrist. Perhaps then she would discover the root cause of her malady and start on the long journey of recovery. In the meantime, she would move in with Donna Lawrence, who would mother her on a more permanent basis.

When the matter of my fee came up, I told Charlie to put it toward Betsy's paid leave. I'd already received payment enough, I said, when I discovered that Eleanor Palladino would make an excellent associate.

"Do you really think I'll be suitable?" my new associate was saying, as we sat with our after-dinner desserts in Lindy's.

"You'll have to get your license," I noted.

"No sweat. Based on my work on the Hemingway case, you already know I can handle a gun…very well."

"That's true," I said enthusiastically. "And if you get your license, I'll take you with me this fall to hunt for my long-lost father."

"Does that license also include a ring?" Eleanor asked.

"A *what?*"

"You know. Comes in a little box, fits on the ring finger of the left hand."

There was a very long pause.

"Eat your cherry cheesecake," I finally ordered.

"Yes, boss," she said, with a happy grin.

"Hmm," I muttered, and began to wonder who the real boss was going to be.

3

THE HAUNTING OF HARVEY HARDWICK

(A Cass and Eleanor Mystery)

Sunday, August 28, 1960

New York City, U.S.A.

During the last week of August, 1960, the weather in New York City was damn hot, but my friend, Charlie Silverman, the Broadway producer, had air-conditioning in his office. Happily, it was working just fine and so was Charlie. *Ravens Cliff,* his Off-Broadway show, was doing respectable business, he was two months away from opening a new comedy on Broadway, and both his daughters were heading back to university with all their bills paid. Life was good.

Then his phone rang.

A half hour later, he was mixing himself a tall glass of Alka-Seltzer and wishing his sister Rebecca had another big brother to call on instead of Charlie. To be honest, Rebecca was not a bad sort, but everything in her life had to be a Big Deal. Sorry, make that a Big Production Number, according to Charlie. He told me *she* shoulda gone into show business, and *he* shoulda become a lawyer or a brain surgeon like his beloved mother wanted. This time, Rebecca was calling because she thought her husband Harvey was having a nervous breakdown.

Right off the bat, Charlie said to her, "So, why are you calling me? I'm no psychiatrist. I'm a Broadway producer, though god only knows there's plenty of nutcases in my business!"

She gave him a blast of static over the phone, and he calmly asked her to explain what was going on. She cooled down long enough to tell him that Harvey wasn't sleeping at night, and that when he did, he had horrible nightmares—the same ones he had when he was a little kid.

Trying his best to sound sympathetic, Charlie asked his sister for details. By the time she finished, Charlie was more than a little convinced there *was* something serious going on with Harvey. The way Rebecca described the situation, it appeared he was being haunted by a childhood incident he barely remembered yet couldn't get out of his head.

Feeling somewhat embarrassed, Charlie asked her a few *delicate* questions, but she quickly let him know there was nothing *sick* or *dirty* about his memories. Respecting her sense of propriety, he dropped that line of questioning like a hot potato.

Rebecca finished her story, and Charlie told her not to worry. Her big brother was on the job, he said, and promised he'd get back to her before poor old Harvey had one more nightmare.

There was no time to lose, Charlie concluded, as he thought to himself, *It was bad enough the poor schmuck had to go through life with a name like Harvey Hardwick!*

Tuesday, August 30, 1960

Flying to Toronto, Ontario

Two days later, I'm flying out of LaGuardia, heading south for Toronto International Airport. With me are two special people—my friend Charlie Silverman, and Eleanor Palladino, my girlfriend and new associate in my private investigation agency.

They're special because Eleanor's dad and Charlie grew up together as kids, and Charlie is Eleanor's honorary godfather. Further, she and I have become more than good friends, and we'd just solved a major problem for Charlie a few weeks ago. We were able to discover what was bugging one of his employees, who was threatening to quit because she was getting too much *romantic* attention at work. You can read about the case of "Too Many Love Letters" in the book *Promises and Other Tales of White Lies.*

Presently, the three of us were flying in a Boeing 707, discussing Harvey Hardwick and his case of the screaming meemies.

"You've definitely captured our interest, Charlie," I said. "So, tell us the whole story."

"I think he's captured more that our interest, honey," Eleanor offered sweetly. "He's got us 20,000 feet up in the air. What're we going to do if we decide to turn down the case? Ask the stewardess for a couple of parachutes?"

"Darling," I calmly replied, "we've already taken the case as a favor to Charlie, as well as a chance to go up to the cottage later, and visit my mother."

"Oh, Cracker Jack!! I plumb forgot about the cottage," she said in a Southern belle's voice. "And I forgot to pack my canoe paddle, as well."

"Are you serious?" I responded.

"No, you goof. I'm just pulling your leg."

"Children, children," Charlie jumped in, "Play nice."

"Sorry, Uncle Charlie," Eleanor said. "Give us the gory details."

And he did. For the next half-hour or so, he repeated Rebecca's story, mostly for Eleanor's sake, as he'd already informed me of how Harvey had been waking up in the middle of the night, covered in sweat and hollering his head off. Some nights, he'd gotten so overwrought that he almost fell out of bed.

"According to my sister," Charlie said, "the dreams are pretty much the same. They just get repeated, over and over again.

"In them, Harvey is a little boy," he continued, "maybe five, likely a little younger. He's walking out of his house with his dad, and after some time, they come to a corner store. Harvey remembers a sign with the little Dutch Girl—the trademark for Schneiders meats—above the entranceway.

"They turn the corner and continue to walk down the street for what, to little Harvey, seems a long way. Then they arrive at a big, tall house, with windows up high and there are two front doors off a big porch."

"It's a duplex home," Eleanor suggested. "We'll be looking for a duplex partway down a street that has, or at least had, an old corner store."

"One that sold Schneiders meat products," I finished.

"What a team!" she enthused.

"And we're only getting started," I said.

"We'll have the case solved in no time."

"Then, we'll be off to Mother's cottage in the woods."

"Cottage in the woods? Goodness, I feel like Little Red Riding Hood!"

"*May I continue?*" Charlie jumped in. And without waiting for an answer from us, he continued to describe Harvey's dream.

"Inside the house," he said, "almost in front of the door, there's a long stairway going up to the second floor. Beside the staircase is a large room. There's no television, but a big, tall box, with lots of knobs and a light, softly playing music."

"It's an old-fashioned, floor-model radio," I suggested. "Likely from the 1920s or early '30s. Made of wood."

"Just what I was thinking," he agreed. "Likely a Zenith or an RCA. What do you think, Eleanor?"

"Sorry, boys. I'm much too young to go back that far."

Eleanor let loose with an unladylike giggle, I sighed, and Charlie went on with his recitation.

"In the room with the old radio, there is a young man and woman who appear to be about the same age as Harvey's father. They are very nice to young Harvey; they tell him that Daddy is going upstairs to visit a friend, and that he won't be long. Harvey's father plants a smooch on the little guy's kisser and heads up the stairs.

"The boy tries to follow, but the nice couple surprise him with a double-scoop ice-cream cone. By the time he's had his first lick or two, and turned back to the staircase, his daddy is nowhere to be seen. The stairway is empty, and the door at the top of the landing is closed.

"Time slides by. The cone is finished, the nice couple and the boy are playing a game of Snap, and everyone is happy.

"When the father comes down the stairs and says, 'It's time to go home,' the little fellow doesn't want to leave. And it's not because he's having a good time.

"'*That's not my daddy!* the little boy cries. And the screaming begins."

Tuesday, August 30, 1960

Toronto, Ontario, Canada

Many hours later, we were sitting in a richly appointed living room in the east end of Toronto. Charlie's sister had picked us up at the airport and driven across town to a two-and-a-half-story house just south of Danforth Avenue and east of Broadview Avenue. Rebecca had talked nonstop all the way, going over the same details that her brother had passed along to Eleanor and me.

Before Rebecca jumped up to start making a three-course lunch, Charlie asked her if she had any idea why little Harvey believed that the man coming down the stairs was not his father.

"It took a long time for me to discover the truth about that," she said, "but it seemed that his father's face didn't look the same anymore."

"What does that mean?" I asked.

"His face was all smooshy," Rebecca replied.

"*Smooshy?*" Eleanor interjected. "Is that a new medical condition?"

"I'm sorry," Rebecca said. "I should have said *scrunchy*. You know, all scrunched up."

"Right, much clearer." Eleanor nodded. "Harvey's father looked like he had been crying."

"Correct!" Rebecca exclaimed. "What a smart girl, Cass. Are you sure she's all Italian? Maybe a little drop of Jewish blood in the family?"

"I'm honored by the suggestion, Mrs. Hardwick," Eleanor said, with a sincere smile, "but I'm afraid not."

I jumped back into the conversation. "So, you think the father had been crying, and that scared little Harvey."

"Of course, dear," Rebecca said. "He had never seen his daddy cry before, and besides, his father's cheeks were wet."

"Well, that solves that issue," I said, leaning back into the plush sofa and stretching out my legs.

For a moment, everyone was quiet. Rebecca ducked into the kitchen to assemble lunch.

Across the living room, out in the mahogany-paneled hall, the family's old grandfather clock struck the hour. The clock's subsequent heart-beating cadence lulled us into a deeper silence.

Eventually, Eleanor got up and toured the room, admiring the framed paintings that decorate three walls. The fourth wall was home to a large fireplace, with a mantlepiece covered with family photographs.

Eleanor took down a pair of framed enlargements and studied them. When she'd finished, she looked up at Charlie and said, "There's a strong family resemblance, Uncle Charlie."

"That, there is, kiddo," he said. "The picture in your left hand is of Harvey and his dad, Weston Hardwick, when Harvey was 17 or so. The other is a shot of Harvey's grandfather with young Weston Hardwick, when Weston was about 17, as well. Strong family resemblance, indeed."

"But *you* don't look at all like them, Uncle Charlie," Eleanor observed, with a rascally twinkle in her eyes.

Charlie decided to play along with her. "True, but Harvey is obviously taking after *his father's* side of the family. Besides, even if I was Harvey's *brother*, and not his brother-in-law, I'd wanna be devilish and enhance the old rumor that went around about *me*."

"What rumor is that, Uncle Charlie?" she asked, in all theatrical innocence.

"That I was born *on the wrong side of the sheets*, my dear."

"You mean your father wasn't your real…oh, Uncle Charlie!" To her acting credit, I think she actually squeezed out a blush.

Later, after a hearty, late lunch of matzoh ball soup, braided challah bread, and a delicious brisket, we sat back down in the living room to plan our strategy to save poor old Harvey.

However, it was hard to get started, as we're all bursting at the seams from overeating. A good nap would fix that, but Charlie's sister was on the prowl.

Rebecca tried to convince us that we needed some chocolate rugelach pastries for dessert. She was greeted with dead silence. Then Eleanor saved the day, politely saying how wonderful lunch was, and suggesting that if we wait for another hour or so, we'd be more than delighted to dig into those heavenly little desserts. Rebecca was happily mollified, and sat down to join us.

Silence ensued. I don't know if everyone was thinking about where to start, or trying hard to resist the temptation to fall asleep. Eventually, I stood up and began pacing about the room. Soon, however, I stopped, turned to face everyone, and got the ball rolling.

"It's obvious that we must find out more about Harvey's childhood —his birth, where he grew up, traumatic events in his past life, that sort of thing. We also need to know more about the house where this red-letter event took place."

"Like what?" Charlie asked.

"Like where it's located, if it's still there. Who lived there at the time Harvey and his dad visited."

"Speaking of Harvey, where is he now, Rebecca?" Charlie asked.

"Oh, he walked to work this morning, dear," she said. "We're not wealthy like you are, you know. Why the taxes on this property alone…"

Charlie allowed a little smile to crease his wrinkles even more, and appeared to suppress the temptation to laugh at her plea of poverty. Instead, he asked her if she knew where Harvey was living when he was four or five, when he experienced his nightmarish events.

"Why, right here, of course," she said, as if Charlie were a little bit daft. "He's lived here all his life."

"Great!" Eleanor said. "That'll make it much easier to find the mystery house."

"Precisely," I agreed. "Now, can you tell us if the family had a car in those days?"

"A car?" Rebecca asked incredulously. "Why on earth would you want to know that?"

Walking over to the two-seater couch where she sat, I joined her, and held her hand. "Because your answer may provide a very important clue for us. You see, if they had a car, but didn't use it to drive to our mystery house, it would suggest that the house was fairly close by. We already know that little Harvey and his father walked through the streets to this house, so that would also suggest that it was close to *their* home. Now, if they owned a car *and* walked, it would *confirm* that the house was, indeed, nearby."

"Weeell," Rebecca tittered, "it *must be* close, then! The Hardwicks have always had an automobile. Harvey says the family bought one of the original Model T Fords!"

"It appears we're off to the races," Eleanor said to our hostess. "Tonight, when he comes home from work, you can tell Harvey he has nothing to worry about."

That night, after another outrageously large meal and a pleasant meeting with the subject of our visit, we headed off to separate bedrooms. Charlie got the special guest room with all the bells and whistles, while Eleanor and I got the one with the small twin beds.

That arrangement was deliberate, of course, as Rebecca was quite a stickler for propriety; she would never think of putting the young, unmarried couple in the same bed. No hanky and no panky allowed in that house, tsk-tsk. To be honest, Charlie even told me later on the QT that he wasn't too old or too naïve to figure that what can be done in a king-size bed can be done just as satisfactorily in a single twin.

Even Frank Palladino, Eleanor's father, had given him strict orders to make sure his little girl remained his *little girl*. After all, she was *only* 25 years old and Daddy's beloved princess. Never mind that after graduating from Dartmouth College, she'd spent the next two years in Sicily doing *postgrad work* with her relatives to help with her father's business—running one of the biggest crime families on the Eastern Seaboard. Perhaps she would even take it over when Frankie retired, because her older brother was a nitwit! Needless to say, during her training in Sicily, Eleanor had developed some very special skills.

If you're interested in discovering how I got tied up with the Palladino *famiglia* in general and Eleanor in particular, I would suggest you read my first two adventures, *The Death Merchants* and *The Man With Hemingway's Face*. They will reveal all.

Wednesday, August 31, 1960

Toronto, Ontario, Canada

The next morning, everyone was up early and well rested. Even Harvey slept through the night without screaming or falling out of bed. As for his visitors, Charlie slept like the proverbial log, and whatever Eleanor and I did in our monk-like cell was our own damn business, thank you very much.

Breakfast was traditional kosher. Neither Eleanor or I are Jewish, but I have to admit that I very much enjoy toasted sesame-seed bagels, kissed by lox, with a healthy slathering of cream cheese, and a touch of diced red onions. Stand well back, folks!

After Harvey went to work, we sat out in the back sunroom, drank our freshly brewed, rich, dark coffee, and divided up the day's work. Harvey had provided us with valuable background information, so we decided that I would check out the local Registry Office, while Eleanor and Charlie would put on their comfortable walking shoes and wander the surrounding streets in search of a corner building that might have been a variety store about 40 years ago.

An hour later, Eleanor and my Broadway producer friend were heading east along Dearborn Avenue to Bowden Street, and then south to check out the streets that ran parallel to that of the Hardwicks' residence. The following is my account of their morning, based on a report that Eleanor furnished when we reassembled later that afternoon.

It was a beautiful morning, not a cloud in the sky, and they were in no particular hurry. It was a fine day for walking, and the exercise didn't hurt after all the eating they'd been doing since yesterday morning.

Behind them, street noises filtered down from the Danforth, but they were almost drowned out by the cries of some angry seagulls that, according to Charlie's patented sense of humor, seemed to have missed a turn somewhere north of Lake Ontario. However, the gulls were not alone in the critter department. Two black squirrels were chasing each other around the well-manicured lawns that they passed, and Eleanor was starting to get the feeling that this just might be an early winter.

The first street they came to that showed any promise was Fairview Boulevard. They were definitely in an older part of town—the homes seemed to range in age from the early years of the century to the mid-'40s or so.

The house on the northeast corner of the street started Charlie's old heart racing a bit. It was a two-story job, with the front door at an angle facing both Fairview and Bowden. On either side of the door, and facing their respective streets, were two fairly large, display-type windows. Over the door was a partially faded sign, with a picture of the Schneiders Dutch Girl!

Eleanor gave her Uncle Charlie a big hug and a serious kiss on the cheek. They paused a moment to decide whether to bask in their success, or continue along Fairview Boulevard. There were no lights on in the place, and what would they ask the owners if they were in? *What happened to the variety store that sold Schneiders sausages?* They concluded that would be a big waste of time!

So, they decided to proceed down the street, walking west along Fairview toward Broadview Avenue. Fairview was an old street, with an eclectic assortment of houses. Some had two stories, others only one. Many were made of red brick, others of stucco and wood. Still others were wood only, painted in a variety of colors.

They checked both sides of the street as they went, looking for a duplex. Yet, as their journey got closer to the end, and they began to see the rush of Broadview traffic ahead, their optimism gradually faded.

Suddenly, Eleanor grabbed her godfather's arm, gave it an enthusiastic squeeze, and said, "There it is!"

Three or four houses down on their side of the street, sat the target house—an aging, two-story duplex. It was a wooden clapboard structure with faded green trim. There was also a lone garbage can sitting out front. They felt like they were one step closer to solving the mystery.

They made a beeline toward the house, but just as they got to the garbage can, Eleanor noticed that on the other side of their target, and slightly behind it, was another, almost identical duplex.

"*Oops*," Uncle Charlie said, or words to that effect. "We've got a complication, already."

"No big deal," Eleanor responded. "One of them has to be the place we want."

So, they headed up the sidewalk, mounted what appeared to be a newly painted set of stairs and checked out the two front doors. Charlie looked at Eleanor, Eleanor looked at Charlie, and both of them shrugged their shoulders about the same time. Eleanor decided to perform a little *eeny-meeny-miny-mo* routine, and the farthest door won. They headed down the veranda, and Charlie let his goddaughter knock for good luck.

She hammers away on the wood, waited for a good 15 seconds, and tried again. There was no answer, so Charlie hauled out one of his business cards, and stuck it between the door and the plate of an old-fashioned, skeleton-key, door handle-and-lock combination. They moved back down the veranda to the first door, and repeated the ritual. This didn't seem to be their day, so Charlie pulled out another card, and they were just about to leave it, when a voice from the sidewalk hollered up to them.

"They don't like peddlers none," the voice said. It belonged to an old man in a baggy suit that would have been in style when the duplex was first built.

"We're not peddlers," Eleanor replied in her sweetest voice.

"They don't like religious callers, either," the voice said.

"We're not religious callers," Eleanor replied. "We're investigators—looking for some folks who lived in a duplex on this street. A long time ago."

The old man paused. He looked up and down the street. Then he said, "How long ago, would you say?"

"About 40 years," Eleanor confessed.

"That wouldn't be them. The people in that place are a young, married couple. They both work during the day."

"What about the other place?" Charlie asked, gesturing to the door at the end of the veranda.

"Nope. She's not around, either."

"She work, too?"

"Not anymore. Up and died a few months ago. Place is locked up tighter'n a drunk on a Saturday night toot."

Eleanor and Charlie exchanged looks. He appeared as wilted as she felt, like that guy in the *Li'l Abner* comic strip who always had a little black rain cloud over his head.

Then the old fellow said to them, "Come on with me," and he headed across the lawn to the other duplex.

They followed him, and within 15 minutes, after a short but revealing conversation, they were on their way back to Harvey and Rebecca's home. The life and times of Harvey Hardwick were about to get turned upside down."

Meanwhile, up on the Danforth, I was working the registry offices, and was having a morning that was as electrifying as that of Eleanor and Charlie. It hadn't taken me too long to discover where the Office of Official Records was—in an old building nestled close to the main drag. I headed up its six steps, swung open the single door, and slipped inside.

The interior smelt of freshly scrubbed floors and polished, wooden wainscoting. The old globe lamps, hanging from the ceiling, appeared to have been around since the late 1800s or early 1900s. I walked under them to get to the information station, about 20 feet away to the right of the front door.

Once there, I asked the neatly dressed receptionist where I could find birth records. She pointed straight down the corridor on her right, and told me to see Mr. McConnell. I thanked the woman for her help, and headed down the corridor to find McConnell.

Two minutes later, I was sitting on a hard, wooden chair that would keep a corpse alert until the end of time. I was not alone. There were a number of other uncomfortable chairs in the waiting area, and many of them were occupied.

Having expected something like this, I'd brought along a copy of Daphne Du Maurier's novel *Rebecca*. I had seen the Hitchcock film in my early teens and fallen in love with the plot. This was my second time through the book, and I was glad I brought it with me, because the bureaucrat on the desk was being extra officious today. It was going to be a long wait.

An hour and a half later, it was my turn, and I approached McConnell's desk with *Rebecca* in my left hand. My bookmark was a $50 bill.

"May I help you, sir?" McConnell said, in a voice that remined me of the butler in that old comedy *My Man Godfrey*.

"I hope so," I said, and told him I wished to see the birth records of Mr. Harvey Hardwick, of Dearborn Street.

He asked me for Mr. Hardwick's date of birth, and I gave it to him. There was a long pause, after which he asked if I am a member of the family.

"No, I'm not," I said with exacting politeness; I've dealt with his type before. "I'm a private investigator, engaged by Mr. Hardwick's family."

"May I see some identification?" he said, his voice slipping more and more into official bureaucratese.

I dug out my license and moved it across the desk toward his folded hands. He picked it up, scanned it with annoying exactitude, gave a prissy, little sigh, and told me that it was an *American* license.

"I know," I said with a smile.

"But *American* licenses have no currency in Canada," he said, emphasizing the nationality as if it were a dirty word. Then he added, "Sir."

I decided not to tell him I have dual citizenship, knowing that would lead to a barrage of heavier sighs. Instead, I looked down at *Rebecca*. The book was facing McConnell; the $50 bill was sticking out toward me. I slowly rotated the book around so that McConnell was looking at the money.

"Is there a water fountain close by?" I asked.

The man heaved a deep sigh of feigned annoyance, pointed across the room behind me, and I excused myself for a few moments. When I got back, McConnell had disappeared. So had the money. Figuring he's snapped up the bait and retreated into the bowels of the records room, I gathered up *Rebecca* and returned to the waiting area.

Almost 15 minutes later, McConnell returned with a smug smile on his face and a piece of paper in his hand. He told me that all the information may be found on the paper, but he couldn't resist the joy of explaining the success of his research. I gave him a knowing wink, and nodded my head.

McConnell started his spiel. "Mr. Harvey Hardwick was born in the old Toronto General Hospital. He was born in 1916, and his father was Winston P. Hardwick. The mother was Margaret Agnes Browning-Hardwick." McConnell paused. His expression suggested that I should provide a round of applause.

"Thanks very much," I managed, and reached across the desk to retrieve the paper. However, McConnell had quick reflexes and pulled it back.

"There's more," he said, raising the paper to his face and reading. "It appears there was a little complication in the life of Mr. Winston P. Hardwick."

"Complication?" I said. "What does that mean, precisely? Was Hardwick already married, or something?"

"Close, Mr. Gentry. Very darn close."

"Hmm." I hummed with a slight nudge of surprise. "Who was it who said, 'Curiouser and curiouser!'?"

"I believe it was Alice from *Alice's Adventures in Wonderland*." McConnell smirked. "But it was Lewis Carroll who wrote it!"

"Indeed, he did," I said, and leaned into the desk, prepared to hear all about the so-called *complication*.

Later that afternoon, Eleanor, Charlie and I met again in the back sunroom. We were enjoying some of Rebecca's Tahini Rainbow Shortbread, along with some specialty coffee, and I don't know which was more delicious. Harvey was still away at the office; Rebecca was busy tidying up the kitchen, and starting to prepare for the evening meal.

The day continued to be warm, the sun had shifted in the sky, and Eleanor and Charlie were about to report their exciting news.

Eleanor went first, and reviewed the trip down Bowden. She described how they discovered the building with the Schneiders meats sign at the Fairview corner, and their trip to the first duplex, with no results.

When the old gentleman appeared on the scene, Charlie took over the tale and revealed how the old man ushered them over to the second duplex.

There, the story started to get interesting.

"They're almost identical," the old fellow had said, referring to the two units in his building, "and that includes the peeling paint. I've been here since I came back from the Western Front, fighting in the Great War. Moved in with my young bride in 1919."

"That's a long time ago," Eleanor remarked, with an encouraging smile.

"You can surely say that again, young lady. A fellow my age starts to slow down, runs out of juice, you know. That's why there's been no painting done for the last 10 years or so."

Charlie nodded his head in the old gent's direction, and the three of them grinned at each other. Finally, Charlie popped the Big Question.

"Do you remember being visited one night, back then," said Charlie, "by a young man about your age then? He had a little boy with him, around four or five years old."

The old fellow was silent for a moment. He was either searching his memory, or deciding to say nothing.

"Perhaps it was the other duplex they visited," Eleanor said.

After a few seconds, the old man said, "No, my friend. It was here. The man and the little boy came to my house."

I grinned as Charlie and Eleanor came to the end of their story, nodded my head as if to say, *It's all coming together.*

"What is it, Cass?" Charlie said. "What's going on in that devious, crime-fighting mind of yours?"

I reached over to the chair beside mine, picked up the piece of paper I'd brought from the Registry Office, and started to read.

I informed everybody that Harvey was born in 1916, that his father was Winston Hardwick, and that the mother was a lady named Margaret Browning-Hardwick. Charlie and Eleanor smiled and gave each other a *so-what's-new-and-exciting-about-that* look.

Then I calmly said, "As you already know, Harvey's parents were both killed during the blitz in London, in the '40s. But there's a slight complication to the story."

Eleanor and Charlie leaned forward at the same time, ready for the punch line.

"It appeared that Winston P. Hardwick was married before he married Harvey's mother."

"Are we talking *divorce?*" Eleanor piped up. "Or *bigamy?*"

"We're talking *death,*" I replied. "The first Mrs. Winston Hardwick died in childbirth, several years before young Harvey was born. Supposedly, the baby died, as well, and was buried with its mother in the same coffin."

That evening, after dinner, Harvey Hardwick was driving his new Lincoln Continental Mark II over the few short blocks to the old gentleman's home on Fairview Boulevard.

Eleanor, Charlie and I had assured him that we had a pleasant surprise for him and that after tonight, he should no longer be troubled by nightmares. Harvey was skeptical, and not a little on edge. His white-knuckled grip on the steering wheel was tight enough to choke a boa constrictor.

We'd told him only that we had found the house in his dreams, and were lucky enough to meet a gentleman who was present back then, when a little boy and his father came to visit. We didn't say that the old fellow remembered playing cards with the little boy, while his father went upstairs to visit someone.

All that Harvey could recall was being convinced that the man who came downstairs was not his father. He couldn't remember going home, and he had no idea why his father had gone to that house in the first place. He even *asked us* if we knew anything more about the visit. We answered by repeating that old chestnut: *All will be revealed.*

Further, we didn't tell him that after the three of us had met in the sunroom that afternoon, Eleanor, Charlie and I had returned immediately to the mystery house on Fairview, sat down with the old gentleman, and put all the pieces of the puzzle together. Then, we made arrangements to meet back at his house at eight o'clock that night—with Harvey P. Hardwick in tow.

At the appointed hour, we knocked on the door, the old man let us in, and introductions were made all around. Seated, I watched our new acquaintance staring and staring at Harvey. Harvey was staring and staring at the staircase that took his father up into the unknown, those many years ago.

Once or twice, the elderly gentleman shook his head, his thinning white hair fluffing about like a delinquent halo. Finally, he spoke.

"Little Harvey, here at last," he said. "I always wondered if we'd ever see you again." Tears formed at the corners of his eyes.

"You were the card man," Harvey said at last. "We played Snap or something. You and I and a lady."

"That's right," the man replied. "She was my wife. We were very young then. She's gone now."

"I'm sorry. She was very nice and gave me ice cream, I remember. That was before my father came down the stairs, and I started screaming."

There was a long silence. No one wanted to break it. Finally, I said, "I think it's time."

The old man looked up to the top of the stairs, and called out a name. The door up there opened, and a man came out of the room beyond. He paused at the top of the stairs, and then slowly began to descend.

Harvey was now standing. His face had turned deathly white, and he murmured one word.

"Father," he managed, and then slumped to the floor.

Thursday, September 1, 1960

Toronto, Ontario, Canada

"I just had the best sleep of my life," Harvey Hardwick said the following morning.

It was another bright, cloudless day, and Harvey, Charlie and I were having our morning caffeine fix in the back sunroom. Everyone had finished breakfast, and Eleanor was upstairs packing for our trip up north to visit my mother at her Muskoka cottage.

Harvey had decided to treat himself to a long weekend at home, figuring he deserved it after last night's astounding revelations.

"Man, I thought I was going to have a heart attack when the guy came down those stairs," he said. "He looked exactly like my father when I was a little kid. I could feel the blood rush to my head, and then I was falling on my face."

"I'm glad Cass was fast enough to break your fall," Charlie said, "or you would have smashed your schnoz to pieces."

"I got more than my nose to thank him for," he said. "He's the guy who found the key to the entire puzzle. If it hadn't been for Cass…"

"We wouldn't have discovered that your father's first wife actually passed away, but the baby *did not die*," I finish."

"When I learned from the registry clerk that Winston Hardwick had been married before, and that his wife and baby had died in childbirth, I followed the trail to the next level. Unable to believe that the baby had been buried with the mother, especially in the 20th century, I checked out the Office of Death Records.

"There, I discovered that the first wife had, indeed, passed away, but that there was no record of a death of any Hardwick child on that date or at any subsequent time.

"The last piece of the puzzle fell into place: the infant had lived, but because the overwrought father couldn't reconcile himself to the death of his wife, the baby was given up for adoption. A young couple, who couldn't have children, gratefully adopted the tyke, and brought him home to their newly acquired duplex.

"And that is why, a number of years later," Eleanor said as she entered the sunroom, "Winston Hardwick and his little boy, Harvey, were visiting the duplex. While young Harvey was playing cards with the happy young couple, Winston was upstairs visiting with his first son. A sad, tearful reunion for the older man."

"I guess it was those tears that scared me so much when he came down the stairs," Harvey said.

"I guess so," Cass agreed. "But I wonder if he ever saw the boy again, over the years."

"Good question," Harvey said. "Perhaps I'll ask my *big brother* this afternoon. Rebecca and I are going over for a family visit."

Ten minutes later, Eleanor and I exchanged good-byes with Harvey and Rebecca. A few moments after that, we were sitting in Harvey's new Lincoln while I leaned out the passenger side window and shook hands with Charlie Silverman.

Harvey had loaned us his wheels for the week. Eleanor and I had tossed a coin to see who drove first, and Eleanor was the jubilant winner.

"Well, guys," Charlie said, "you've come to my rescue again. I'm very grateful."

"Don't mention it, Uncle Charlie," his honorary goddaughter said. "The bill will be in the mail as soon as we get back home."

"Crumb, she's beginning to sound like you, Gentry!" Charlie said.

"Just teaching her the ropes," I said. "These rich women have to learn the value of the almighty dollar."

"Look who's talking," he shot back. "The mystery man with an unlimited pot of money." He paused. "Where does it all come from, anyway?"

"One of these times," I said, "I'm going to open a new file and find out: *The Case of the Missing Father.*"

"Sounds exciting," Charlie said. "When do you start?"

"This December," I replied, "but first, we must have a few more cases to pay for all the travel expenses."

Eleanor turned to me and said, "No, darling, first we must have this little vacation, and before we leave, there's something very important that I must get."

"What's that, honey?" I said.

"You told me there will be some canoe paddling up north. I'm informed that every Canadian voyageur had his or her own canoe paddle, and I need to get mine. Uncle Charlie, do you know where there's a sports store close by?"

"For Pete's sake, Eleanor," I moaned. "Knock it off!"

"Don't tell me to knock it off. I'm dead serious."

"No, you're not. You're just pulling my chain!"

"I am not."

"You are so."

"Am not."

"Are—"

"Children, children," Charlie interrupted. "Just say good-bye and get outta here, already!"

As we pulled out of the driveway and roared off toward Broadview Avenue, the two of us were laughing like a couple of delinquent teenagers who'd just kicked over a farmer's outhouse. However, it wouldn't be long before we were on our way up north, and to be perfectly honest, I had a strange feeling that our little vacation would be interrupted by a very unusual mystery.

4

—————

TURNABOUTS

(A Cass and Eleanor Mystery)

Thursday, September 1, 1960

Orillia, Ontario, Canada

Eleanor and I had just pulled off Highway 11 and entered the Golden Dragon Restaurant in Orillia, Ontario. It didn't take us more than a few seconds to figure out something was seriously wrong. The place was half-crowded with lunchtime customers, but there wasn't a sound in the room. No conversation, no scraping of knives and forks on plates, no music on the jukebox. The tension was heavier than four wrestlers in a tag-team match.

79

We looked at each other, and I wondered if we'd just walked onto a movie set, waiting for the director to yell "Action!" Perhaps this eatery was something out of *Invasion of the Body Snatchers,* and everyone had been turned into those zombie-like pod people.

Parking ourselves on a pair of high-backed swivel chairs along the right-hand bar, we looked around for a waiter, but no server appeared. Then Eleanor nodded across the aisle to one of the booths along the left wall, and we saw why the room was as quiet as a cemetery.

There were three men at an end booth. One of them, a little guy, was seated, while the other two stood around the table staring down at him. The seated fellow was crying.

"So, what's it to be, creep?" one of the standing guys said loudly. "You gonna get lost, or you gonna wait 'til Ronny gets out of the john and throws your freaky ass outta here?"

"But I'm not hurting anybody," the little man cried. "I'm just minding my own business."

"That's not what Ronny says," the other standing guy countered. "Ronny says you're a creep, and you *offend his sensibilities.*"

At this point, I looked at Eleanor, and we both twigged to the situation. The crying man was small, well-dressed, and spoke with a gentle, polite voice. He was an easy target for these hulking thugs, and likely had been since high school. I shook my head, while Eleanor glanced back at the scene in the corner. I imagined a tiny flame igniting in the back of her eyes.

Near the end booth, another person had joined the standing delegation. Tall and broad-shouldered, he appeared to be the dreaded Ronny of the offended sensibilities.

"What's the decision?" the newcomer asked. His voice was modulated, but clear and loud enough for everyone in the restaurant to hear. "Are you leaving, you little snot, or do I have to kick your ass outta here?"

"Come on," the little man begged. "I've just started my meal, Ronny. Can't you and the guys sit at another booth?"

"No, creep, we can't. This is our favorite booth, and you're sitting in it. So, either you pretend it's a take-out lunch and you take off with it, or you'll be wearing it as I throw your little fairy ass out the door."

At this point, two things happened in rapid succession. Ronny started to bend down to pick up the little man, and Eleanor slid off her chair and called out in a very loud, very New Jersey-accented voice: "Leave the little guy alone, shithead!"

Earlier that morning, we'd left Mr. and Mrs. Harvey Hardwick's lovely home just south of the Danforth in Toronto. Eleanor and I had flown in from New York a few days before, and just wrapped up a case to help her honorary godfather's sister, who had been worried sick about her husband Harvey. He had been having serious nightmares for weeks, and Eleanor and I got the nod to assist in finding a solution.

I confess to being smitten with Eleanor, whom I've known for a year. She worked with me on the *Too Many Love Letters* case, and did such a fine job that I decided it wouldn't hurt to have her aboard my detective agency.

What can I say? She has some special skills that come in handy in my line of work, and she comes by those skills honestly. Her father is Frank Palladino, and if you don't know who Frank Palladino is, you better not be asking the wrong people, as he runs one of the five major *families* on the East Coast. And I don't mean the *Father Knows Best* kind of families like on TV.

After Eleanor graduated from Dartmouth, she took off for Sicily, where she stayed for almost two years with her blood relatives. Thinking she might go into the family business, she prepped herself with various types of postgraduate training—if you know what I mean.

With the Toronto case solved, we borrowed one of Harvey's cars—a smooth-driving Continental Mark II—and headed north to visit my mother who was just finishing up with summer at her cottage up in Muskoka. The day was bright, warm and full of promise.

We made one stop before leaving the city. Eleanor had insisted that if she was going to do some canoeing up north, she needed to get her own paddle.

"You gotta be kidding," I said.

"No, I'm not. I'm dead serious," she replied. "It's what I've been taught."

"Horsefeathers! Who taught you that?"

"An old friend of the family. Someone very special."

"Who?"

"As a matter of fact, it was *your mother*. She told me last fall, on the way down to Miami with Ernest Hemingway."

"Hah!" I scoffed. "That's a lot of bull. She'd never say anything like that."

"Actually, what she said was, 'Love many, trust few, always paddle your own canoe.'"

"Damn, you're right," I admitted, feeling a little chastened. "She always told me that, too."

"So, if I'm not using my own canoe, I could at least use my own paddle. Besides, I can't resist messing with your head a little."

I shook my messed-about head and told her to keep driving. After all, she had won the toss to see who got to test drive the Lincoln first. So far, it looked like I was batting zero for two for the day.

"By the way," she continued, "I think because you lost that argument, you should buy lunch."

"Yeah, yeah," I said, but really thought *zero for three*.

"Where will we stop?" she asked sweetly.

"I was thinking of a place in Orillia. It's about halfway up Highway 11, has great Chinese food, and is usually very quiet."

Little did I know.

Ronny, the bully who had just been dubbed a *shithead*, slowly turned around. and menacingly muttered, "Who said that?"

"Me!" said Eleanor Palladino as she stood there in plain sight. "Are you blind, as well as a shithead?"

Ronny made a big production number out of hitching up his pants, squaring his shoulders and sticking a menacing sneer on his face. Then he clomped over to us in his highly polished Wellington boots. His two colleagues obediently followed, after repeating their leader's hitching, squaring and sneering routine. In the meantime, Eleanor moved into the center aisle and quietly waited. I sat back and shook my head.

Like the uncle said to Pat Boone in the movie *April Love*, "Showing's better than telling!"

The trio of punks stopped a few feet away from Eleanor and quietly practiced their sneers. Eleanor stood her ground as the dreaded Ronny slowly advanced toward her.

"You got a big mouth!" he growled.

"So what?" Eleanor said, and I knew she was grinning at him.

"So, you think your pretty boyfriend over there is going to protect your smart mouth?" Ronny grunted.

"Is that the best you can do, shithead?" Eleanor responded.

"Man, I'm really going to enjoy smacking you in the mouth, bit—"

"Wrong answer!" interrupted Eleanor, and promptly kicked him in his privates.

As the gasping Ronny sank to the floor, Eleanor smacked both her hands against his ears at the same time, with such force that the resulting cracking noise was heard all over the restaurant.

Ronny's eyes rolled up in his head, while his mouth shot open in surprise and pain. Eleanor followed up with a hard knee to his chin. His head jerked back so fast; I thought I could hear the punk's neck snap.

Ronny was down for the count, but his buddies—who looked like adult versions of the Bobbsey Twins with their matching black leather jackets and tight-fitting blue jeans—were moving one step closer to the action. Eleanor moved forward and made some rapid motions with her hands and arms that reminded me of my karate combat training.

The terrible twosome stopped. Eleanor remained motionless, rigid, waiting.

The two punks looked at each other, decided they should stay clear of Eleanor's hands, and quickly pulled out switchblades from their leather jackets.

I stood up. They snicked open their blades. I opened my black, summer-weight suit jacket.

"I wouldn't do that," I said. They looked over at me and saw my hand resting on the gun in my holster rig. The punks glanced from Eleanor to me, then pocketed their knives and turned back to assist Ronny.

Five minutes later, Ronny and his two bozos were history. The owner of the restaurant, Mr. Way Lem, introduced himself, thanked us profusely and took our orders. Soon, the restaurant was full of talk and laughter, and Bobby Darin was singing "Dream Lover" on the jukebox. We joined the little man at his table and introduced ourselves.

As it turned out, Eleanor and I had been correct. The little fellow, whose name was Jeffery Reid, had gone to public and high school with the three thugs, and they had, indeed, made his life one long, miserable ride. Nothing much changed after they became adults. When Jeffrey returned home to Orillia after college, the bozo brigade was there to welcome him and continue to make the little guy's life hell.

"Actually, I'm not really a gay man," Jeffery said. "I've always been small, and was brought up to be polite, quiet and comport myself as a gentleman. Ronny and his circus clowns have always taken advantage of my gentle nature."

"There's nothing wrong with being gay, Jeffery," Eleanor said. "In fact, it would be a better world if more men, gay or not, practiced being polite, quiet and gentlemanly. Just ask my friend, Cass." She had a twinkle in her eye. "He's a real gentleman, but a deadly killer."

"Really?" Jeffrey turned to me, with a touch of fear on his face. "Have you really killed people?"

"Only in the Korean War, my friend. And perhaps a few other thugs along the way."

"Goodness," cried the little man. "Are you a gangster or something?"

I turned to Eleanor, shot her a cheeky grin, and said, "Close, Jeffrey. Very close. Actually, I'm a private investigator, working out of New York City. I'm here on vacation, visiting my mother on the Lake of Bays."

"Well, I'm very pleased to have met you, Cass. And very glad that you and Eleanor came along when you did."

As the jukebox started playing Canada's own Paul Anka singing "Put Your Head on My Shoulder," Eleanor and I finished up our sweet-and-sour chicken balls, chicken chow mein and fried rice, while Jeffery Reid sipped on a Canada Dry ginger ale and picked away at his stir-fried meal. Time slipped by in pleasant conversation, as the music played and the restaurant's lunch crowd slipped out. Some folks even stopped by the booth to thank us for our intervention.

At meal's end, I gave our grateful new friend one of my business cards after scribbling on the back. "I want you to keep this, Jeffery," I said before leaving. "It's my card, and on the back is my mother's cottage phone number. If anything comes up in the next few days that needs our attention, don't hesitate to call us. We always look after our clients. Past, present and future."

"But, Cass," said the little man, staring at my card, "I'm really not your client."

"You are now, my friend."

"You look wasted away," my mother said, by way of a greeting. "You haven't been eating."

"You say that every time we meet, Maggie." I replied.

"Doesn't make it any less true."

"Nope, but why don't we start with something a little less argumentative."

"Like what?" Maggie asked, smiling.

"How about this?" I gathered her into my arms, gave her a serious squeeze and planted a loud smooch on her cheek. Maggie grimaced to suggest she didn't approve of such outward displays of affection, but she couldn't fool me or Eleanor.

"Let's sit out on the patio," Maggie said as she disentangled herself. "We can enjoy the last of the summer day."

Ten minutes later, as we lounged in late afternoon warmth, we looked over the shaded expanse of pine and silver birches, and the sparkling water below that linked boaters with nearby Lake of Bays. I was nursing a bottle of Black Label beer, Eleanor was sipping on a Lime Rickey, and my mother was treating herself to her favorite—single malt scotch. Everyone was enjoying the peace and quiet of our natural surroundings. Even the cries of an unhappy-sounding seagull seemed to blend in perfectly with the serenity of the day.

As I drifted on thoughts of my last visit here the previous autumn, I was reminded of how I'd discovered Ernest Hemingway, the famous American writer, hiding out on Bigwin Island, disguised as none other than…Ernest Hemingway. What do I mean by that? Check out my case book *The Man With Hemingway's Face* for the answer.

Meanwhile, Eleanor and Maggie were reminiscing about how the two of them had driven from New Jersey to Miami with Hemingway that fall, disguised as a family of tourists returning home from visiting relatives in the Garden State. It was a pretty exciting case, if I do say so myself, and it explains why the government of the United States was, for a time, trying to assassinate the Nobel Prize-winning author.

Maggie suddenly changed the conversation. "I'm very glad the two of you are here."

"What's up, Maggie?" I know the dear soul sometimes has a hidden agenda lurking up her well-tailored, 5th Avenue suit sleeve.

"I might have a mystery for you two to solve."

"I thought this was going to be a little vacation," I said.

Maggie smiled adorably, raised her voice a half octave to emulate a little girl's voice, and innocently cooed, "There's no law against mixing a bit of business with a lot of pleasure…sweetheart."

"Sweetheart?" Eleanor raised her eyebrows.

"That's me," I joined in. "Particularly when she *wants something*."

"Just a teensy-weensy favor," Maggie purred.

The teensy-weensy favor involved a retired scientist, Dr. Norman Middleton, who had a cottage on the point, down from Maggie's summer home. A widower, he had two adult children—a married daughter who lived and worked in Toronto, and a son who lived on the family homestead in Simcoe County. She wasn't sure what either of the adult children did for a living.

"So, what's the problem?" I asked as Maggie took a moment to light up one of her Parliament cigarettes. She inhaled, then sputtered and coughed.

"He didn't say," Maggie managed, letting out a disgusting mouthful of smoke.

I shook my head, proud that I had been off ciggies for more than a year, while overlooking that I had become a charter member of the Holier-Than-Thou Club.

"However, he knew you were a private detective," Maggie finished, with another slight cough.

"And how did he find out that little bit of information?"

"Everyone knows, darling. You're famous around here. Ever since you closed *The Death Merchants* case."

"Is that what they're calling those murders he solved?" Eleanor piped up.

"Indeed, it is," said my mother, taking another drag on the recessed cardboard filter of her smoke. "I'm so proud of him."

"Mother!" I interrupted. "Thanks for the plug, but I'd really like to learn more about this Dr. Middleton. Does he want to meet with me, or what?"

"Of course, darling. He can't wait, and he says it could be a matter of life and death."

"And I suppose you've already set up an appointment for me?" I asked, feeling my little holiday with Eleanor was slipping away.

"Naturally, darling. Tomorrow morning at 9:30."

Friday, September 2, 1960
Lake of Bays, Muskoka, Ontario

The following morning at the appointed time, Eleanor and I arrived at the summer home of Dr. Norman Middleton, a scientist who, according to my mother, has a PhD in both physics and mechanical engineering.

Once he'd welcomed us into his cottage, something out of *Town and Country* magazine, he conducted us to a solarium, which had a clear view of Lake of Bays, and then set about taking our orders for coffee. Eleanor, who was used to living in rural opulence, threw me a look of impressed surprise, while I quickly changed my mind about our host being a musty academic living in relative poverty. Wrong, dead wrong.

It turned out that Dr. Middleton had been born with a silver spoon in his mouth, as well as a wealth of brains. Once we were suitably introduced to one another, we started to indulge in some exquisite shortbread, washed down with an exotic blend of coffee. Middleton didn't waste much time in getting down to explaining his problem.

Middleton had been a lead scientist working for an undisclosed company in Canada assigned to build certain engine parts, also undisclosed.

"Before you go any farther, Dr. Middleton," I interrupted, "I have to ask you if, during your employment with this company, you had to sign a nondisclosure agreement."

There was a long pause, and then a simple, "Yes. I did."

"Then, I have to ask if you are still bound by that agreement?"

"Why do you ask, Mr. Gentry?"

"Because, if you are still bound, you may find yourself in a world of hurt if you violate the agreement. Legal hurt. Perhaps worse."

Middleton made no response.

"Okay," I said. "Let me make several assumptions, if you don't mind. First, let's suppose that you were working for a company called *Orenda*."

Middleton said nothing, but busied himself with choosing a special shortbread cookie. "Next, let us suppose that this Orenda company was making jet engines for a company called A.V. Roe."

The good doctor stopped searching for the special cookie and took a long swallow of coffee instead.

"Then, let us suppose that this Canadian company called A.V. Roe was building the world's fastest interceptor fighter jet."

"The Avro Arrow," Dr. Middleton admitted. "The CF-105. You are well informed, Mr. Gentry."

"I am, Dr. Middleton," I said, as I held the engineering scientist's steady gaze. "After my tours of duty in Korea, I spent time in Washington. I still have some special clearance there."

"Yet, you're a Canadian."

"Dual citizenship, sir. I have clearance in Canada, as well. Therefore, I, too, have to be very careful with matters of security."

I suggested that we proceed with caution, and Middleton nodded. Setting down his coffee cup, he seemed to relax somewhat. He settled back into his chair, crossed his legs, and began to speak.

"At the time the CF-105 Arrow was rolled out in October, 1957, it was the fastest, most deadly supersonic jet on the market," he said. "Nothing could touch it. It could almost reach Mach 2, twice the speed of sound, and could fly faster than 1,200 miles an hour." He paused. "It would have become legendary, if it hadn't been for international politics. I'm sure you must know something about that, if you were in Washington."

I just sat there and continued to stare at him.

"You can't say anything about that, Mr. Gentry? Or won't say anything?"

"Same thing." I muttered, and took a sip of my coffee.

Middleton only smiled, and continued with his story. "As you likely know, a year ago last February, our prime minister, John

Diefenbaker, canceled the entire program, and put 25,000 Canadians out of work. Some people say he caved to pressure from the United States, because the Arrow was a far superior jet to the American F-86 Sabre and F-100."

"To be fair," I added, "they'd all be obsolete if they couldn't adapt to warding off enemy attacks from ground-to-air missiles."

"Of course," Middleton countered, "but the Americans wanted to get their Bomarc antiaircraft missiles into Canada, didn't they?"

I laughed. "*Touché,* my friend."

Then Eleanor spoke up. "Okay boys, you've had your little pissing contest. Now, can we get down to business? Are you getting death threats, or not?

Middleton looked over at Eleanor. "Is Miss Palladino a partner of yours, Mr. Gentry, or is she just along for the ride?"

"She's a full partner, and a personal friend. Further, she has a set of skills that are equal to, if not greater than, my own. Now, if you want our help, Dr. Middleton, I'd suggest we forget about the history lesson, and get on with why we're here."

For almost a minute, the three of us sat in silence, save for the steady ticking of a classic grandfather clock that stood in the entry hall. It could have been manufactured by the Howard Miller company in the States, but it could have been any brand. They all look the same to me---old, stately and criminally expensive.

Finally, our host sighed and began. "There were rumors of the plant closing as early as the year of the rollout. Our scientific community was pretty close-knit, and the so-called *jungle drums* had been beating since the summer of '57."

"None of this was leaked to the general public," I offered.

"Definitely not, but all of us at Orenda were on edge. In fact, I was more than a little convinced that the politicians and carpetbaggers would have their way and shut us down. As a result, I started to prepare in the early months of '58."

"How so?" Eleanor said, taking more of the shortbread.

Middleton paused, made up his mind, and quietly muttered, "In for a penny, in for a pound."

"I beg your pardon?" I said, but I needn't have bothered. I knew where he was going with his story.

His wife dying of cancer in the summer of 1957 was all that it took to push Dr. Norman Middleton into violating is nondisclosure agreement with Orenda, and, in turn, the Canadian government. He took an early retirement from Orenda in the late winter of 1958, received the traditional golden handshake, and went home to start writing an exposé of what happened to the CF-105 Arrow. He had even smuggled photographs and notes about the miracle jet out of his office, in order to embellish the book and to assist his memory.

In the eyes of the law, if he were caught, he'd be a criminal, but he never considered himself to be anything but a scientist.

As well, he thought he had nothing to lose in proceeding with the exposé. Both his children were adults, his wife was gone, and he was financially well-off.

Naturally, his manuscript was going to be published by a small underground press under an alias. He hadn't decided what that *nom de plume* would be, but he wanted to have a bit of fun with it. Among the candidates were John Otherwise, Johnny Moniker and even Johan Deaf N. Bungler. I thought they were all pretty sophomoric, but secretly smiled at the last one, as the Canadian prime minister had been dubbed John Diefenbungler by his detractors.

For more than two years, Middleton worked steadily on the project. Some days, he put in in excess of 18 hours; other days, he slept and recharged his batteries. During the winter, he toiled at the family homestead in Simcoe County, often using the local library and the Metropolitan Library in Toronto to add to what he recalled. In spring and summer, he stayed at the cottage, often rewriting earlier drafts of the manuscript. Then something happened.

"Earlier this week, I got an anonymous phone call," Middleton explained. "The caller made no attempt to disguise his voice, but in any event, I didn't recognize it." He paused, and poured himself another cup of coffee before continuing. "The caller suggested that he had in his possession a recent draft of the book, my set of notes, and the photographs."

"At which point," Eleanor chimed in, "you suddenly developed a sinking feeling in the pit of your stomach."

"I'd rather describe it as that early warning sign of nausea," Middleton responded, giving her a wry smile.

"I can appreciate your situation," Eleanor said. "I'd have felt the same if somebody broke into my house and stole what could amount to my life's work."

"Not to mention the fact that what they stole is highly confidential and illegal to possess," I added. I stood up to walk around the solarium. "I suppose there was a blackmail threat to conclude this alarming phone call."

"Needless to say," the scientist agreed. "It involved a very large sum of money."

"And what if you don't pay up?" Eleanor asked.

"Simple. They send the complete package to our security service, the Royal Canadian Mounted Police, with a copy to the offices of A.V. Roe. Then, they pay me a visit to kill me, and they make damned sure my death looks like *suicide.*"

The ticking of the grandfather clock suddenly seemed louder and more ominous in the ensuing silence.

Finally, I asked, "You know for a fact that those draft papers are, indeed, missing?"

"Yes. I immediately drove back home, and checked the safe. I found it wide open, and all the papers and photographs missing."

"Anything else gone?" Eleanor inquired.

"A small amount of money and gold coins that I was hanging on to."

"How long have you got?" I asked.

"I will get another phone call tomorrow morning," Middleton replied. "He will tell me the time and place of the exchange. I have already visited the branch office of my bank in Huntsville, made the withdrawal for the ransom money, and will travel back to the homestead tomorrow after the call."

"Won't your son be there, or does he work Saturdays?" Eleanor asked.

"No, he's off on a holiday in Florida. He and some friends are staying at the Eden Roc in Miami, and then taking in some horse racing at Hialeah Park," the scientist answered.

"Does he know about the blackmail?" Eleanor continued.

"Neither of my children knows anything about it. Chris and Judi think I've been working on a history of Canadian aviation. Nothing else."

Eleanor and I exchanged glances. I made a little after-you gesture, and Eleanor said, "How would you like some company tomorrow?"

A big grin spread across Middleton's face as he offered us another cup of coffee. Who could turn down such a lovely blend, not to mention the finest shortbread since my mother was on a baking binge, back when I played with my tin soldiers on the front veranda?

While we enjoyed the goodies, Dr. Middleton talked about his family, showed us some group photographs, and bragged about how well his daughter was doing teaching graduate-level math at the University of Toronto. We *oohed* and *aahed* at the family portraits, commenting on the good looks of his son Chris and his daughter Judi. Eleanor even managed to suggest how much Judi looked like her late mother.

Back in the car, on our way home to Maggie's cottage, Eleanor said, "He sure was proud of his daughter Judi, wasn't he?"

"Yeah, and funny how he never mentioned anything about son Chris."

"I know," Eleanor agreed. "But what can you say about a grown man who wears a black leather jacket, carries a switchblade, and hangs around a shithead like the dreaded Ronny?"

Later that night, after dinner, Eleanor finally got hold of her father at the family compound near Teaneck, New Jersey. Her request was simple—order his employees at the Esprit Royale Hotel in North Miami Beach to contact their associates at the Eden Roc Hotel in Miami to find out if any guests registered there were from Ontario, Canada. One of the Canadians might be named Chris Middleton. She then provided a description of all three thugs who had made a nuisance of themselves at the Golden Dragon Restaurant.

Her second request of her father involved Hialeah Park; she wanted to know if the horses were running at this time of year. I suspected the track would be temporarily closed for the season because all three legs of the 1960 Triple Crown had been run.

It took a couple of hours to get a response, but the wait was definitely worth it.

Saturday, September 3, 1960

Simcoe Township, Ontario, Canada

By noon the following day, Middleton, Eleanor and I arrived at the Middleton family homestead in Simcoe Township. We used Middleton's station wagon because we figured it would be more familiar to our expected visitors, and didn't want to alarm them with some strange vehicle.

The homestead itself turned out to be of French rural design, built sometime during the first decade of the century. It stood in two-story splendor, rectangular in shape, and covered with a mansard roof that sloped steeply down all four sides and ended in a delicate upturn.

Above the recessed front entrance was a set of French doors, which led out onto a small, wrought iron balcony. Both the balcony and the front entrance were flanked by tall, imposing windows with wooden, shake-covered shutters.

Off to the side stood a double garage, which had been a carriage house during the early 1900s. After a brief discussion with the good Doctor, we concluded it was best to leave the wagon inside the garage, as per normal.

Once we'd passed into the homestead, Middleton gave us a tour of the house. The central hall led to a general living room on the left, a family/television room on the right, and a kitchen and dining room at the back of the house. All rooms were spacious and tastefully appointed. Upstairs were three very sizable bedrooms, a bathroom and Dr. Middleton's private den.

Inside the den stood a wide-open wall safe. On the floor, below the yawning safe, sat a rather forlorn-looking oil painting that had normally covered the safe.

We again discussed calling the police, and once more rejected the notion. Then it was time to plan for the arrival of our "guests." The blackmailer had called Middleton early that morning, and ordered him to be at the Simcoe homestead at seven o'clock in the evening. It was during our drive down from Middleton's summer home in Muskoka, we began to tell him what we'd learned. He wasn't overjoyed.

"First of all," I said, "from the photographs you were showing us at your cottage, my colleague and I immediately recognized your son, Chris, as one of three fellows who were picking on a young man in Orillia on Thursday. That, and three other clues, led us to surmise that your blackmailers are a thug named Ronny and his two companions. One of them, as I said, is your son, who may or may not be a willing participant in the theft."

Middleton sat expressionless and silent.

At this point, Eleanor picked up relating what we'd learned.

"The second bit of evidence, although not conclusive, is pretty compelling," she said. "We received information from the management at Miami's Eden Roc Hotel last night advising us that there is no person registered there who resembles your son or his two friends. We have that on very reliable, very personal authority."

Eleanor continued, "The third clue is the fact that there is no horse racing this week at Hialeah race track. Therefore, put clues number two and three together, and it would be fair to say that your son was lying to you about his little vacation in Florida."

"I see," Middleton said, in a subdued voice. "And your fourth clue would be the city of Orillia itself."

"Precisely," I confirmed. "When I realized that Orillia was also in Simcoe County, and only a few miles away from your family homestead, the picture started to become very clear, indeed."

"And how did you ascertain that?" Middleton asked.

"That was easy," I replied. "I simply asked my mother where the township was located, and she told me. She also said that you told her where you were brought up. Born in North Bay and moved to a lovely rural home in the woods of Simcoe Township, just outside of Orillia, Ontario."

"Your mother is an amazing woman, isn't she?" Middleton said.

"That she is, Dr. Middleton. That she is."

"As for Chris," Middleton added to the evidence, "he was only aware I was working on an aviation history, but he could see that I was being pretty tight-lipped about it. Never wanting to discuss it, always locking my research and writing away in the house safe."

"Further," I added, "all he had to do was wait for you to move to the cottage, and then go rooting around for the combination of the safe. Upon opening it, he discovered your project, including the photos and various drafts, and realized how important it was to national security."

"It really wouldn't have been too difficult to discover the combination," Eleanor said, "no matter how carefully you hid it. There are only so many places to hide a slip of paper. Taped to the bottom of a drawer, stashed in a plastic bag hidden in the water tank of your toilet, affixed to the bottom of—"

"All right!" Middleton snapped. "I get the picture." He took a moment to compose himself. "Let's assume the blackmailers *are* my son and his friends. How harmful can they *really* be? Would my son be a party to death threats, even if they don't mean to carry things that far?"

I thought for a moment about the scene in the Golden Dragon Restaurant, the relentless bullying and the ugly brutality of Ronny. Then I thought about the switchblades.

"I'm not sure," I admitted. "They could just be young men playing power games, and you're an easy target. On the other hand—"

"On the other hand," Eleanor jumped in, "they can be deadly serious. And, to quote a rather quaint Barbadian saying, 'You don't die---you just wake up dead!'"

Seven o'clock came and went. So did eight o'clock and eight-thirty.

By then, Norman Middleton was pretty agitated. He had been sitting in the family and television room to the right of the front door, expecting the blackmailers to arrive at any moment. By seven-thirty, he tried reading a book to tamp down his jitters, and when that didn't work, he turned on the TV. However, the only program that interested him was *Perry Mason,* which was well into its second half hour. Nevertheless, he sat blankly watching an episode that made very little sense to him.

Meanwhile, I was across the hall, sitting quietly in the living room, leafing through some well-worn *National Geographic* magazines, my Sig Sauer P210 on the sofa beside me. Eleanor was stationed in the kitchen.

Shortly before nine o'clock, the suspense came to an end. There was a tentative knock on the door. I grabbed my automatic and slipped behind the partly closed living room door. I could hear the television being turned off and Middleton heading out into the hall. The knock was repeated, and the scientist, who was now in position, opened the door.

"Chris!" Middleton exclaimed. "What are you doing here?"

"May I please come in, Father?" Chris sounded subdued. "I haven't much time, and they'll be here within the hour."

I heard the sound of boots on the hardwood floor of the hallway, father and son enter the family room, and the door close. However, I could still hear their voices.

Chris said, "I told them I'd meet them here. I told them I'd make sure the door was unlocked and the ransom would take place with no hitch."

"So, it's true," Middleton said in a low but firm voice. "You're one of them. You're going to rob your own father."

"I'm sorry, Dad. They're making me do it. They found out about me, and they're forcing me to do it, or they'll tell everyone about me."

"What have you done, Chris? What are they holding over you to blackmail me?"

"I can't, Father. I'm too ashamed to tell you."

As the silence deepened, I figured the situation was going nowhere fast, so I put my gun back into its holster, and entered the family room.

"Okay, kids," I said, "let's play a little game of Show and Tell."

Chris immediately recognized me and almost fell over. He turned to his father. "Wha—what's he doing here?" he gasped.

"Sit down, Chris," the scientist muttered, and his son collapsed into the couch. "This is Cass Gentry. He's a private detective. His mother is a friend of mine, and brought him up here to help me."

Chris's face turned very pale; he was either going to faint or start to cry. His father sat down beside the young man, who no longer resembled the cocky bully he was portraying only two days ago.

"There's nothing for you to be afraid of," I began. "I'm pretty well convinced that you've gotten yourself into a bad situation. One that you feel is almost hopeless to escape."

Young Middleton hung his head and tried to say something, but managed only a strangled croak. His father put his arm around him and tried to ease the boy's pain.

"Tell me," said Middleton, as he drew the broken young man into his arms. "Tell your father what you've done that they're holding over your head."

After a short cry, young Middleton let it all spill out. He, Ronny and the other fellow had been friends throughout elementary and high school. Ronny was the tough guy, the leader in everything they did. They often got into minor scrapes, were involved in a little theft, and beat up smaller kids and vulnerable peers who didn't measure up to Ronny's standards of being *a man.*

They went their separate ways after high school, with young Chris ending up at college. There, he discovered another lifestyle, one that didn't fit in with the norms of his old gang. Upon returning home after graduation, he found a good job in Orillia, and renewed his friendship with his boyhood chums. Everything was perfect, until Ronny discovered that Chris was gay.

"From then on," Chris continued, "Ronny was always on my case. Laughing at me, making fun of me, and even getting me to pick on other gay guys like the one you and that woman saved the other day."

"Actually, we found out that Jeffrey Reid, the little man, isn't gay at all," I said. "It's just the way he talks and behaves. We assured him that in our books, there's nothing wrong with being gay."

"You're kidding." Chris smiled and started to perk up a little.

"Not at all. It might not be a popular sentiment in 1960, but a time will come, Chris, when being gay will be accepted in our society. Frankly, there are communities of gay folks, today, living in Toronto, New York and other large, urban centers."

Chris started to weep again, his shoulders shaking with emotion.

His father comforted him as best he could, saying that he understood his predicament, and forgiving him for breaking into the safe and stealing the documents and manuscripts.

Suddenly, someone began to knock loudly at the front door and rattle it vigorously.

"Holy crap!" Chris cried out. "I forgot to leave the door unlocked!"

"Never mind," I ordered. "I'll get it."

With that, I quickly crossed to the hall door and opened it so fast that the other Bobbsey Twin, standing there alone, had no time to react. When he saw me, he made a feeble attempt to raise the gun he was carrying, but he wasn't nearly as ready as I was.

With my right hand, I seized his neck under the chin, while at the same time grabbed his gun hand around the wrist with my left hand. I dragged the punk into the hall, keeping a strangling grip on his throat. Then I forced his wrist downward and slammed the gun hand against the wall several times; the gun flew out of his grip.

I immediately spun him around to my left, smashing him into the wall with my hand still around his neck. As he sputtered for breath, I drove my left fist into his right side, over and over again until there was no breath for him to expel. Only then did I let up the pressure on his throat. As he started to sag to the floor, I gave him a sharp knee to the groin.

Kicking the door closed, I was bending down to pick up the punk's gun, when my attention shifted sharply to the other end of the hallway. There stood Ronny, with one arm around Eleanor's neck and his other hand holding a gun to her head.

"Guess who I found hiding out in the kitchen?" he said.

I shrugged my shoulders a few times, trying to stay loose while weighing my options.

"Yeah, buddy, who's the *shithead* now?" he continued, with his patented, loopy smirk. "Here's me, sneaking into the kitchen from the old cold-cellar entrance out back, and what do I find? Little Miss Bigmouth hanging around in the dark. So, what do you think I should do with her?"

Looking at Eleanor, I shrugged one more time, then shot her a look that said, "Do you want to do it, or should I?"

In response, a beatific grin spread across my partner's face. Then Eleanor went into action.

Late the following morning, we explained to Maggie how father and son had been reunited, and how we had let Ronny and his fellow goon off the hook in exchange for their promise not to pick on vulnerable people like Jeffrey Reid and Chris Middleton. My mother asked how we were going to *police* the bad boys' behavior, from New York City.

"With much difficulty," I said. "There will always be thugs in the world. The best I could do was give my card to Jeffrey and Chris, with a promise to stage a return engagement if trouble started up again. And I'd bring Eleanor with me for good measure. The threat of Eleanor seemed to have some effect on them!"

Maggie laughed, then said, "Tell me again, Eleanor, how you got away from that Ronny person."

"I simply told him, as he had me around the neck with a gun to my head, I had enough of his crap calling me the B-word," Eleanor said.

"Naturally, he started to use it again, so I kicked his shin as hard as I could with the back of my foot. At the same time, I slipped straight down to the floor as he cursed and hopped around on one foot. While I was down on the ground, I kicked up into his stomach. and when he was deciding which hurt more, his gut or his shin, I rose up like Venus from the shell and drove a straight-arm punch into his throat."

Eleanor continued, "By the time he finished gaging and coughing, I had his gun in my hand, Cass had taken possession of all the black-mail documents, and we had given the terrible twosome our farewell address. As they drove off into the moonrise, we had a nice little family reunion, and discussed what Dr. Middleton was going to do about his book."

"So, what did Norman decide to do?" Maggie asked.

"He's going to cool it for a little while," I said. "Take a bit of a break. Do some fishing, some boating, go out to Bigwin Inn, have a nice dinner."

"Ooh, that sounds lovely," Maggie declared.

"If you play your cards right," Eleanor added, "maybe he'll ask you to join him."

My mother blushed ever so slightly, and quickly changed the subject. "What are you two planning for the remainder of your visit?"

"Maybe a little boating, try to get the last of the summer sun," I said. "Perhaps a trip over to Bigwin Inn, ourselves, and have a lunch or dinner."

"Don't forget the canoe," my mother interjected.

"That's right, Maggie," Eleanor said. "I've even brought my own paddle."

"Good girl," Maggie said. "Don't forget what I taught you: Love many, trust few—"

"Always paddle your own canoe!" Eleanor and I chimed in together.

5

———

HALLOWEEN DEATHTRAP

(A Cass and Eleanor Mystery)

Tuesday, October 18, 1960

I was enjoying a peaceful autumn morning thinking about Halloween. I'd just finished a second cup of coffee, and was reading a collection of short stories that tickled my interest in the season of ghosts and goblins.

The coffee was a traditional Moroccan dark roast and the collection was by Washington Irving. The tale that held my attention was "The Legend of Sleepy Hollow," which I'd read at least two dozen times. I'd also seen the Disney version about Ichabod Crane many years ago in my youth. I'd always been a sucker for Halloween.

Then the phone rang. If I could have foreseen the future, I would have ignored the damned thing.

The call was from Archie Kohl, a penny-ante crook who hung around Manhattan's Greenwich Village, near Washington Square. With the help of a couple of dim-witted gunsels, he emptied the wallets of unsuspecting NYU students, providing them with drugs and women for a very short ride to Neverland.

Kohl wanted to see me as soon as possible. He sounded scared—genuinely scared. Frankly, I don't take jobs from creeps who operate outside the law, but Kohl projected such raw fear that I started to waver. Stupid me.

"You gotta help me, Gentry!" I sensed he was near tears, and I could almost see snot dribbling from his nose as he tried to plead his case.

I mustered as little enthusiasm as I could. "What's the problem?"

"They're gonna kill me!" Kohl blubbered.

"Who's going to kill you?"

"I don't know, man. They've already killed Rick, shot him from a car last week as he was leaving a movie theater." He paused and sniffed. "Then, last night, they knifed Jamie as he was coming out of the Green Tiger, down near the docks." With that, Kohl stopped talking, and took a long, hiccup-punctuated breath.

"So, what do you want me to do, Kohl?" The answer was obvious, but I asked anyway to give myself time to think up a good excuse to tell him to take a hike.

"Like, what do you think, man?" he whispered. "They killed my two guys, so who do you suppose is next on the menu?"

"That would be *you*."

"You got it! That would be me, and I need protection."

"Sorry, Kohl. I'm already working on a case."

"Please, Gentry. I'm begging you! I've got money. I've got lots of money. Just name your price, man."

I didn't need the money, but let a long moment pass without saying a word. I could hear Kohl sniffing and snorting on the other end of the line, and I guess I felt sorry for him. He said *please* several more times, and like a dummy—an amateur dummy, at that—I finally told Kohl that I'd meet him and hear the whole story. There had to be a lot more to Archie Kohl's woes than he was letting on.

His gratitude seemed truly heartrending, but I still didn't know whether to believe the creep. Then, he informed me that he'd gone to ground at a motel in the Lower East Side. He gave me the address and room number, and set a meeting time for eight o'clock that night. I looked up the location later, and found it to be close to a sleazy area near the East River.

As I hung up the phone, I shook my head. I was a jackass for even agreeing to see the guy, let alone hearing him out. In the end, I decided to have another coffee and discuss the situation with my friend and mentor, Zuni Smith.

Willard "Zuni" Smith, a full-blooded member of the southwestern Zuni First Nation, had been my combat instructor during the Korean War. We'd become good friends, and after the conflict, he joined me in my double apartment in Greenwich Village, just west of Washington Square. His preference was to become my majordomo and run the household for me; my preference was to retain him as a friend and confidant. Combining the two jobs made a successful relationship.

That afternoon, we were discussing the possibility of my taking on Archie Kohl as a client, when we were interrupted by the street-level door buzzer. The visitor was Stuart Montgomery, my art collection guru, who owns *The Golden Palette,* a modest but high-end art gallery.

I buzzed him up, and soon the three of us were sitting in my den.

Montgomery is a tall, rake-thin, British expatriate who looks like the film actor David Nevin and speaks with a slight upper-crust British accent. He has become a trusted friend.

He handed me his latest addition to my personal art collection. "You're going to like this one, Cass."

I knew I'd like the new offering, as Montgomery has never steered me wrong, and had provided me with a number of excellent works. My hobby is collecting original art used to illustrate classic novels or movie storyboards. In the past, he'd help me acquire originals from such books as Anthony Hope's *The Prisoner of Zenda*, Dickens' *Bleak House* and Baum's *The Wonderful World of Oz*.

Quickly unwrapping the package, I was delightfully surprised to discover a storyboard print from the 1949 Disney movie *The Legend of Sleepy Hollow*, featuring the Headless Horseman seated on his black stallion and carrying a fiendishly grinning jack-o'-lantern. To top it all off, the piece was signed by the original artist, Mary Blair.

"This is fantastic!" I enthused. "Where did you find it?"

Montgomery only tapped the side of his nose and gave me a sly wink.

"Okay." I smiled. "Let me ask you another question."

He spread his open hands in my direction, as if to say, "Help yourself."

"What are you doing here at this time of the day? Who's minding the shop?"

"That's two questions," he said, in his dry, British manner. "Nevertheless, I'll answer both. I've left my assistant, Gloria, in charge."

Then he paused. "I have something to tell you two gentlemen."

Mr. Smith and I exchanged glances. I settled in, expecting to hear about something more serious than art delivery. Mr. Smith inquired if we'd like some coffee, or something more stimulating.

"I think my information will be stimulating enough," Montgomery began. Then he proceeded to tell us what had happened to him last night at his shop, shortly before he put out the Closed sign.

When he went to lock the door, two thugs forced their way into the shop. One of them secured the front door, while the other drove a solid punch into the pit of Montgomery's stomach. Before he could throw up, the intruder hustled him into the office, pushed him into the desk chair, and began a short but not so sweet lecture. Luckily for Gloria, it was her day off.

The theme of the punk's dissertation was Montgomery's desire to sell *The Golden Palette*. The shocked art dealer said that he had no intention of selling his business, whereupon the second guy delivered a resounding slap to the side of Montgomery's left cheek that almost knocked him out of the chair. Then, he was told that he had less than 48 hours to consider their offer.

"Or what?" Montgomery had gasped.

"Or we burn the place down!" the stomach puncher had said. "With your dead body inside."

For a few seconds, the only sound in my den was the ticking of an Astonia American mantle clock. Then Zuni Smith broke the silence. "Did they give you any idea why they want the shop?" he said.

"Not a word," Montgomery muttered. "They just said they were representing a party that wanted the business, had all the necessary papers already drawn up, and if I didn't sell within 48 hours, I'd be a smoldering corpse inside a blazing building."

"Did they give you a time for this transaction?" I asked.

"They just said 48 hours."

I looked over at Mr. Smith, who nodded, almost imperceptibly. "We'll be there," I promised. "The entire day, if necessary."

Stuart Montgomery sat back in his seat, sighed in relief, and noted that the Disney print was a gift of his gratitude.

I reminded him of Yogi Berra's dictum about nothing being over 'til it's over, while Mr. Smith got up and silently slipped into the kitchen. He returned carrying a tray with three glasses and a special bottle of Aberlour single malt whisky to seal the deal.

Later that night, just before I went out to meet Kohl, Stuart Montgomery phoned to tell me that while he'd been here, the thugs had returned to *The Golden Palette* to remind him that he only had 24 hours to sign the transfer papers.

They were a little disappointed to have missed him, but were delighted to meet Gloria. They took her into the office to deliver a more dramatic message. The bigger of the two punks beat hell out of her. Montgomery would be running the shop by himself for the next little while.

Shortly after 8 p.m., I pulled up in front of Kohl's Lower East Side motel. I parked my '57 Jaguar XK-140 beside the only other two cars in the lot, locked the doors, and zipped up the tonneau cover. I scouted around 'til I found the correct room number on the second floor.

As I'd figured, the place was a bit of a dump, but I felt secure. I'd strapped on my gun and holster rig before leaving the Village.

After rapping on the door, I waited in silence. No response. I knocked again, and after another long pause, I tried the door handle. Just like in the movies, the door swung open easily.

I pulled out my Sig P210 automatic and stepped inside. The room appeared to be a regular, low-rental motel room—plain and simple, complete with washroom, dresser, television, a few cheap pictures on the walls, and a bed.

An old Gene Autry movie was playing on the television, the pictures were hanging slightly askew, and the bed was occupied. Figuring Kohl had drifted off while waiting for me, I walked over to him and gave him a shake.

He grunted something that sounded like, "Leave me alone." I shook him again, more vigorously this time, and he responded with a garbled order that told me what I should do to myself.

Knowing that was a physical impossibility, I squeezed out a wry smile and started to give him a more vigorous cue to wake up. It was then that I got smacked one hell of a blow on the back of my head, and I descended into a rush of ink-black nothingness.

When I came to, I had a skull-numbing headache, and my eyes quickly slammed shut. Yet, in that split second of wakefulness, I realized I was no longer in the motel room.

I was sitting in a jail cell.

Wednesday, October 19, 1960

"Well, Howdy Doody, kiss my patootie!" It was a familiar voice, one that I hadn't heard in more than a year. "Daddy-o, I always knew you'd end up in the can!"

"Why's that?" I grumbled, as I slowly sat up from the bed. It was next morning, and I felt like yesterday's garbage.

"Easy deduction, man." He smiled as he smoothed his hair down over his forehead. It was one of Inspector Danny Mullen's trademarks. "The way you hang with gangsters and dead bodies, man, it just stands to reason."

Mullen is a New York City cop, who talks and dresses like a West Village beatnik. Recently, he'd been working on an exchange program with the Ontario Provincial Police up in Ontario's Muskoka region. There, we'd met and worked together on a series of murders, in what I'd tagged as *The Death Merchants* case. From my experience, he was a very good cop.

While one of the officers opened the cell for Mullen, I slowly shook my head as I checked out my guest. It was always beyond my understanding why his bosses allowed him to switch a suit, shirt, and tie for a pair of dark, stovepipe pants, matching jacket, and turtleneck sweater. It might have had something to do with his professional efficiency, or maybe he had some kind of pull from upstairs—and I'm not talking about the guy who operates the Pearly Gates. But who knows? I was happy to see him, even though I would never admit it to him.

"So, are you here to let me out, Mullen, or do you just want to stand there and make me feel like a donkey's ass?"

While the turnkey locked up, I nodded for Mullen to take the only chair in the cell. He did, smoothed down his hair again, and we sat shaking our heads at one another for a few seconds.

Finally, I said, "What are you doing here? I thought you were up in Muskoka, writing out traffic tickets."

"That gig is gone, man. Like Elvis' hair, when he joined the army. I'm back in the city. Reassigned to the 5th Precinct."

"Congrats, Inspector," I said, trying to be a little hospitable. "That place has history."

"Right on, *amigo*. Established in 1881, it's one of the oldest in the city. And by the way, chum, I don't have the title *inspector* anymore. Here in the U.S. of A., that would have put me in an executive position. I only wanted to do what I do best—being plain old *Detective* Mullen."

Smiling at his history lesson, I rephrased my question. "Why are you here?"

"Long story, man!"

"It seems I have the time," I said, looking around my cell.

Here's what he told me.

The night clerk of Kohl's motel having heard a pair of gunshots in the vicinity, decided to investigate. He found one of the room doors wide-open, and an unconscious man lying on the floor with a gun in his hand. The rest of the room was empty, but on the bed, there was a significant amount of blood.

The clerk rushed back to the office, reported his findings to the cops, and was told to return to the room, touch nothing, but make sure that the man was still breathing.

Within minutes, a police cruiser arrived, accompanied by an ambulance, a detective, and several uniformed officers. One of the officers accompanied the clerk back to his office and took down his statement. The clerk said there were only two other rentals that night, both couples of legal-consent age, lodged at opposite ends of the ground floor.

Upstairs, ambulance personnel checked the body for life signs, and concluded that the man was still alive, but possibly suffering from a concussion, judging from the lump on his head and the trickle of blood around it.

Meanwhile, the police detective and the other cop concentrated on the gun. The detective figured there was something hinky about the weapon. Its positioning seemed awkward, staged.

Less than 10 minutes later, the body—identified from papers in his wallet as being Cass Gentry, Private Investigator—was on its way to the hospital, accompanied by one of the cops. Following an examination by an overworked doctor on a busy night, he was declared to be okay for transportation and was summarily shipped off to the local cop shop. He was pretty groggy, and slept most of the way before being deposited in a precinct cell.

At the same time, the detective and the other officer had made several discoveries of interest.

"There were two reported shots," Mullen said, looking me straight in the eye. "One of the bullets was found buried in the wall over the head of the bed. The other one was found under the bed, lodged in the floorboard directly below the blood on the bedspread."

"What happened to my gun?" I asked.

"Carefully placed, with rubber gloves, in a plastic bag," Mullen explained. "The discharged bullets were placed into two other bags. They've gone to the lab for analysis, along with a sample of the blood found on the bedspread. The cops also performed a down and dirty paraffin test on you."

I mulled over what I'd just been told, remembering my phone call from Kohl, our arrangement to meet, and the few moments I'd spent there before the lights went out.

"Hey, man!" Mullen interrupted. "Are you interviewing your brain, or what?"

"Ever hear of a hood named Archie Kohl?" I said, snapping back into the present.

"Punk," Mullen said. "Small-time operator. Hangs around your neck of the woods hustling drugs and hookers. Runs with a couple of gunnies who think their tough."

"Not anymore. According to Kohl, they got iced, and he was next on their hit parade."

"Do tell," Mullen said.

As he crossed his legs and picked at something invisible on the knee of his stovepipe pants, I gave Mullen a miniversion of Kohl's phone call, his pleas for help, his blubbering and snot-blowing, and my final mistake of agreeing to meet him at the motel dump.

"Dumb move," Mullen said, as he manicured his pant leg.

I continued to recite my tale of woe—the unlocked door, drawing my gun, Kohl's zonked-out body on the bed, and his mumbled reluctance to indulge in adult conversation.

"Was he drunk?" Mullen asked, looking up from his knee.

"Hard to say. I didn't smell any booze, but I didn't stick my nose in his face. It could have been drugs. I really didn't have time to learn anything else."

"Why's that?"

"Maybe because somebody tried to hit a home run using my head for the ball!"

Mullen smoothed down his hair again, and related a few interesting tidbits of his own.

My gun really didn't appear to have been held in a normal position. If someone had been slammed in the head with as much force and remained unconscious as long as I had, the gun would have flown out of his hand, or the victim would have squeezed it with such force, because of the blow, that he'd still be gripping it when the cops investigated.

"Instead," Mullen said, "your mitt was loosely covering the rod, like it'd been carefully placed in that position."

"Has it been checked for prints, other than mine?"

"No results yet. Should get them back from the lab soon. Then, there's the bullet in the wall. That's also weirdsville."

"How do you mean?"

"The bullet hole was high up on the wall. I remember Kohl being a little punk, an inch or so under average. Even if the shooter was trying for a headshot, the vic would have been seven feet tall! This was more like a warning shot."

I thought about the whole situation for a minute—the unrealistic gun placement, the hole in the wall, the murdered body on the bed. "Like you said, it's all kind of bizarre!"

"I said *weirdsville*, dude. Not *bizarre*. There's a difference."

"You're kidding," I said.

"No way, *amigo*." He shook his head. "Big diff between the two! *Bizarre* means strange, something very unusual. *Weirdsville*, on the other hand, means wrong, out-of-place, something that makes a dude feel like saying, *'No way, man. This ain't right.'*"

I was about to protest the overlap of meanings, when the turnkey interrupted us. He unlocked the cell and told me I was free to go, but that the captain wanted to see both of us in his office. Pronto.

After collecting my personal belongings, Mullen and I were sitting in a couple of hard, wooden chairs in front of the captain's desk. His office was about as uninviting as the damned chairs. The walls were decorated only with a few framed photographs, a banner with the precinct number emblazoned on it, and a picture of President Dwight Eisenhower.

As for the man, himself, Captain Luis Botero was a big guy, well over six feet, with broad shoulders and clean-shaven. He wore the look of a man who hadn't slept in more than 48 hours.

On the way to his office, Mullen informed me that Botero had come out of one of the toughest Hispanic ghettos in the city, managed to complete his Grade 12 studies at night school, and realized a boyhood dream by becoming a cop before he turned 23. Intelligent, hardworking and street-smart, he rose through the ranks, and before he was 42, he'd made captain.

"Thanks to my counterpart in the West Village, Gentry got himself a glowing recommendation." Botero's voice was low, authoritative, no accent. "Captain Stewart thinks you're the best private dick in the Village, the entire Washington Square area."

I gave him a nod of thanks, and he kept on going. "Did you used to work for Stewart, or do you pay him a monthly retainer to keep your reputation gold-plated?"

I cracked a smile, but said nothing. I'd known Captain Grant Stewart for quite some time, and we'd worked in concert on a couple of cases over the past few years. Born in Scotland, he worked as a constable in Edinburgh before migrating to America, and starting a new career in Midtown Manhattan. There, he worked his way up the ladder to head his own precinct. I was grateful for his support, but right now, all I wanted to do was get the hell out of Botero's office and stand for 20 minutes under a warm shower.

"Of course," Captain Botero continued, as he turned to Mullen, "this detective's assistance didn't hurt at all. When he arrived, we received a full background report on you, and although he made a few wisecracks along the way, we were almost convinced you weren't the killer."

"Almost convinced?" I said.

Mullen cleared his throat, and Botero wiggled his right hand in a *comme ci, comme ça,* gesture. "Nobody's perfect, Gentry." He squeezed out a small smile. "But there doesn't appear to be any tangible proof that you're guilty of a crime."

"Why's that?"

"No body, no blood, no prints on the gun."

"That's crazy," I said, more than a little surprised. Mullen was right: something weird *was* going on.

"The last thing I remember," I continued, "is looking down at my client's body on the bed. He was muttering nonsense, but he was very much alive. At the same time, I was holding my automatic in my hand. My prints would've been all over the thing."

"Nope. The lab report just came back," Botero said, picking up a piece of paper from his desk and handing it to me.

A quick glance at it confirmed the captain's statement. The automatic was as clean as Old Mother Hubbard's cupboard.

"Whoever whacked me over the head, must have wiped off the entire surface of the gun. What about the paraffin test?"

"Negative," Botero said. "You weren't holding the weapon when it was fired."

"And the bullets?" Mullen jumped in. "Did they match up to Gentry's piece?"

"Yes. Both of them. And his weapon had been fired very recently."

Mullen cleared his throat. "If there were no prints on it, we can't prove that Gentry pulled the trigger."

"Precisely," Botero agreed. "Besides, there are other anomalies about the shooting. The bullet in the wall was too high up for the vic. I've had dealings with Kohl before, and he was a little punk. So, it must have been a warning shot."

Botero shuffled some of the paperwork in front of him. "But why do you fire a warning shot if you're going to kill the guy?"

Mullen and I exchanged glances.

"What about the bullet in the floor, under the bed?" I asked.

"Also an anomaly," the captain replied. "Chances are it wouldn't have passed through the vic, and on through the mattress and into the floor. As both of you know, it would more than likely have hit bone and rattled around inside the body."

"You said there was no blood," Mullen offered. "Yet, when I arrived this morning, last night's report differed. It said there was plenty of blood."

"That's right, Detective. There was blood, all right."

"So, what's the punch line?" Mullen asked.

"It was pig's blood!"

Fifteen minutes later, I had retrieved my weapon, and we were on our way back to pick up my car at the motel. Mullen was driving his dark blue '58, Chevy Bel Air. It was a modest-looking hardtop, but had a very big motor under the hood and a top-of-the-line radio inside.

The sweet and swinging sounds of the Dave Brubeck Quartet were compliments of his favorite jazz station, the same one I play, WKCR out of Columbia University.

"You recall talking about this music when we met a couple of summers ago?" I asked.

"Sure do, man. I thought you were sucking up to me, pretending you were a jazz enthusiast. Do you remember the title, or was that just a lucky guess?"

"No guess, my friend," I replied, as we turned into the motel's depressed neighborhood. "Almost his signature piece, 'Take Five' appeared on his album *Time Out,* and was written by the quartet's sax player, Paul Desmond."

Mullen took his right hand off the steering wheel, performed his hair-smoothing ritual, and gave a little throat-clearing chuff.

"Desmond also wrote 'Blue Rondo à La Turk,'" I continued. "He was inspired by—"

"I know, already," Mullen interrupted. "It's the friggin' time signature of the music! So, you're a jazz enthusiast! Big deal!"

Having ticked him off for the first time in our relationship, I shook my head and changed the subject. "May I ask you a simple question or two?" I said, barely disguising my sarcasm.

He grunted something that sounded like a *maybe*, and I fired off the first one.

"Back in Botero's office, I noticed that his precinct pennant wasn't your precinct's number."

"Well, bingo!" Mullen grunted. "I'm at the 5th, precinct, like I told you, dude. We've just left the 7th!" He pulled into the motel's lot and parked beside my Jag.

"So, my second question is, why would the cops know we were friends and you could vouch for me? I still thought you were up north near my mother's summer cottage."

"Easy-peasy, man. When you were unconscious, the detective in charge went through your wallet, found your PI ticket, and among other things, there was my old Ontario Provincial Police business card.

They called up north, discovered I was transferred back to Manhattan, and eventually, I got rousted out of bed to come and cover your ass. Cool with that?"

"Cool!" I offered him my hand. "And I'm damned glad you're here."

He skinned my hand, palm to palm, and we got out of his car.

The rest of the lot was empty, but, more importantly, the tonneau cover on my Jag was still in one piece.

"Natch!" Mullen said, when I expressed my surprise. "The guys from the 7th gave the night manager the word from the herd—keep an eye on your wheels, or they'll bust this dump for running a whorehouse."

I walked around my car. Not a scratch. As Mullen joined me, I unzipped the cover and reflexively checked my pockets for the keys.

"Lose something?" Mullen dangled them in his hand."

I suggested that he was a lower portion of the human anatomy, and he suggested that I was an amateur detective. I had a snappy comeback, but decided to thank him for his assistance, instead. We shook hands, for real this time, and we agreed to a breakfast meeting tomorrow at my greasy spoon in the Village. I'd buy.

Tonight, I had some serious business to attend to uptown. I had to deal with a man or two about the sale of an art dealer's gallery. There was also the matter of a woman named Gloria who'd received a severe beating. Someone would pay for that.

Later, after having brought Zuni Smith up to date on my adventures in the slammer, we discussed the various components of my experience in the motel.

"Given the weird stuff we have in this particular case," Mr. Smith said, "I'd suggest we're missing a few pieces of the puzzle."

"Tell me about it," I said. "It seems that the gamemaster is missing a few bits, or the guy is using pieces from another game."

Mr. Smith thought about that for a few moments before breaking the silence.

"What do we have?" he quietly began. "You get a call for help from someone who doesn't want to speak with you when you meet him. Then there's a theoretical body in the room that doesn't exist."

"A pool of blood where the body was lying," I added, "but no body. The kicker is that the blood that was there wasn't human blood."

"A bullet is found in the floor, below the pig blood where the body should have been."

"Another bullet is in a wall, nowhere near where the body *was* located, but far too high on the wall to match the height of the supposed victim."

We sat quietly as Zuni Smith's voice faded away.

Eventually, I broke the silence. "Let's suppose the bullet in the wall was not intended for human consumption. Let's say it was a warning shot."

Mr. Smith thought about *that* for a moment longer. "Let's say *all* the pieces of the puzzle *combined* to provide a warning shot."

"If that's the case, Mr. Smith, my client wasn't in any danger at all. He was a pawn in a larger scheme to lure me to the motel."

Silence engulfed the room once more. Then I snarled, "So *I* was the object of the entire exercise!"

"Makes perfect sense," Zuni Smith agreed. "*You* were the target."

Checking my watch to see how our time was for the rendezvous at Montgomery's gallery, I stood up and started pacing the room.

"The problem with that theory," I said, "is why did they knock me out? Why didn't they kill me when they had the chance?"

"Because they didn't want you dead. They didn't even want the cops to think that you fired the gun."

"Of course!" I snapped. "That's why they wiped all the prints off the gun. That also explains why they left my hand resting on the weapon, instead of forcing it into my hand while I was unconscious."

Zuni Smith summed it up neatly: "They performed the whole charade as a warning, Mr. Gentry. A warning that they could get to you any time, any place, and anyhow they wanted!"

Moments later, I was thinking about what Mr. Smith had said while I changed into a fresh set of my usual clothing. My girlfriend, Eleanor, who is also my business associate, once called my clothes a *uniform*. I guess she's right, as I usually wear an outfit consisting of a Brooks Brothers suit, Rene Lacoste polo shirt and imported Dolcis Vincenza leather slip-ons. Everything is black, solid black. And I have numerous sets of the entire ensemble.

The only exception would be a formal occasion tuxedo.

That may seem a little *bizarre* to you, not to overuse the word, but I made a conscious decision about my wardrobe a number of years ago. Black is always serviceable and always in fashion. Furthermore, it takes me no time to make up my mind each day as to what I'm going to wear.

As Mullen would say, *easy-peasy*.

By 4:30 p.m., I was dressed, fed, and driving uptown in Zuni Smith's '57 Ford Thunderbird. He's very proud of the vehicle, an acknowledgement of his heritage. There were no worries about expense, due to his army pension, and, further, I treat him well in the wallet department. We didn't need to toss a coin to see who'd drive on this assignment.

We headed up Broadway until the traffic started to get too heavy, then cut over to Madison. Traveling at a moderate speed, Mr. Smith tooled up Madison and then hung a right on East 76th, where we cruised until we got close to the gallery.

While I'd been holidaying in the 7th cooler, Stuart Montgomery informed Smith that the meeting between the creeps and himself was set for 8 p.m. He was ordered to be there and not be seen with someone who drove a black Jag XK-140.

That information gave us plenty of time to arrive and get set up at the gallery. It also told me that the bad guys knew about Montgomery's association with a PI named Gentry.

Forewarned is forearmed.

The Golden Palette is located on East 76th Street, between Madison and Park avenues. Although not a large gallery, it is ideally located, and sufficiently roomy for monthly exhibits of up-and-comers. It is also the temporary home of some very fine pieces of art—not in the Picasso and Modigliani class, mind you, but it's displayed an occasional Benton, Wood, and Rothko, and even an O'Keefe and a Pollock. Once, I got within six feet of the Pollock piece.

Arriving in good time, Smith dropped me off about a half block from the front door, and drove on to park the Bird in an underground lot. On returning, he would find an alleyway to the left of the shop, the rear door unlocked, and our plans already in motion.

Arriving at *The Golden Palette*, I made like a tourist, peering in the windows, pretending to admire the artwork inside. Stuart Montgomery was alone, standing beside a small display of modern art, and appeared to be rehearsing the part of a stone statue in some Off Broadway show.

I walked in. The bell above the door gave out a polite tinkle. I approached Montgomery. He remained frozen, a study in fear.

A deep voice growled, "Can I help you out?"

The voice belonged to a heavyset man big enough to play fullback for the New York Titans. As he stood up from behind a display case, I knew that we'd been foxed. They'd *expected* us to arrive early.

"Why would you want to help me out?" My question seemed to stump the guy.

"Whad'ya mean?" he managed.

"What I mean is, why would you want to help me *out,* if I'd just *come in?*" Nothing registered with the mug. He just stood there with his mouth slightly open. "I've just *come in to buy something.*"

"Ask him what kind of car he drives," said another voice from the back gallery. A smaller man carrying a gun stepped into view.

The big guy's confusion seemed to clear, and he obediently asked what kind of car I drove.

"A Yellow Cab," I said.

"You're a cabbie?" the fullback asked.

"Shut up!" the gunman said. He slowly walked over to me, and stopped less than a foot away.

We spent close to 10 seconds smelling each other's aftershave. I'd have bet that he didn't know I was wearing 4711, but I sure as hell knew he was doused in Sail.

"Answer the question, wiseass," the smaller punk said. "What kind of car do you drive?" He tapped me on the chest with his revolver.

"Do that again," I said, with no emotion in my voice, "and I'll take it away from you, stick it in your left eye, and blow the back of your head off."

My response seemed to amuse him so much that he looked over at his mute partner with a wiseass grin. It was just enough time for me to sweep the gun out of his hand, and backhand him across his right cheek. He lost his balance and started to stumble to the floor; I helped him on his way with a sharp kick to the solar plexus.

When he hit the deck, I followed up with a solid stomp to the side of his head. His eyes did some kind of hula dance, while the rest of him didn't move at all.

I picked up his revolver, and turned to his mute partner. The goof's mouth was still hanging open, and he gave no indication of moving. Taking a moment to walk to the door, I locked it, hung out the Closed sign, and returned to the big guy.

"Okay, shit-for-brains," I started. "Let's play a little game. I ask you a question, and if I like the answer, I give you a present."

"What kind of present?" he asked, and a sly grin slowly blossomed across his face. Suddenly, I saw him in a different light. Take away the three-day growth of beard and the fattened nose that may have been broken a number of times in the boxing ring, and he may have been handsome at one time. Maybe a lot smarter, as well.

Perhaps I was being unfair to the guy. I paused to consider whether he was really that naive, or putting me on.

"Okay," I said, "let's say I ask you who's your boss. Who sent you here? You tell me the answer, and I give you 50 bucks."

"That's an easy one," the fellow replied, and started to giggle."

"What's so funny?"

"That was two questions," he replied. "If I answered them both, you'd owe me a hundred bucks!" He laughed. "Get your money out, and ask me the questions."

"I can't," I said, "because I'm holding this gun."

"Well, give the rod to me," the guy said, still laughing. "I'll hold it for you."

Suddenly, we were both laughing, and shaking our heads at each other.

When I'd had enough merriment, I cracked open the revolver, emptied out the bullets, put them in my pocket, and threw the gun away.

As I walked up to him, neither of us was laughing. He took a roundhouse swing at me. It was a lot faster than I thought possible for a big man.

I ducked with only a split second to spare.

Then I slammed him in the breadbasket. Doing that reminded me of hitting a tree when I was toughening up my knuckles back in my youth. He only grinned and tried to catch me with a right-handed straight-arm. I blocked it with my left arm, and hit him in the throat with my fist.

The blow was hard enough to get him gasping and coughing, but not enough to kill him. While he was dancing around, holding his throat and grunting, I landed a couple of hard kidney punches. That brought him to his knees. He remained bent over, coughing up his guts and sucking in air. At that point, I decided to use his chin for a football and kicked a pretty solid field goal that sent him over and onto his back.

"That's for Gloria!" I muttered, and walked over to Montgomery, who sighed with relief.

He was about to say something, but I interrupted him. "Find some rope or electrician's tape. Anything that can tie up these clowns before they wake up and I have to shoot them."

Less than 10 minutes later, the two thugs were bound hand and foot, mouths gagged. Only Harry Houdini could escape those bindings, and I was pretty sure that his ghost wasn't about to make any surprise appearances.

By the time Montgomery had turned off the showroom lights and we'd retreated to the back office, Zuni Smith made his appearance. He was a little embarrassed. "I had to park the damned Bird halfway to the East River."

I told him to forget about it, replayed the last half hour, and asked him to go out front to keep an eye on the trussed-up turkeys while I phoned for the cops.

Seconds later, I was talking to the desk sergeant at the Greenwich Village station and asking if Captain Stewart was still there.

"Who wants to know?" came the terse reply.

I identified myself, told him I'd just defused an attempted robbery and extortion, and needed to contact the precinct closest to my location. I gave him the address on East 76th.

"Captain Stewart has gone home for the day, Mr. Gentry," he said, "but I can phone it in for you, if you'd like."

"I'd like very much, Sergeant. As soon as you can, if you don't mind."

"Roger that, sir.

I thanked him and added, "And please give my respects to Scottie."

"Pardon sir? Scottie?"

"Sorry. I mean Captain Stewart."

"Yes, sir!" the desk sergeant said.

"And, Sergeant, I would advise you never to call him *Scottie,* unless you'd like to get busted down to a beat cop.

"Ten-four, Mr. Gentry. I read you loud and clear, sir."

Thursday, October 20, 1960

The next morning, Detective Mullen and I were meeting for an eleven o'clock breakfast at *Bistro on the Square*. It was Danny Mullen's day off, and I was quite happy to sleep in.

As for the term *bistro,* the name is a bit of a misnomer—it's more a family restaurant than a bistro. The eatery is at least a half block away from Stanford White's famous arch that heralds the beginning of Washington Square and the end of Fifth Avenue.

All that aside, it's my favorite restaurant in the Village, and only a few minutes' walk from my apartment. Naturally, I have my special seating spot.

Upon entering the bistro, a client will find that the room is divided in half. On the right-hand side, there are a number of spacious booths that run down to a service area, behind which is a clearly visible kitchen. On the left is a wider space that provides a number of tables and chairs to accommodate families, as well as smaller units more suitable for couples. Between both sections is the checkout counter and a home station for the servers.

At the back of the restaurant, and to the left of the kitchen, there is a hallway that leads to the restrooms, as well as two booths that are a little more private. One of the booths is my favorite home away from home. Presently, it was already occupied.

"Good morning, Detective Mullen," I said, as I parked across from him.

"Morning, Gentry." He folded up his newspaper and stashed it on the bench seat.

"Anything interesting in *The Times?*"

"How do you know it's *The Times?*"

"I recognized the typeface," I said. "Your paper is written in Times New Roman. It has been for years."

He smoothed down his hair and muttered "Smartass!" just as our waitress appeared.

Helen is a young woman in her late 20s, but appears to be much older. Her employer once confided in me that she had been an abused housewife. Beaten up regularly. When her husband discovered she was pregnant with their second child, he disappeared into the night. However, it was rumored he sometimes returned to extort money from her.

Every time I think of Helen's husband, I tell myself I'd like to get him alone in a locked room for about five minutes. Instead, I always leave her a tip that almost equals the amount of my bill. Eleanor, my girlfriend and associate, helps out, as well. She contributes to Helen's monthly income. Usually, it's enough to cover the woman's babysitting fees for the week.

This morning, Helen appeared more tired than usual. There were dark circles under her eyes, and for the first time, I was able to notice some gray hairs peeking out from under her saucy little bonnet. No matter how trying her life must be, she was always neat and clean, her waitress' uniform smartly laundered and ironed. Today, however, even her clothing seemed wilted.

"You okay, Helen?" I asked.

She shook her head, in a way that implied she didn't want to talk about it. Instead, she smiled at me as if to suggest that everything was cool, and nodded at Mullen, her pen poised over her order pad.

My guest, a stranger to Helen, ordered a plate of bacon and eggs. Two eggs, to be exact, partnered with four strips of bacon, crisp, almost to the point of being burnt. Rye toast, don't spare the butter, and a big mug of black coffee.

"Keep the coffee coming," Mullen concluded.

Helen looked over at me, squeezed out a smile that tried to dispel any concerns, and asked if I wanted the bacon and eggs special, or the pancakes. I opted for the pancakes, and she was off to the kitchen to place our orders.

"Is she really okay?" Mullen asked softly.

"I don't know," I said. Something had occurred recently—something that she wasn't prepared to talk about in front of a stranger.

While we waited for our orders, I told Mullen about last night's adventures at *The Golden Palette*. He listened attentively, asked a few questions, but offered no comments.

Over breakfast, he opened up and added some curious news of his own.

"That's the damndest thing!" he said, as he cut one of the strips of bacon precisely in half. For a guy who often acts and sounds like a beatnik instead of a cop, he's a very fastidious eater. Most fellows I know, including myself, cut up their eggs with a knife and fork, but usually pick up the bacon and eat it with their fingers.

"What's the damndest thing?" I asked, before popping a syrup-laden piece of pancake into my mouth.

"Your tale of extortion," he said. "It sounds like something I heard about this morning. A colleague of mine near the Garment District phoned me up and told me about a weird visit a local clothier got from a couple of goofballs."

Mullen paused in an effort to slide his fork under the half piece of bacon. He wasn't having much success.

Setting aside my knife and fork, I was suddenly all ears.

As he continued his efforts to corral the troublesome bacon, he said, "The two bozos told the merchant they represented a certain party who wants to buy his clothing store."

Leaning back in the booth, I asked if their offer came wrapped up in a threat.

"Precisely," Mullen said in a low voice. In frustration, he picked up the bacon and put it on his fork. A second later, it was in his mouth, and I was smiling at him.

"Don't you ever use your fingers?" I asked.

"Never. It's ungentlemanly."

"Did your mother teach you that?"

"No!" he said vehemently. I must have struck a nerve. He then tried the same routine with the other half of the bacon strip—slipping his fork under the piece of crisp meat and trying to scoop it into his mouth.

"Do you ever eat Kentucky Fried Chicken?" I asked, trying to sound innocent as I watched him have the same luck with the other piece of bacon.

Concentrating on the bacon-and-fork operation, he nodded *yes*, and I asked him how he went about eating it.

He put down his fork in exasperation, looked hard across the table at me, and muttered, "I don't pick it up like a cannibal and munch on it, if that's what you're getting at. That would be too ungentlemanly, as well."

I started to grin, and he continued, "If you really must know, I hold the leg in one hand, and pick off the meat with the other. Now, are you satisfied?"

"Don't you find that way too messy, as well?"

Danny Mullen slid out of the booth, asked where the washroom was, and told me Helen could clear his side of the table. As he walked away, he mumbled, "Like, man, you're exhausting, dude!"

I just shook my head. Detective Mullen must have had one hell of a strict mother. Munching on a chicken leg and getting your hands a little messy is one of the great culinary joys of life.

As Mullen disappeared around the kitchen exit, I continued to eat my pancakes. However, within seconds, I was joined by Helen.

She asked if everything was satisfactory, I nodded, and quickly asked her, "Are you sure *you're* okay?"

She gave me a sheepish smile that wasn't quite sincere. Before I could say anything else, she dropped a small piece of paper on the table and gently pushed it over to me. It was not the bill.

"Please," was all she said, and quickly retreated to the servers' station.

Walking back to my apartment on Jones Street, I was thinking about Helen's note. At the same time, I couldn't shake the last part of my conversion with Mullen, after his washroom break. His information was not only revealing, but it grabbed my attention like a sudden kick in the privates.

Helen's note was short, but definitely not sweet. It simply read, *Help me! Call after work at....* She had scrawled her phone number in a small, adolescent script.

While I waited for Helen to get home from the restaurant, I hopped into my Jag and headed north on 5th Avenue. There was a definite nip in the air, so I decided to leave the top rig up and not pretend I was Johnny Cool with the top down on a chilly autumn afternoon.

While opening up the Jag a little, I maneuvered around some slower traffic, and got on the tail of a Yellow Cab. That was always good sport, as it allowed me to dodge in and out of traffic at the cab's speed and dexterity.

It also kept in sync with my brain, which was racing along with what I'd just learned from Danny Mullen.

It appeared that the plot to hustle a store out of business in the Garment District was a carbon copy of the scam that had just been tried on Stuart Montgomery's *Golden Palette* art gallery.

What made this more personal was the fact the merchants in question were two brothers who owned and operated a thriving fur business near 25th and Sixth Avenue. I sometimes play poker with Aaron Saltzman and his younger brother Marty.

A year ago last July, I helped Marty out of a jam when he got involved with buying into a Broadway theater production. The only problem was his financier was connected to the Mob. Ironically, that crime family would eventually become very close to me in another way —the Don's daughter is now my girlfriend and business associate.

Back on the streets, the Yellow Cab seemed to make traffic dissolve and time evaporate. The Jag's radio helped the trip speed along, as well, thanks to WNBC on the dial, I was entertained by such hits of the day as the Everly Brothers' "Cathy's Clown," Elvis's "It's Now or Never," and even a silly ditty, Bryan Hyland's "Itsy Bitsy Teenie Weenie Yellow Polka Dot Bikini."

I shook my head at the bikini nonsense, but was glad I hung in and didn't turn the radio off. Right after, the station played Percy Faith's rendition of the theme from the romantic tearjerker *A Summer Place.* That raised my spirits. These days, I was in a romantic mood.

"Cass Gentry!" Aaron Saltzman cried, as I walked through the doors of his fur emporiums. "My absolute favorite, number one detective!"

Overstatement is one of Ari's vices, and at the same time one of his best virtues.

"Come give this tired old merchant a big hug," he cried.

I complied with his request and was soon receiving a mighty bear hug from a man who was as tall as he was wide. Ari only came up to my chin, and I could have easily rested my head on top of his noodle.

When he released me, I could see that he was emotionally drained.

His curly hair seemed much grayer, and even his bushy eyebrows appeared to have wilted. His eyes confirmed the stress he was under, and it was obvious that he hadn't slept well last night. Usually as bright as twinkling twin stars, today they were dull, looking like they belonged to an old man who had just lost all hope of living.

"Ari," I said in a stern voice, "you have to get hold of yourself."

"If you only knew," he moaned, as if he were the last man on Earth and had just lost his mate.

"I *do* know," I said, with an attempt at encouragement. "That's why I'm here."

"*Baruch Hashem!*" his brother, Marty Saltzman, called out as he hurried down the stairs from a second-floor display room. "Thank God!"

"*Emmanuel!*" replied the older brother.

"God is with us," Marty echoed.

Soon, they were both hugging me and jostling me in a kind of primitive dance. I didn't know whether to push them off in embarrassment, or start to hum along to "Hava Nagila."

When the rapture of the moment faded, Marty's oldest daughter, Miriam, took over the main floor of the store, while the three of us secured ourselves in the office.

I started by telling them how I'd heard about their harrowing experience. I told them their plight was not unique, that there'd been at least one other such scam in recent days.

I never mentioned any names.

Then I learned that the two men who's threatened them were not the two thugs who'd tried to scam Stuart Montgomery. One of these creeps was not much taller than the Saltzman brothers, but he was powerfully built and had an old scar down the side of his left cheek. The other bozo was rake-thin, average height, and had a bald head that was complemented by a thin mustache and a natty Vandyke beard.

Their story was the same as Montgomery's—introductory meeting, filled with threats; 48 hours to decide to sell. If, on their return, the answer is No Sale, the Saltzman brothers end up victims of an industrial accident.

In the final analysis, Aaron and Marty Saltzman wanted to know what they were going to do.

"Nothing," I said. "Sit tight, and try not to worry. I'll be here tomorrow, long before the deadline time. I won't be alone, and I won't be unarmed. If anything changes, let me know. You've already got my number because of the poker games, but just in case, here's my business card. Keep it on you at all times."

Just before I left, the boys wanted to have another three-way hug, but I managed to get out of that. I still had a phone call to make to find out what was troubling our friend Helen from the restaurant.

"What are you doing later tonight?" I asked my lady friend as soon as she picked up the phone.

"Who wants to know?" Eleanor responded. Her voice was low and husky, a good imitation of the movie star Lauren Bacall. It was the voice she liked to use when being playful.

"Humphrey Bogart," I replied, making the best of a poor imitation of the actor.

"Sorry, Bogie," she said. "I'm all booked up for this evening. I'm expecting Kirk Douglas any moment."

"The guy with the big dimple in his chin?"

"Same fellow," she said. "You wouldn't take me to see his movie *Spartacus* at the DeMille last week, so I phoned him up. He'll be here any moment."

"In the flesh?"

"Dimple and all."

"I'm happy for you," I said, dropping the Bogie accent. "But I'm worried about our friend Helen. She's in trouble."

"Helen? You mean Helen the waitress?"

"Yes," I clarified. "Helen, the waitress at *Bistro on the Square*."

"Where do you want to meet?"

I gave Eleanor an address in Greenwich Village, a small two-bedroom flat that Helen was renting from a friend, who was taking courses at the Sorbonne in Paris. I also suggested a rendezvous time that evening, giving her plenty of opportunity to blow off Kirk Douglas and get over to Manhattan from her house across the river in Jersey.

At nine o'clock that night, Eleanor and I were sitting in a plain but neat and tidy living room in the Village. Eleanor was trying to comfort Helen, while I sat in an overstuffed armchair that had seen better days. While Eleanor comforted her, I was trying to figure out how to protect this extremely upset woman whom we'd taken under our wings.

Earlier, Helen and I had spoken over the phone, and, between sobs that bordered on hysteria, she revealed that her ex-husband had called her the night before. The one-way conversation was short, but sharp as an ice pick. He made it perfectly clear that he was going to make a return visit. He said he wasn't staying long, but he wanted money. If she didn't fork it over, he vowed that she wouldn't be able to go into work for a week or two.

While Helen sobbed and hiccupped, I wandered over to the window and contemplated the situation. Helen's apartment had benefits, as well as problems.

The main point in its favor was the location on the third floor of the building. Her ex-husband had to turn into Superman and fly to her window, or morph into Batman and scale up or down the outside walls to her chambers.

But the premier negative was the lack of security in the apartment complex. No buzzer-intercom system. The creep could simply open the street door, walk up the stairs, and pound on her apartment door. There was little doubt in my mind that Helen would definitely admit him—she was terrified of the animal. If she did refuse him, he'd most likely break in through the door, and then take pleasure at breaking up Helen herself.

In the end, it was decided that Eleanor would stay the night with the woman; I would go home, and return the following morning to install a new, single-cylinder dead bolt. This worked out well, as Helen had the morning shift off, and there would be no finer protector for the frightened waitress than my lady friend, Eleanor Palladino.

Friday, October 21, 1960

As the Scottish poet Robert Burns once wrote: *The best-laid schemes o' mice an' men gang aft a-gley.* Hardly anything we'd planned turned out right.

The dead bolt took longer to install than anticipated. Eleanor couldn't stay another night with Helen due to a family celebration, and I had to attend to the Saltzman brothers' problem. Finally, our reception plans for the thugs went off the rails from the start.

Specifically, when the two punks knocked on the door at nine o'clock, Ari and Marty were supposed to let them in and lock up. When they entered the office on the ground floor, they would be met by Zuni Smith, while I appeared out of the downstairs showroom behind them. Mr. Smith and I were amply qualified to handle the two bozos, and while that was going on, the Saltzman brothers would perform a swift and silent disappearing act.

However, that's not how events unfolded.

Instead of two visitors, there were *three.* Two of them appeared to be muscle, while the third was holding a serious-looking semiautomatic handgun. Later, I would learn that it was one of the relatively new Smith & Wesson Model 39s.

When the trio of hoods reached the office with the Saltzmans, the brothers made their exit, I jumped the guy with the gun, and Mr. Smith took over entertaining the other two cowboys in the office.

Although there was a thunderous clamor of scuffling and crashing coming from in the office, I was fully occupied with the fellow identi-fied as the leader of the troops. My first objective was to disarm him, which I did with a sharp, hard kidney punch from behind. His gun arm automatically went up and slightly to his right.

Grabbing him around the neck with my left arm, while at the same time putting an iron lock on the wrist and hand with the gun, I helped him to perform a snappy, military salute. I forced his gun hand up and smacked it into the right side of his forehead. He dropped the gun, and I followed up with a choke hold around his neck. He passed out, I let him go, and he slumped to the floor.

Leaving the gunman for the moment, I went into the office to find Mr. Smith and the two thugs locked in a tangle of three standing bodies—the two thugs making a Zuni sandwich out of Mr. Smith.

Crossing to the one with his back turned to me, I kicked him in the back of his left leg, just behind the kneecap. He immediately let go of my partner, and dropped to the floor in a paroxysm of pain. I grabbed his hair, spun him around, and drove a straight-arm into the bridge of his nose. It shattered, blood spurting all over his shirt and jacket.

Still being held by the other criminal, Zuni Smith, thanked me for my assistance. "But I will take it from here," he concluded. And, indeed, he did, with speed and dexterity that I could never muster in the next 40 years.

When it was all over, we performed the same ritual that Stuart Montgomery and I had enacted a few nights before—bound and gagged the men, called the police, received our friends' gracious thanks, and tore out of the shop.

On my way out, I picked up the Smith & Wesson Model 39 as a souvenir. I still have it in my personal collection to this day.

Saturday, October 22, 1960

The harsh jangle of the telephone instantly woke me up. If that wasn't enough, I had forgotten to close my bedroom drapes last night, and the sun's brilliance almost elicited a stream of vulgarities from me. Almost, but not quite. I gave a guttural growl, and snarled "Yes?" into the receiver of my rotary dial phone.

"My, my," Eleanor said in a cool voice. "Who knocked over *your* bowl of Rice Krispies this morning?"

"Sorry," I mumbled, trying to shake the cobwebs from my head. "Give me a minute." I made a valiant effort to clear my head, eyes and throat, all in the space of 10 or 15 seconds.

Feeling slightly more human, I said, "Sorry, Eleanor. I had a long night after looking after the Saltzman boys."

"How did it go?" she said. "The Saltzmans and the long night?"

"The Saltzman caper was fun, but over too soon. The good guys won."

After a significant pause, she said, "And how was the long night, and what were you doing to make it so damned long?"

It was my turn to pause. Finally, I said, "She looked an awful lot like you, my sweet one. Remarkably like you, as I lay there in my lonely bed, thinking of your golden hair, your lithe and athletic body, and daydreaming of all the lovely things we could be doing if you were only here."

"Liar," she said, but I imagined a pleased smile crossing her face.

"Okay, my love, would you believe that Zuni Smith and I stayed up for hours, discussing various possibilities of what is going on with these attempted takeovers?"

That sounded reasonable, and she asked me for details. Briefly, I synthesized my late discussion with Mr. Smith. As I drew my theory to a tentative conclusion, I suggested she and I take a little drive over to Queens to visit one of my poker buddies. Eleanor had already planned to stay that night with Helen, the threatened waitress, so we agreed to meet at my apartment within two hours.

My parting advice to her was from Shakespeare: *Before the game is afoot, thou still let'st slip.*

Loosely translated—before things really start a-poppin,' let's get a move on!

It was less than two hours later when Eleanor and I left the Village, traveled north on Broadway, and headed east into the borough of Queens to meet my poker pal, Nicholas Speropolous.

Nick is a middle-aged Greek entrepreneur, whom I've known for a number of years. Among other things, he owns a nightclub on Gleanne Street in Queens. A very hot spot, *Nick's Tavern* is especially popular on Friday and Saturday jazz nights. The Greek's favorite slogan is: *The room heats up when the music gets cool.* Dave Brubeck and Stan Kenton have already played a few sets there.

Speropolous is a regular go-getter—curly, dark hair, flashing eyes that never stop moving around. He has the kind of personality that always lands him in the middle of some new excitement—some lucrative scheme that will make him more of the green stuff.

Needless to say—but I will, because he's a pretty fine guy, and a gentleman, to boot—Nick's a hit with the ladies. He's also not a big partyer. He enjoys a good time, but never drinks to excess. When he does imbibe, his favorite libation is champagne. Naturally, he's been given the nickname Nicky Champagne.

"Hey, man!" Nicky greeted me with genuine enthusiasm as we shook hands. "How's it goin'?"

"Round and round," I said. "Just like the Indy 500."

"Cool, dude. You were always a man in motion, my brother," he replied. Then turning to Eleanor, he inquired, "And who is this fair damsel?" His voice was smoothly polite, but his eyes were dancing.

I introduced Eleanor as my lady friend and business associate. Nicky gave an old-fashioned bow, and paid his respects, recognizing the Palladino name and knowing her father's reputation.

Moments later, we were ensconced in Nicky's leather-and-mahogany office and enjoying ice-cold Virgin Caesars, compliments of the swift-moving bartender on duty.

After a brief catch-up exchange, we got down to the reason for my visit.

"Has anyone offered to buy *Nick's Tavern* from you?" I asked. "Lately?"

Nicky shrugged and shook his head. "I've received a few offers, over time, but nothing lately."

"This would be fairly recent. Two guys. Messenger boys that look more like muscle."

Nicky took a sip from his drink, set it down, and leaned forward. "What's this all about, Cass? You didn't come all the way from Washington Square to ask about the state of my business affairs."

"No, I didn't, my friend. But I've got a hunch that your turn at bat may be coming up. Soon."

"What the hell does that mean?" he said, then glanced over at Eleanor to apologize for his language.

"I've heard a lot worse," she replied, then gave a demure smile.

"I'll bet you have." Nicky winked, and we all laughed.

With the mood lightened, I went on to relate what had recently occurred with both of our acquaintances and poker buddies.

After a short pause, Nicky said, "It could be coincidence. After all, both Montgomery and the Saltzman boys own successful, Manhattan businesses."

"I know," I replied. "And it's possible they have mutual friends, even if one is Church of England and the brothers are Jewish."

"That's why we're here," Eleanor chipped in. "Seeing if you've received the same kind of offer. Cass will also check on other mutual friends. The only other poker person that ever broke into the group was my brother, Joey. He only made one appearance and never returned. Besides, he's now residing in Sicily with some relatives."

Nick Speropolous gave a little chuckle. "I believe I heard about that, Eleanor."

"Yes," she confirmed. "He'd been a bad boy, and was sent to the old country to get a little...*reconditioning,* shall we say."

Eleanor looked over at me, I looked across at Nicky, and all of us sat silently for a few moments.

Finally, Nicky broke the silence with a sudden clap of his hands. "Look, you kids, why don't you take some time away from playing Ellery Queen and Miss Marple and visit *Nick's Tavern* for the night?"

Eleanor and I exchanged glances, knowing that the interview was over. As all three of us stood, Nicky said, "Come to the tavern early. Food and drinks on the house, and I'll put you up for the night. Whad'ya say?"

"It's a very generous offer," Eleanor said. "I'm all in, Nicky. But, do I have to bring *this* guy?" We all had a good chuckle.

On my way out, I stopped at the bar and gave the bartender a ten-spot for his trouble with the drinks. I know these guys really make their living from customer tips, and I don't mean what nag's going to win in the second at Hialeah Race Track.

"Holy mackerel, dude!" Nicky cried as we approached the door. "Are you awash in dough? Giving the barkeep a sawbuck for making a few Virgin Caesars?"

"Gotta keep the help sweet," I said.

"Jeesh, man. If I kept them that sweet, they'd be owning the joint in a coupla years!"

We all laughed, promised to make the overnight visit soon, and exchanged hugs and handshakes. On our way back to the Village, I couldn't help but think that Nicky was prepared for the worst if he had some uninvited visitors.

As for me, I was receiving a completely different message—one that was a lot closer to home. And it didn't please me one bit.

Sunday, October 23, 1960

The next day, Zuni Smith did his regular housecleaning and hung up my Halloween picture from the Disney studios.

After our visit with Nicky Champagne, Eleanor spent the night with Helen, and everything was peaceful in the Village. In the morning, she helped Helen make breakfast for the two of them, and then accompanied her to the restaurant in time for her eleven o'clock shift.

Helen was going to fly solo tonight, while Eleanor went back across the Hudson River to her home in New Jersey, where she lives with her father, the notorious *Don* Palladino. Her house, a magnificent Neo-Tudor mansion, is also home to a number of servants and some very trustworthy *associates* who take turns guarding the lord of the manor.

As for me, I had a little business to attend to up in Brooklyn. It was going to be long and tedious, but was part of a standing arrangement with a lawyer who was trying to stay on the right side of the law while defending people with questionable reputations. It was a nasty job, but a lot cleaner than divorce work. That was where I drew the line. No sneaking around in the shadows with a camera in the middle of the night for me!

Later that evening, after crossing back over the East River via the Brooklyn Bridge, I returned home. It had been a long day, and I felt tired and a little dirty. However, I'd manage to keep on the right side of the angels and my own personal code of honor. The drive also gave me some time to mull over a few developing theories I had about the buyout hustles.

Tired as I was, I joined Zuni Smith in his private chambers. He was still up, reading a book of history that concerned the development of the First Nations' belief systems of life. He gently set the book on his night table, and invited me to sit down.

I did, and immediately shared my evolving theories with him.

Mr. Smith listened attentively, never interrupting. When I was finished, he asked a few questions, made several adjustments to my assumptions, and eventually gave me the green light to continue with my present lines of logic. I am always grateful for his intelligence, as well as his fatherly advice and friendship.

After the discussion, I retired to my den, made a few notes on my business day, and took a long, hot shower. Then I slipped on the top of my black, silk PJs and fell into bed. A glance at the clock told me it was after 1:30 a.m. I closed my eyes, and within seconds, I was fast…

The phone rang.

"It's happened!" was all Eleanor said. I immediately knew what she meant.

"Around eight o'clock," she continued, "Helen's husband smashed the door off its hinges, and beat her to a pulp."

Monday, October 24, 1960

After Eleanor's report, I tossed some water on my face, quickly dressed in a fresh set of blacks, and headed down to the underground garage. Discovering the night had turned suddenly cool, I returned up-stairs and donned my Irving Schott leather jacket. If it was good enough for Elvis. Marlon, and James Dean, it was good enough for me.

Reentering the garage, I ripped off the tonneau cover and booted up the ramp, where I sped south toward the hospital. The autumn air kept me awake and helped me to organize my thoughts. Along the way, I started developing a plan to avenge our friend, Helen.

Shortly after 8:30, I was permitted to join Eleanor in the waiting room at Saint Vincent's Catholic Medical Center, in the Lower West Side. Eleanor had been there for some time, and had already learned some pertinent details. As she spoke, the entire picture started to come into focus.

After the attack, Helen had mustered up enough strength to phone Eleanor, who immediately called the emergency number at St. Vincent's.

After waking me up, and giving me a brief rundown, she'd left the Palladino compound in Jersey and headed directly to the hospital to join the ambulance when it arrived. If she was late, at least she'd be in the hospital and available to supply any background information to the staff and police.

We'd both known that Helen was Catholic, and would be more at home in that medical center. She would put up less of a fuss about going there and reporting the incident to the authorities.

I learned that Helen had suffered extensively. Both eyes were almost closed. Her mouth was bleeding where her husband had punched out some teeth. She was sure that one arm was broken; the other was barely functional. When she used the second arm to phone Eleanor, her hand hurt like hell, as did several other parts of her body. As for any internal injuries, that would have to be determined by the professionals.

While the hours dragged by in the waiting room, Eleanor became more agitated, not knowing how our friend was doing. No one had informed us of her present condition. The thought of serious internal injuries was haunting both of us, and the numerous cups of coffee the hospital provided in the waiting room wasn't helping.

Finally, a nurse came into the room and spoke to us in low, guarded tones. Helen was comfortable, but presently speaking with the police. Evidently, there was no internal bleeding or discernable injuries. However, the one arm was definitely fractured; the other would heal within a few weeks, but feel quite painful for several more days.

Two teeth had been knocked out during the savage beating. As for the eyes, her right one appeared worse than it actually was, but there was some concern for the other. A specialist had been summoned for further examination and consultation with the hospital's staff.

"Did she say anything about the perp?" Eleanor said, with nothing but payback on her mind.

"Perp?" the nurse asked.

"Her husband. The son of a bitch who did this to her!"

The nurse stared at Eleanor, clearly torn between sympathy and distaste for my girlfriend's language. Finally, she said, "You'll have to speak with the police about that. I'll send them in to see you when they are finished questioning Mrs. Grise."

With that, the nurse disappeared from the room, while Eleanor and I were left trying to sort out our emotions. Eventually, I gave Eleanor a twisted, little smile and a shake of the head.

"What?" she demanded.

"We'll have to be a little more subtle when talking to the cops," I said.

"Why?" she demanded. I could see the spirit of her Italian ancestry—not to mention her father's famous temper—rise up in protest.

"Because, my love, I have a plan. And you'll love it!" I gave her a wink.

She was definitely torn, wanting to know what I had up my sleeve, but still too steamed up to ask. So, we hung around for another long time, one of us sitting on a well-used leatherette couch, while the other paced back and forth and pretended to stare out the window. After a while, we'd trade places.

Eventually, when I could sense that Eleanor was about ready to lose her cool, a plainclothesman walked in, with a uniformed cop in tow.

"My name's Detective Angelo Rossi," he said without preamble, "and this is Officer Frank Andreas." As he spoke, he offered identification, including his badge. His partner just stood there; the metal buzzer on his chest served as sufficient ID.

"I'm Cass Gentry," I said, and hauled out my own shield and ticket. "We're personal friends of the victim, Miss Grise."

Meanwhile, Eleanor was making a production number out of inspecting Rossi's papers—very up close.

"Whatsamatta, lady?" Rossi demanded. "You think I clipped 'em? Ya think they're phonus bolonus?"

In a voice dripping with sarcasm, Eleanor said, "I'd never, in a million years, think you'd stolen them, or faked them, *sir*." Smiling sweetly, like a Shirley Temple doll with dimples flashing, she finished, "Let's just say I've been cooped up for hours in this room, waiting for you gentlemen to show up, while my poor eyes have gradually become short-sighted, Detective Rosey."

"It's Rossi, lady. Pronounced ROSS-EE, with the accent on the first syllable. Now, it's your turn. Who are *you*?"

"The name's Palladino. Eleanor Palladino. Perhaps you know my father—"

That's when I interrupted.

"Darling, I believe that Detective Rossi is only interested in *us*. You and I, and what we can add to the case that the officers are compiling as we speak."

We stared at each other. I gave her another wink and sat down on the couch. She took in several deep breaths, and joined me. Disaster may have been averted.

Within moments, the two policemen had pulled up chairs from other spots in the room and sat facing us.

At first, they wanted to know how we knew Miss Grise. I explained how I frequented the *Bistro on the Square*, where she is a waitress. Through that connection, she and I had become friends. When I'd found out about her abusive husband, and how he had recently threatened her, I'd brought in Eleanor, my associate.

Eleanor continued by explaining how she had stayed overnight at Helen's several evenings in order to keep her safe. She also mentioned strengthening the security locks of the apartment door. The rest was very recent history.

"Did either of you meet this husband of hers?" asked Rossi, a tall, well-dressed detective who would have been considered a perfect male model—he resembled the movie star Burt Lancaster

—except for his withered look and unshaven growth of beard. It was obvious that he hadn't been to bed for several days.

"Neither one of us has had the dubious pleasure," Eleanor answered. "I wouldn't know him if you stuck him in a lineup with only three suspects."

"Would you have any idea where he lives, miss?" Rossi continued.

"No clue. The only thing we learned about him was he's a bully and a physical brute. He regularly beat her up most of their married life."

"Do you know where he lives, Mr. Gentry?"

"I've no idea, officer. Did Helen Grise tell you?"

Rossi looked over at Officer Andreas, who gave a little shrug.

"The only thing I know for sure," I offered, "is that even after leaving her, he'd sometimes return unexpectedly—demanding money from her, and threatening to beat her severely if she didn't fork over her meager savings. This time, he went too far."

There was a pause in the questioning. At last, Rossi gave each of us his business card, and said to call if we remembered any relevant details. Then he thanked us for our co-operation, and silently left with his foot soldier.

When they'd gone, Eleanor snorted my words back at me: "*This time, he went too far.*"

"It's okay, kiddo," I said. "We got out of them all we needed to know."

"What's that?"

"Officer Andreas's little *tell—his shrug.* You can bet your next five paychecks that the cops have no idea where he lives. If they didn't get her husband's present whereabouts out of Helen, then we must get her to confess."

"And then?"

"And then, my plan for Helen's revenge starts to fall into place."

As long as I'd known Eleanor Palladino, I'd never seen her cry. Today was the first time. She took one look at Helen—with her eyes covered in gauze, her left arm in a sling, and a tube running from an IV drip into her arm—and the tears began to flow. I believe it was the gauzed eyes that really got to her.

As we stood just inside the doorway to the patient's room, tears slowly rolled down my girlfriend's face. Helen seemed to sense our presence and stirred. She mumbled something.

While I stood by in silent empathy, Eleanor moved to the victim's bedside, gently picked up her free hand, and quietly sobbed.

After some time, Eleanor spoke softly in our friend's ear. I moved closer to the other side of the bed, trying not to get tangled in the hanging medical paraphernalia.

Helen mumbled something barely audible, but I believed that she was asking if I was there.

"Dear Helen," was all I could manage.

"Come closer," she whispered.

I did, and she tried to clear her throat. Eleanor and I exchanged looks and there were still tears in my partner's eyes.

"I...I didn't tell them," she said in a hoarse croak.

"What didn't you tell them?" Eleanor said, struggling to keep her tears under control.

"His address. They don't know where he lives."

"We heard," I whispered into her ear. "The police talked with us, and we were just as ignorant as them."

Helen took a long break. "I'll tell you. I had to change his mailing address. Find him and make him stop."

"We will," Eleanor breathed into her other ear. "I promise he will never touch you again."

Helen Grise squeezed out a tiny, painful smile. Then she gave us her tormentor's address.

Letting our friend sleep, Eleanor and I returned to the waiting room to discuss how we were going to proceed. Both of us wanted to stay and be present for Helen throughout the day, while at the same time, we felt a strong urge to locate Grise and make damned sure he never laid a finger on Helen again.

"He's not going anywhere," Eleanor reasoned. "Probably shacked up in some dump on the Lower East Side, and got the money he wanted from Helen. Likely pretty satisfied with himself, the pig."

"He might have gotten his fill of kicks last night," I added, "but we'll make damned sure his punching bag days are over."

Sitting once more on the leather couch, I outlined my plan to Eleanor *sotto voce*. By the time I was finished, there was a smile on her face.

In the end, it was decided that Eleanor would stay at the hospital with Helen, throughout the day and night if need be. Meanwhile, because I had the shorter journey back to my digs near Washington Square, I would return there, make certain arrangements with Zuni Smith, and then look after any private business that had sprung up during the day. If there was none, I'd return to the hospital to relieve Eleanor. She'd then drive back across the Hudson River in her MGA sports car for a fresh change of clothes and a good night's rest at the Palladino estate.

A warm hug and a kiss sealed the deal, and I was returning to Jones Street in the West Village.

Back home, Mr. Smith wasted no time in bringing me up to date on my messages. The first was from Nicky Champagne, and he hadn't sounded like his usual Mr. Congeniality self, according to Smith.

Something serious had arisen that sounded like what we'd discussed the other night at his tavern. He wanted a return call ASAP.

The other message was also urgent. Mr. Smith didn't recognize the gentleman's name, but he described him as an older-sounding person with an Italian accent who identified himself as the owner of *Casa Romano*, a small Italian restaurant in West Englewood, on the Jersey side of the Hudson.

Thanking Zuni Smith for his information, I headed into my den, puzzling over why on Earth *il proprietario* of the *Casa Romano* wanted to speak with me. He wasn't one of my poker buddies, although I had met him on a number of occasions. In fact, Eleanor and I had our first date at his restaurant.

Letting that mystery slide for the moment, I phoned Nick Speropolous. Almost immediately, Nick's house manager answered and, without the customary small talk, put me through to the boss's extension.

"You weren't just whistling Dixie!" Nick declared immediately.

"Don't know the tune," I said. "Whistle me a bar or two."

"I can't, buddy. My mouth's too dry," he fired back.

"Aha!" I cried. "You've had some *visitors*."

"As you recently suggested I might."

"How long have you got?"

"They're coming back later tonight. After closing time."

"And if you don't sign?" I prompted.

"They'll burn *Nick's Tavern* to the ground, with me in it."

I thought for a moment. "How many bouncers do you normally have on hand?"

"It depends on the day of the week," he said. "If those hoods return tonight, like they promised, I'll only have three of my guys."

"Are your guys armed?"

"Come on, Cass. You know as well as me it's not legal."

"Are they *armed*?" I repeated.

"All right, already! They're armed!"

"Good thing," I muttered. I proceeded to recount what Mr. Smith and I had encountered at *The Golden Palette* and the Saltzman brothers' establishment, particularly the appearance of a third thug wielding a gun. The last detail got Nicky's attention.

"So, these birds are actually serious!" Nicky exploded. "They may start a firefight. Might even bring more troops!"

"Anything can happen, Nick," I said, "but to be honest, I don't think they're really sincere about buying out your business."

"The hell you say!" He was still angry, but there was a trace of relief in his voice.

That's when I told him my theory about all this nonsense. The whole gambit had nothing to do with buying or selling business establishments; the real target was something else entirely.

I proceeded to suggest that he order his tavern boys to stick around after closing. In turn, I promised to make the trek back to Queens within the next few hours, and we'd set up a housewarming party for the so-called purchasers.

By the time I ended the conversation, Nicky felt a tad more optimistic.

Next, I called up the hospital and left a message for Miss Eleanor Palladino, a very close friend of Mrs. Grise in the emergency ward. Miss Palladino was to be informed that Mr. Gentry would not be able to return this evening, but would be pleased to join her for the *vigil* before noon tomorrow.

Following my call to the hospital, I had an interesting conversation with *Signore* Marcello Romano, owner of *Casa Romano* in West Englewood. He told me that two strangers had dropped into the restaurant a few days earlier and asked him if he knew a man named Cass Gentry.

"I said I didn't know anyone by that name," Romano explained. "Then they showed me a picture and a newspaper story about you."

"Shit!" I exclaimed, and immediately thought of an interview I'd done for a local weekly called *The Village Beat*. The small, independent paper featured squibs on notable events and persons from the beatnik and jazz scenes of a few years ago. The publication's now defunct, but evidently some stories have a long shelf life.

"These guys," Romano continued, "looked pretty tough, and wanted to know if you ever showed up at my restaurant."

"And you told them...?"

"I told them nothing. I told them I see a lot of people. *Casa Romano* is a very popular spot."

"How did they respond to that?"

"They told me to think real hard about the picture," Romano replied. "One of the guys gave me a hard poke in the chest and told me they'd be back in a few days, to see if my memory had improved any. If it hadn't, they'd use some carpentry tools to help me remember."

We both knew that I had frequented Romano's restaurant a number of times, always in the company of Eleanor. Apparently, someone else had taken note.

"So, *Signore* Romano," I surmised, "you phoned up *Don* Palladino, explained your predicament, and received, in turn, my phone number."

He agreed, with a touch of pride.

Seeing the possible tie-in between *Casa Romano, The Golden Palette, Nick's Tavern,* and the Saltzman brothers' store, I told Romano to sit tight. I had another important engagement tonight, but I would send him a trusted associate of mine, one on whom I would stake my life.

Romano was extremely relieved and grateful for the assistance. Time was of the essence, so I quickly rang off.

Finally, I huddled with Zuni Smith. Informing him that I had to return to Queens to help out Nick Speropolous, I asked him to fire up his Thunderbird and head over to Jersey.

I gave him the scoop on *Casa Romano,* and the street address on Queen Anne Road. I advised him to arm himself, just in case. If all went well, we'd rendezvous back at Jones Street sometime before sunrise.

Putting my leather jacket on, I headed into the night wearing a shoulder rig, complete with my Sig P210 semiautomatic. Under the right epaulette of the jacket, I'd secured a short-bladed combat knife. I was ready for battle.

Tuesday, October 25, 1960

By 1:30 a.m., *Nick's Tavern* was closing up. The house musicians had zipped up their guitar, bass fiddle and sax, while the keyboard player had lovingly tucked the piano in for the night.

Nicky's soloist had traded her sequined dress for a tight-fitting pair of jeans and a bulky knit sweater that had a saucy-faced pumpkin on the front. The pumpkin's eyes were strategically placed on her chest, while its mouth was stretched wide in an unmistakably salacious grin.

Back in the office, Nicky, his three bouncers, and I put the finishing touches on our plans before heading into the tavern itself, each to his assigned place. Nicky and I would be sitting at an empty table near the stage, sipping a colorful concoction with no alcohol. On the table were a few phony papers that masqueraded as business documents, and we'd be pretending to have a marketing discussion.

Meanwhile, the bouncers would be waiting for showtime behind closed doors—the office, the women's washroom, and a discreet storage closet. These points of entry had been deliberately chosen as each of them opened onto the restaurant and entertainment center itself.

By the time all of us were settled in, it was well past two in the morning, according to the Howard Miller grandfather clock on the downstage wall near the piano.

As the minutes ticked on, Nick's men waited in their assigned locations. They were armed and, according to their boss, looking forward to a little bit of action. The doorman had been instructed to allow the thugs to enter unimpeded and to escort them to the restaurant section.

Meanwhile, my car was safely stowed away in the double garage at the rear of the building, while I sat with my back to the entrance of the room. Nicky sat facing me. Neither of us said anything. We knew what had to be done.

At 2:43, according to my Rolex, there was a pounding on the front door. Seconds later, I could hear thumping feet entering the room and heading straight for our table. Nick Speropolous stood up. I remained seated, my back to the visitors.

Nicky muttered, "Welcome back."

There was a shuffling of feet, the clearing of someone's throat, and a short statement.

"We're not staying long."

The voice was soft and pleasant. "Just two questions," it continued. "Number one—are you willing to sell *Nick's Tavern* to the person we represent?"

I watched Nicky, as his straight face dissolved into a wide smile. "Are you really serious?"

"You can be well assured that I am, Mr. Speropolous. Otherwise, you're a dead man and your business will be a burnt-out shell." The voice paused. "Unless..."

"Unless what?" Nicky fired back, his quick temper suddenly breaking through his quiet facade.

"Unless you hand over your friend, *Cass Gentry*."

Everything went silent, save for the ticking of the Howard Miller clock. Then I stood up and slowly turned to face the voice. It belonged to a stranger.

Wearing a black, full-length overcoat, with a matching felt homburg hat, the man was tall, clean-shaven, good-looking, and fully composed. However, what made his appearance so arresting was his blossoming grin, surprisingly wide and glittering. It not only appeared genuine, but seemed to invite whoever he met to smile right back.

"Mr. Gentry, I presume," he said smoothly. Behind him, less-than-polite guffaws sounded from the three other men in the party. Two of them I'd met the preceding nights.

"And, you are...?" I asked, being equally polite.

The man's smile remained intact. "A friend...of an acquaintance of yours. Someone who wishes to renew his association with you at the earliest, possible convenience."

I grinned and nodded. "So, the purchase of these various businesses was only a ruse. A way to flush me out into the open to meet with this *unnamed* acquaintance."

"Perfectly so," the man in the homburg replied.

"And this acquaintance has no name, for the moment?"

"That is also true. The person is particularly shy."

"And if I say *no* to such a reunion?"

The man gave a theatrical sigh. "That would be most unfortunate for one or two of your poker pals. And their businesses."

"Well, in that case, I believe I'll have to take your invitation under advisement, and give it some serious thought."

The only sounds in the room were the ticking of the grandfather wall clock, and the clicking of the man's perfect teeth as he shut his mouth with a sudden snap of displeasure.

"Was there anything else?" I asked.

"Unfortunately, *yes*," said the man, as he pulled out a gun from his coat pocket. "I'm afraid you will have to come with us, Mr. Gentry. Now."

Knowing full well he wouldn't shoot his client's target, I drew my Sig from its holster. "I really don't think that will be possible."

Then things moved very quickly.

The three clowns behind Homburg Man pulled out their pistols.

Nicky called out the prearranged signal for his bouncers. "Party time!!"

Three doors opened, and three men appeared, ratcheting their automatic weapons.

"Welcome to this evening's entertainment," Nicky said. He pulled his own weapon out from under the phony papers. "Nine guns at a Mexican standoff!"

The room went silent before Homburg Man slowly returned his weapon to its resting place, and his crew followed suit. The bouncers and I remained at the ready, our guns still very much in evidence.

Homburg Man leaned in toward me and almost whispered, "You're making a foolish mistake, Mr. Gentry. Because you're refusing a little discussion with an old friend, you're jeopardizing the businesses and perhaps the lives of your poker buddies."

Then he backed off, ever so slightly, gave me one of his thousand-watt smiles, and snapped the fingers of his left hand. His men performed an about-face and headed for the door. My antagonist stood grinning at me for a few more seconds, and I was sorely tempted to smash that million-dollar grin into a pile of enamel dust.

As he left, he said, "I'll be back to get your *final* answer. If there is none, the deaths and burnings will begin. And don't forget, I also know where your girlfriend lives, as well as…"

The door slammed on his retreating figure, but the last words sounded an awful lot like *your mother.*

"That's not very sporting if they bring your mother into play," Zuni Smith muttered.

It was now past five in the morning, and Mr. Smith and I were back on our home turf in the Village. Both of us were extremely tired.

"Not to mention my girlfriend," I added. "They obviously don't know who they're threatening. If Eleanor's father ever caught wind of this, he'd have his hoods out there with tommy guns."

The usually straight-faced Willard Smith cracked a small grin before continuing on a more serious note.

"At least you're making progress, knowing your theory was correct," he said. "*You* were the target all along. *You* were the common denominator for all scams. As the friend of Montgomery and the Saltzman brothers, then Nicky and Romano, you were expected to come to their rescue. However, you ended up turning the tables on each attempt."

"At least, that's gratifying," I muttered, as I sank into the soft leather couch. "But who's hiring them? That's the question."

"It must be someone connected to a former case," Mr. Smith mused. "Someone you were instrumental in sending to jail."

My fatigue was catching up with me. I started to nod off when Zuni Smith began describing his meeting with the owner of *Casa Romano*. Snapping back into the present, I heard him quote *Signore* Romano as saying, "It was a pretty quiet day. No visitors, thank Mary, mother of Jesus."

I readjusted my position on the couch and jumped back into the discussion. "The problem is simple. These creeps are prepared to punish friends of mine if they don't deliver me into their hands."

"How is there a problem?"

"I don't have enough colleagues to cover all of the potential victims. There's Nick Speropolous, the Saltzman brothers, Stuart Montgomery and *Signore* Romano. That's five possible victims, not counting my mother up in Canada. In reality, there's only you and me, and perhaps Eleanor, if I decide to put her in harm's way."

"She's a pretty capable detective, Cass. She has skills as good as you and me, and she's also as competent with a gun as either of us."

I acknowledged the wisdom of his statement, but still had second thoughts. I didn't want to lose her.

"What about your detective friend? Would Mullen be up for a little freelance action?"

I had to admit I really didn't know, but I wondered if a cop with his experience and rank was allowed to perform freelance work.

"I can always ask him," I said, but deep down, my gut told me the probability of such an assignment was slim to zero. However, I told Zuni Smith that I'd suss out the situation with Mullen. "He can only say *no.*" I reasoned.

Shortly after, we broke up the meeting, and I retired to my bed for a few hours' sleep.

By two o'clock that afternoon, I was showered, shaved, and on my way to Saint Vincent's Catholic Medical Center.

Checking in with the duty nurse on Helen's floor, I was informed by Sister Rose that the patient was resting peacefully, off the support paraphernalia, and being entertained by her visitor, Miss Palladino. I thanked the nurse, and was permitted to join the visitation down the hall.

A solid hug and a lingering kiss with Eleanor were followed by a gentle embrace with the patient. We shared a congenial chat, and I was pleased to note that Helen seemed to have made substantial progress since I saw her last. Although wearing a cast on her broken arm, the eye bandages had been removed. Happily, although the eyes and the areas surrounding them were badly bruised, she was able to see out of both of them.

Helen assured me that the attending physician had declared there would be no permanent damage to either eye, although a follow-up examination with a specialist had been arranged for a month from now. Helen was expected to be released within a week, and would be going back to stay with Eleanor in Jersey, while the door to her apartment was repaired and the living room was returned to normal.

Later, over coffees and an early supper in the hospital's cafeteria, Eleanor and I planned how we were going to deal with Helen's estranged husband. The *beast* would be our dessert for the occasion. As it turned out, his new den was on the Lower East Side, just outside of Chinatown and a few blocks within Little Italy.

Not knowing if he was shacked up with a new lady friend, Eleanor had used some of her time with Helen to phone information, get Grise's new number, and make several phone calls. The device was always answered by a man's voice. I had to smile when she told me she had the greatest desire to ask the *voice* if that "shithead Grise" was in." Fortunately, the cretin didn't have the opportunity to answer that question.

I phoned Zuni Smith, and gave him Grise's address, along with Helen's description of today's honorary *shithead*. Mr. Smith would stake out the address and discover as much as he could about the man. Most importantly, did Grise have a live-in partner? We didn't want to visit him to offer our unique kind of *respects* if there was any chance we'd be interrupted during the festivities.

After our supper at the hospital café, Eleanor and I sat in her MG for a quarter of an hour, planning our next moves. Both of us would drive to our own apartments, have a solid twelve hours' sleep, get an appropriate change of clothes for our plan, and then rendezvous back at my place in the Village around midafternoon tomorrow.

By that time, we should be well rested, and have gotten all the strategic details from Mr. Smith after his stakeout. It was important not only to discover if Grise was flying solo at home, but also details about the neighborhood, the target's house itself, and whether it was indeed a house or an apartment. If it was the latter, what floor was he on and what room number did he occupy?

"You think of everything," Eleanor murmured, as she leaned over toward me.

"Not quite everything," I said, my voice suddenly more husky.

"Are you going to stay for the fireworks when we get to his place?" She moved in as close as she could get, the stick shift on the floor between us.

"Only if it's a house." I nuzzled her neck. "If it's an apartment, I'll camp outside the door. In case of nosy neighbors."

"And what would you tell them if anyone came asking about all the noise going on inside?"

"I'd say that Grise and his girlfriend were having some serious sex."

"Sounds like a good idea to me," she said with a little catch in her voice.

"What?" I whispered. "Standing outside the door, or having some serious sex?"

"Definitely the serious sex part," she whispered back, and followed it up with a very, serious kiss.

A few minutes later, I was standing outside waving goodbye to her on a surprisingly cold night. Some ideas are great, but some great ideas have to wait for later.

But not too much later.

Wednesday, October 26, 1960

"You've gotta be yanking my chain, man!"

"Wouldn't think of it," I said to Mullen, as I listened to him grind his teeth over the phone.

"You want me to go on a private assignment to protect one of your friends from thugs?"

"You got it!"

"Because you're busy protecting other friends."

"Right on!"

"And you don't have enough associates to go around."

"I couldn't have said it better myself."

"You did," growled Mullen. "Twice! I was listening both times."

"And your answer to the $64,000 question is…"

"I'm a cop. A detective of police. I work for the great State of New York. I like my job. I'm reasonably well paid, and I want to continue working for the great State of New York. Does that answer your question, Gentry?"

I paused for a few seconds. "Is *no* your final answer?"

"Let me think about it." And he hung up.

As I looked at the dead phone in my hand, Zuni Smith came into the den, carrying two cups of dark Turkish coffee.

"And his response is negative?" he offered, passing one of the cups to me.

"He said he'd think about it," I replied, nodding my thanks for the fresh brew.

Smith had arrived home late from his assignment, and both he and I had slept in. By the time I started working in the den after my shower and shave, Mr. Smith was already a man in motion. Indeed, coffee was more than welcome.

My friend and confidant settled in one of my brown, leather chairs and we sipped our coffees as he proceeded with his report.

"You may be happy to note," he was saying, "that Grise actually lives in a modest, neat-looking bungalow. No slum, just a nice district, fairly close to Chinatown."

"Well lit street?" I prompted.

"Reasonable. Old-fashioned lamp standards—fluted bodies, like miniature pillars, topped with globe lights the size of basketballs. They're spaced about 30 yards apart, and give off a warm, subdued glow."

"So, the area isn't lit up like Time Square."

"Definitely not," my friend agreed. "It's a modest, middle-class neighborhood. Didn't hear any dogs barking, either. It should be relatively safe for prowling."

"So far, so appealing," I offered. "Yet it makes me wonder what a jerk like him is doing in a neighborhood like that. He must have some kind of regular employment, besides extorting money from his wife."

"Ahh," murmured Smith. "Good point. Actually, I believe that he does have a job. Shortly after I started my surveillance, I saw him come home. At least, I figure it was him, as he walked straight up the sidewalk, mounted the few steps, unlocked the door, and went straight in. Seemed very familiar with his surroundings. Besides, he was carrying a lunch pail in his right hand. Dressed like a dockworker."

"Any idea about a girlfriend, or live-in lady friend?"

"If she was living with that cretin, I'd hesitate calling her a *lady*," Smith said, with a rare sardonic smile. "However, the fact he used a key would suggest he was alone at that time of the evening."

"And the rest of the night?"

"I'd highly doubt any company. I hung around until five o'clock. He had no visitors. He didn't leave the house."

"It sounds encouraging."

"Maybe, but it may mean nothing. Perhaps a friend works a night shift, or Grise might have a visitor tomorrow night, or the night after."

Finishing my coffee, I set it down on the side of the dark walnut desk and jotted a few notes. "Tell me a little more about the neighborhood," I prompted.

"Definitely comfortable, middle-class," Smith began. "Some two-story buildings, but a lot of one-and-a-half-story jobs—Craftsman bungalows, with a single, large gable on the sloping roof, most likely the master bedroom. Rather dates the whole area from the 1920s onward."

He took another sip of his dark roast and continued. "The Craftsman bungalows have varied sidings—wooden shakes, clapboard, stucco. The larger homes have a lot of red brick. They're mixed in with the wooden siding and stucco buildings. Some have driveways, many don't. Short runs of grass out front, some with bushes framing the house fronts, some with trees at street level."

"How close to the street are the houses located?"

"Close. Twenty feet, 30 at most."

"Doesn't sound like there are any hiding places," I grumbled.

"As for Grise himself, he's a big guy," my friend continued. "About your height, perhaps a little taller."

I shrugged.

"Definitely a bloody big guy. Either he was wearing a linebacker's padding, or he's got impressive shoulders, and a set of arms to match."

"I could always bring my elephant gun—the Remington 30-06," I responded.

"Seriously, Cass, do you think Eleanor is really up for this brute?"

When Mr. Smith uses my first name, I know he's deadly serious.

I couldn't fault him for his concern, but in response, I shot him a steely look. I didn't have to say a word. He and I both knew how much Eleanor wanted to punish Grise.

After a moment, Smith nodded his assent, and then quietly cleared away the coffee cups. The die had been cast.

Thursday, October 27, 1960

Eleanor and I parked about a block from Grise's home in the old Italian suburb near Chinatown. This time, we were driving my wheels instead of her MG, in case we needed to make a fast getaway. The Jag might have been more easily identifiable, but it had twice the number of horses beneath the hood if we needed them.

It was shortly after 2:30 the next morning, and the area was as dead as Jacob Marley in *A Christmas Carol.* We were just a short walk away from Grise's house, but it was even darker than Mr. Smith had noted. It appeared that one of the globe lamps had burned out in the last 24 hours, and the scene was as dark as some of those *film noir* classics that were so popular in the '40s. Eleanor whispered that it felt like one of Orson Welles' recent movies; indeed, *Touch of Evil* had more than its share of disturbing and moody night scenes.

Clad in deepest black, both of us had dressed for the adventure. I was wearing the same getup and holster rig as I'd donned during my last visit to *Nick's Tavern,* while Eleanor, also clothed in solid blacks, was armed with a set of burglar tools and her well-trained pair of hands. For the caper, she'd also suitably sharpened her fingernails and painted them bloodred for the hell of it.

On our arrival, we reconnoitered Grise's abode one last time, then quietly strolled up the sidewalk and tiptoed up the stairs. Eleanor went to work on the lock, and within seconds, we were inside.

Once we got accustomed to the gloominess of the house, we were able to make out an old-fashioned living room to the left, a short hall-way that led straight to what appeared to be a kitchen, and a set of stairs to the right that presumably ascended to the bathroom and a couple of small bedrooms. It was not necessary to chance the aged steps whose creaks and groans might have given us away; the lord of the manor wasn't upstairs.

A quick glance around the living room told us that the place appeared to be dressed out in the same tired furniture it had when the compact bungalow was first built. It also told us that it was presently occupied.

The wifebeater was happily snoring away, as he lay stretched out on an ancient three-seater couch across the room from us. Lying asleep in his underwear, his work clothes carelessly tossed off, he'd apparently been pursuing one of his favorite indoor sports. With the aid of a small end table lamp, he'd been perusing a well-thumbed magazine. We slipped over for a closer look.

"*Playboy*," Eleanor whispered.

"Current issue," I whispered back.

"How do you know *that?*" she asked, her whisper getting a wee bit louder.

"It's open to the centerfold—Kathy Douglas."

"*And how do you know THAT?*" Eleanor demanded, her voice loud enough to wake the dead.

It was evidently loud enough to wake up Grise.

He popped up straight off the couch. "What the fu—"

I cut him off. "Naughty, naughty! Ladies present!" I cautioned him playfully.

"Who the hell are you two assholes?" he challenged.

I opened my leather jacket, displaying the gun and holster rig. Grise sat back down on the couch.

For 10 long seconds, nobody moved—Grise on the couch, Eleanor and I standing a few feet away from him. Eleanor was still looking at me, Italian fire shooting from her eyes to mine.

Finally, Grise broke the silence. "What the hell are you guys doing in my house?"

I smiled at Eleanor. "Do you want to tell him?"

She turned to the slightly bewildered wifebeater and calmly stated, "I came here to kick the shit out of you!"

Grise paused, then started to laugh as if he were watching a Three Stooges' movie. "Why?" he finally said. "You don't even know me?"

She took a step toward him. "You used to live in a Greenwich Village apartment with your wife. Her name is Helen. You were leasing it from a friend of hers who is studying in Paris. Helen works as a waitress in a restaurant near Washington Square. It used to be named *Best in the Village*. Now it's called *Bistro on the Square*. She works long, hard hours, brings home the paycheck, and you take most of it from her."

"That's a lie!" he snarled.

"No, it's not," she continued in a dangerously quiet voice. "She gives it to you, or you beat the living crap out of her. Right?"

He paused and looked over at me. I was now sitting on an old chair that obviously had come with the couch.

Turning back to Eleanor, he sneered, "So what? You gonna hit me with your purse? Beat me to death with your powder puff, while this jerk threatens me with his gun?"

Eleanor smiled. "No such luck, *schmuck.* The other night, you beat Helen so badly that you broke one of her arms and almost punched out both of her eyes."

"Tough shit!" He grinned. "If it wasn't for Silent Sam over there, I'd do the same to you. Then, I'd use you like a whore."

With that, I got up off the chair, zipped up my jacket, and started for the door. "He's all yours, kiddo."

"Hey, punk!" Grise shouted, when I'd almost reached the hall.

I turned around and watched him stand up and strike a belligerent pose. He really was a big son of a bitch.

"Why don't you take out your popgun," he said, "put it on the floor, then come back here and sit down?"

"Now, why would I do that?" I said, in my mild-mannered voice.

"So you can watch me give this broad a good beating, before I do the same to you!"

"Perfect," I said, and did exactly as he'd suggested.

Leaving the gun on the floor in the middle of the hallway entrance, I returned to my chair and settled in for the entertainment. As planned.

"Comfy, Mr. Slick?" Grise asked, as he hitched up his boxer shorts.

"And cozy," I replied with a smile.

Grise ignored me and took a menacing step toward Eleanor. She took a step backward, extended her right arm toward him, and opened her hand to signal *Stop!* He immediately stopped.

Swiftly taking off her leather jacket and tossing it over in my direction, she performed some ritualistic movements with her hands and arms, then immediately dropped into a slight crouch.

"What's this?" he smirked. "Some kind of karate crap?"

Maintaining her crouch, she extended both of her arms straight out to her sides, and curled the fingers of each hand into bloodred claws. Holding that pose, she began to sway from left to right, right to left.

Left to right, right to left, the sway never varying.

"What's this garbage?" Grise grunted. "Karate voodoo? You gonna cast a spell on me?"

Left to right. Right to left.

"It's called the *Dragon's Claw,*" I volunteered.

Left to right. Right to left.

Grise spat out an obscenity and took a step toward her.

Eleanor continued her side-to-side motions, never changing the rhythm, always moving.

Grise took another step.

Eleanor continued the same shifting cadence, but her right hand moved in toward her body and changed from a claw to a fist, the knuckle of the middle finger extended toward her attacker.

"You will note," I volunteered, "that her right hand is now in a different position. It's called the *Dragon's Fang.*

Left to right. Right to left.

Grise took another step, which brought him within striking distance.

Immediately, the claw of Eleanor's left hand shot out and raked her deadly nails across his right cheek.

His right hand grabbed his now lacerated face, four tracks of blood dripping from his cheek.

Before he could back away, Eleanor drove her right hand's *Dragon's Fang* straight into Grise's left eye.

Dropping forward in a ball of agony, Grise howled in pain and anger. He directed a barrage of curses and vulgar epithets at Eleanor, but she remained calm. Her hands were now up in a defensive pose as she lightly danced around his wounded figure, waiting for him to retaliate.

After a long moment, he slowly straightened up, blood streaming down his maimed cheek and a slight dribble of yellowish-red liquid issuing from the corners of his closed left eye.

Eventually, he rose to his full height, and lunged toward her.

She easily sidestepped his attack, slamming a sharp karate chop to the back of his neck as he passed her. His body teetered for a few seconds before he turned back to face her.

Eleanor didn't waste a moment. This time, her right-hand *Dragon's Claw* shot out and opened up Grise's left cheek, a punishment that was immediately followed by the *Dragon's Fang* of her left hand. The *fang* slammed into the wifebeater's other eye, with a pulpy smack that drove him to his knees, in a ball of tortured agony.

The pain was too much for him. His eyes wept tears of blood, and his cheeks ran with rivulets of red that soon stained the tired old rug beneath him.

I stood up and slowly went over to Eleanor. "Are we finished here?"

"Not quite."

She bent down and grabbed Grise's outstretched right arm. Holding him by the wrist, she extended the arm full-length. Giving it a quick, ratcheting twist in one direction, she then snapped it back around in the opposite direction. The cracking of the forearm bone was loud and sickening. Grise bellowed in torment.

Before he passed out, Eleanor whispered so softly into his ear that I almost missed the words she muttered. But I didn't. *If you ever lay another hand on Helen, I'll come back here and cut out both your eyes.*

I totally believed her.

Friday, October 28, 1960

By 6:30 the following evening, Eleanor and I were pulling into my favorite, underground parking lot—the one I always use when I dine at Sardi's, or go to the theaters in that area.

After our encounter with Grise last night, I'd returned her to the MG, and she'd driven back to the family mansion in Teaneck Township. There, she'd had a half-decent rest, and changed her clothes for a night on the town. We'd rendezvoused in time for our trip into the theater district.

Securing my custom-made hardtop for the Jag, we walked down 45th Street, past the Martin Beck Theater, soon rounded the corner, and cut over to 44th.

As we passed the St. James Theater, I started to drool. Laurence Olivier and Anthony Quinn were starring in the English translation of Jean Anouilh's masterpiece, *Becket.* Tickets were harder to find than the proverbial hen's teeth.

I paused to check out the enticing poster, but Eleanor tugged me away. "Not in your lifetime, big boy, unless these two guys stay in the show for years. You'd have to spend a small fortune for a pair of tickets."

"Who's getting the other ticket?" I said, which earned me a playful punch in the arm from Eleanor.

Arriving at Sardi's, we were effusively greeted by the immaculately dressed *maître d'.*

"Welcome back to Sardi's, Mr. Gentry," he said, "and the ever lovely Miss Palladino!" He even bowed to her.

Flashing a smile, I shook his hand and slipped him a little something. "Thanks for taking our reservation on such short notice, Emilio."

"My pleasure, sir," he enthused, as his hand disappeared into a tuxedo pocket. "It's always delightful to see both of you. Please permit me to show you to your table."

We placed our wine order, and were soon sipping a delightful Cabernet Sauvignon from Bordeaux. Soft, romantic strings were serenading us from the speaker system, and we were momentarily intrigued watching a middle-aged man with a young fellow beside him.

The man sported a handsome, graying beard, and was slightly shorter than his companion, a teen of about 17 or 18. The youth stood tall, was very thin, and had flowing, golden hair. There was a striking family resemblance between the two, and, as we soon learned, they were, indeed, father and son.

At the moment, they were checking out Sardi's celebrated collection of caricatures of famous Broadway personalities, from singers like Pearl Bailey, to movie directors like George Abbott, to film stars like the wonderful Katharine Hepburn. Over the years, the display has changed, and the celebrities that have graced the walls of Sardi's now number in the hundreds.

The pair seemed to be enjoying the display, especially the blond teen, whose reaction to many of the pieces was glee and admiration. We later discovered that the young man was fascinated by illustrated books, comics, and caricature art.

Interrupting the scene, however, was our waiter, who excused himself and politely asked if we'd decided on our appetizers. We had, and gave him our order.

"Excellent, Mr. Gentry. Superb, Miss Palladino," he exclaimed. "They'll be right out. Thank you for your orders, Mr. Gentry." With that, he bowed, clicked his heels and hurried off.

"Too much!" Eleanor murmured. "He's going to have to calm down the Mr. Jeeves routine, or he won't last long."

As I grinned across the table at her, I noticed that the father and son had left the celebrity caricatures and were heading in our direction.

"Excuse us for interrupting," the man declared when they arrived. He had a flat Canadian accent and a mischievous twinkle in his eyes. I judged him to be close to 50, and a man of business, very sure of himself.

"May I help you?" I asked.

"Sorry to interrupt," the man said, "but we couldn't help overhearing the waiter mention your name."

"Yes, he was rather…effusive, shall we say," I offered. "Do I know you?"

"No, but I'm familiar with the name Gentry. You *are* Cass Gentry, the detective who helped save Ernest Hemingway last October?"

I looked a little surprised and turned to Eleanor with a Gallic shrug.

"Not many people know that historical tidbit in this country," I responded.

"If we may sit down for a few minutes," he said with a smile, "I'll be most happy to explain myself."

"Of course," Eleanor chimed in. "We'd love to have the two of you join us."

Summoning our enthusiastic waiter, we asked him to hold the appetizers, and to bring our guests a drinks menu. They declined, as they had their own reservations near the back of our section. When they were settled in, the man proceeded with introductions.

"This is my son," he began. "His name is Max, and we're in town for a specialty art convention."

Following handshakes, I asked the boy, "Does Max stand for Maxwell or Maximilian?"

The young man grinned. "Just plain Max, sir." He gave a cheeky wink, and all of us laughed.

It was the father's turn. "I'm Trevor Andrew Benson," he said. "My family calls me Andrew or Drew, not to be confused with my father, who was also a Trevor."

Another round of handshakes ensued, and then Eleanor jumped in.

"If your family calls you Drew," she asked, "what does everyone else call you?"

The man gave a grin very much like his son's. "Somewhere down the line, some smartass stuck the first initials of my three names together, and started calling me *Tab*. Not wishing to be confused with the actor, Tab Hunter, I started writing my street name with two *B*'s. So, call me *Tabb*, with two *B*'s."

Both Eleanor and I shook hands with him as we tried out his street name.

After a brief round of laugher, I asked him, "Are you also in show-biz, like Tab Hunter?"

"Right on cue, Mr. Gentry," the amiable Tabb said. "That's why I know about you and the safe return of Hemingway to Cuba. I believe you called that adventure of yours *The Man With Hemingway's Face*."

"How do you know all this?" I asked our guest.

"Simple, my friend. I'm a television producer for the CBC in Canada. Last year, we had a stringer, a freelance journalist, working an assignment on modern-day piracy."

I sat back in my chair, took a sip of the cab-sauv, and glanced over at Eleanor. I realized where this was going.

"The stringer," Tabb continued, "just happened to be covering the exploits of a scallywag named Captain Stevenson, out of Cat Island in the Bahamas."

Eleanor smiled at me. She knew the story all too well herself.

Tabb carried on. "While doing his research on piracy, the stringer earned his keep aboard Captain Stevenson's ship. It was there, one day, that he made a most newsworthy discovery during one of his trips. Much to his delight, the freelancer recognized Ernest Hemingway, the Nobel-winning author."

Our narrator paused and looked around, apparently wishing to order a drink to wet his whistle. while he talked. Fortunately, our eager-to-please waiter was in our area, and I motioned him over. Minutes later, Tabb and Max were hoisting chilled bottles of Pabst Blue Ribbon beer, and the CBC producer was finishing up the tale of Hemingway's adventure on the high seas.

"During Hemingway's voyage to Cuba, our guy not only met the heroic writer himself, but also a detective named Cass Gentry, who had helped expedite the author's escape, which included an exchange of gunfire with an American Coast Guard vessel."

Tabb took another swig of his beer and wrapped up his yarn. "The story was sold to our network, and Hemingway and this guy Gentry became a bit of a TV sensation in Canada. At least until the next news cycle!"

All of us laughed at the producer's punch line, and then sat chatting pleasantly until the *maître d'* politely interrupted.

"So sorry to bother you folks," he apologized, "but I have an urgent phone call for you, Mr. Gentry."

Less than five minutes later, I was back at the table, shaking hands with Tabb and Max and preparing to leave a tip, and pay our bill.

I looked over at Eleanor, my heart still beating faster than usual.

"What is it?" she said, barely above a whisper.

"That was Zuni Smith on the phone. He got a call—with a message for me."

Eleanor looked concerned. "What message?"

"They have my mother."

Saturday, October 29, 1960

Late the following afternoon, we were picked up and shuttled from the Toronto International Airport to a modestly comfortable motel on the outskirts of Canada's second-largest city. Unfortunately, we were unable to get an early Sunday flight from LaGuardia, but when we landed in Toronto, our driver was able to drop us at the motel where we were staying overnight. Happily, our chauffeur was the newest member of our rescue team.

At first, there were three of us—Eleanor and I, along with Zuni Smith, who adamantly refused to remain in Manhattan. In Smith's mind, Maggie Gentry's life was at stake, not to mention that of her vengeful son.

Almost immediately following my phone call at Sardi's, Eleanor and I paid our bill, left before our meal had been served, waved goodbye to Tabb and Max, and returned to my apartment in Greenwich Village.

There, I brought Mr. Smith up to date, argued with him for almost 20 minutes, and finally consented to let him join us in our attempt to rescue my mother. Sometimes he loses, but most often my friend and mentor wins debates. Actually, it wasn't much of an argument. When Eleanor sided with Smith, it took me only a few heartbeats to throw in the towel.

With his usual stoic demeanor, Zuni Smith headed off to the bedrooms to pack our bags. Eleanor made a short shopping list of clothes she would buy in Canada, and I made a call to the after-hours order desk at LaGuardia Airport to book the earliest flight out to Toronto the following day.

While Mr. Smith gallantly gave up his bedroom for Eleanor (I lost this discussion, as well), I carried on with plans for more backup. The first phone call was to Mullen's police station to ascertain his availability. But I was out of luck—he was working undercover with the New Jersey State Police on a sting operation in Atlantic City. That beatnik daddy sure gets around.

Following that disappointment, I thought of someone I'd worked with in Canada on a similar case to Mullen's Atlantic City gig. Only that time, I was the imported talent helping out on a sting.

Briefly, this person was ideal for the job. In her past, she'd worked a dozen years for the local police in my mother's hometown, and being familiar with the area was a major plus. She was tough, talented, knew her way around weapons, and had combat skills that made her a perfect recruit for our team.

Another plus was that Mara Lombardi was presently a partner in a private detective agency in Toronto. If she had the time and inclination, Mara could pick us up at the airport in Malton, join the team, and convey us to my old homestead in Riverton, a three-hour drive from Toronto.

As luck would have it, Mara had the inclination, took the time, and met us at the Malton airport.

Later, at the motel, the four of us checked into our two rooms, Eleanor and Mara staying in one, and Mr. Smith and I in the other. Mara had decided that it would be more convenient and streamlined if she stayed with us, rather than driving across town to her own digs and then back.

After freshening up, the four of us met in my room for a council of war, and the first item on the agenda was the distribution of weapons. We hadn't wanted to chance bringing our own across the border, so Lombardi agreed to supply our arsenal.

From the small collection she brought in, Eleanor chose a Colt .38 Special, and I selected the Colt M1911 semiautomatic pistol with an extra clip.

Zuni Smith picked up an old Winchester 94 lever-action rifle. "My favorite .30-30," he muttered.

"Good choice," Mara said with a smile. "That baby can drop a moose from across town."

Smith nodded and hefted the Winchester, cradling it. He smiled, as if greeting an old friend, and tried out the lever. Seeming happy with its performance, he said, "Does it have a scope?"

"In the car. Wasn't sure you'd need one."

"Depends where they've stashed her."

Mara agreed, and opened up another satchel and dumped out a selection of knives. "Help yourselves," she said. Once we had, she packed up the unselected weapons.

"What are you using, Miss Mara?" Smith asked, as he leaned the Winchester against the wall beside his bed.

"A slightly used service revolver," she replied. "Smith & Wesson .38," she and Zuni Smith said at the same time.

The two of them laughed and grinned at each other.

Eleanor and I did a slight double take and exchanged looks that said, *Wow! Do you think it's possible?*

Still smiling, Mara packed up the rejected weapons, as Eleanor asked, "What's next on the agenda?"

"A tour of my mother's house---the information may be valuable to you," I said, and proceeded to describe the layout of 33 Lansing Crescent in the little city of Riverton, Ontario.

Specifically, my old homestead and my mother's current residence—when she isn't at the cottage on the Lake of Bays—is a one-and-a-half-story Craftsman construction, with a single, large gable on the second floor. It's located on a short block, with only one house on either side of it.

The ground floor is made out of Ontario fieldstone, while the gable is dark, stained clapboard. A walkway approaches a couple of steps leading to the front door. To the right, another path goes to the side door and a driveway that ends at the mouth of a single-car garage.

Inside the front door, a hallway runs straight ahead to the kitchen, while to the left is the living room. Across the hall, to the right of the entrance, is a set of stairs leading to the second floor. Fairly standard design for a Craftsman of the period---just like Grise's home.

Upstairs, there is a bathroom to the immediate right, and the master bedroom to the immediate left. That room is quite large, and is housed within the central gable of the building.

There are two smaller bedrooms—mine, which is straight ahead at the top of the stairs, and a guest room behind it. After my father sent me off to military school in upstate New York, and I decided to go to college at New York University, he turned my old room into a den and a business office away from our textile factory.

Now, my parents' room belongs to Mother alone, and has for a number of years. My father suddenly disappeared when I was studying at NYU, and we've never seen him since.

Back downstairs, at the end of the main hallway, but before reaching the kitchen, there is a door off to the right, leading to the side door and to the basement below. Off to the left of the kitchen is a dining room, which has a door that opens onto what my mother fondly refers to as the family room. It is decorated with soft, leather couches and chairs, and photographs of numerous special occasions on the walls.

Most of the photos involve Yours Truly in various stages of development. Not too spoiled, I might modestly add, but Eleanor, who has visited the homestead, has another take on that point of view. She once pointed out that it'd be more appropriate to describe the youthful *me* in three words— *spoiled little shit.*

The family room opens out through a solid, interior-locked door onto the backyard, which has six-foot-high privet hedges separating the property from our neighbors at the back and on either side of us. In front of these hedges are carefully tended flower beds and rosebushes, maintained by my mother with the help of a hired gardener.

A large, specially designed gazebo takes up residence in the middle of the backyard. Measuring 12 feet in diameter, it is constructed of oak beams and paneling, and the screening was specially imported from Europe. My mother wanted the best, and although she spends most of her summers at the cottage up north, she wanted something akin to the northern residence in order to enjoy the shoulder seasons of spring and autumn when the weather is agreeable.

But whenever it was time to mow the lawn, our usually amiable gardener cursed the structure, saying things like, *This ding-dang giz-e-boo makes it too ding-dang hard to cut the grass!*

As for the front lawn and the boulevard between the street's sidewalk and the road, there is no problem for the poor man—not a tree or a *giz-e-boo* in sight; there's only a standard, period globe-topped, streetlight on a tall, fluted lamppost. Result—Mr. Gardener is content as he tootles around the lawn with his gas-powered mower.

"What about the basement?" Mara Lombardi asked, as I finished my spiel.

"Good question," I said. "It's vulnerable to entry. It can be accessed from inside the house, as I've already explained, and from three different points outside—the side door to the right of the house, a ground-level window just to the right of the side door, and another ground-level window to the right of the kitchen window at the back of the house.

"Both of these windows are not only low to the ground, but they're also small, only large enough to admit a kid or a short man. In the past, the one by the side door was used for the coal chute, before my mother converted the furnace to oil. Both of them serve as an outdoor light source, and as ventilation in warm weather before my mother installed air-conditioning."

There was a long pause. No questions. Perhaps too much information at one time.

"Let's take a break," I said. "There's a diner across the street, and the tab's on Eleanor."

"Like hell it is!" she said, and told me what I could do with that suggestion.

We all laughed, stowed our weapons away, and headed for the diner. The remainder of the night was going to be for rest and relaxation. In the morning, on our way to Riverton, I'd go over the floor plan again, as well as explain everyone's personal assignment. There were going to be a lot of angles to cover.

Sunday, October 30, 1960

"Tell me," Zuni Smith asked Mara at lunch the next day, "how did you manage to get on the Riverton police force? Most small cities are populated with male cops."

Smith posed his question during a lunch break in the town of Dundas, having spent our trip from Toronto going back over the floor plan of my mother's house. He sat beside Mara in the restaurant booth, with Eleanor and I facing them. In spite of their age difference, they appeared to be getting along like the proverbial blazing house. Eleanor had nudged me with her knee more than once during the meal.

"To be honest," Mara answered Smith, "the police didn't have much choice."

"How do you mean?" Smith had turned sideways, glancing at her with sincere interest and a noticeable sparkle in his eyes.

"Simple. A colleague of my father's had a little talk with the chief of police. Naturally, I was inducted into the force, without ever showing a training certificate or my graduate degree."

"Amazing!" Eleanor said, and there was a big smile on her face. She knew the routine.

By now, all of us suspected that Mara Lombardi was closely related to a certain head of a criminal organization. Very closely related.

Her dad is in the import/export business—a polite euphemism for the same kind of trade Eleanor's father runs. You know what I'm talking about. *The Man* says, "You listen to why I've *imported* you to this crew, or else my boys will *export* your body to a very deep and very damp place. *Capisci?*"

Mara's father is Mateo Lombardi, the head of a mid-level Mafia crew in Hamilton. He's sometimes affiliated with the Luppino Mob, because of their connections with the syndicate in Buffalo. However, Lombardi tries to keep out of the way of the Musitano and Papalia families. Those guys are the real thing, heavy hitters of the first degree.

Not much later, we were driving up the Clappison Cut on our way to Riverton via Highway 8. The Cut was steep and a challenge to drivers back in the day when cars had to be slipped into low gear to make the climb.

However, this was no problem for us. Mara was driving her 1956, two-tone green Dodge Regent—the one with the needle-sharp tail fins and the push-button gear changer to the left of the steering wheel. "This baby has lots of scat—big V8 engine," she declared.

During the ascent, she hummed along to Bobby Darin's hit, "Mack the Knife," while the rest of us remained silent, checking out the steep wall of rock on our right, and the long drop-off on the other side of the road.

Fifteen minutes later, we were at Clappison's Corners, the junction of Highways 5 and 8. I didn't need to cue Mara on which way to go. She'd done her homework, and drove straight across Highway 5 and headed for Riverton on what used to be called King's Highway 8. From there, it was an easy drive, as we passed sleepy villages such as Rockton and Sheffield.

They were picturesque, little communities off the highway, and they always reminded me of when I was a young teenager and allowed to borrow the family car. Today, I had flashbacks to the quaint, tiny church in Rockton, helping a girlfriend rake up leaves for a Halloween bonfire, and buying ice-cold Cokes at the old general store in Sheffield whenever we played ball against their team.

It wasn't long after that when my father, having pulled a few strings, shipped me off to Eagle Ridge, an American military school west of the Hudson River in New York State. It was a prep school for young American men hoping to get into West Point, but my father didn't give a damn about that. All he wanted to do was toughen me up, make a man of me—and Eagle Ridge succeeded.

After graduating, I left home for good, went on to take a degree at NYU, and then entered into the Korean War. When the conflict ended, I stayed in the States, got a green card, and have worked there ever since.

But now it was time to get down to business, and after a few more miles on old Highway 8, I started to discuss assignments with my team.

The instructions I'd received over the phone at Sardi's were short, not so damned sweet, and very explicit. *Go to your mother's house in Riverton. Be there at eight o'clock on Sunday night. Come alone, or we kill the old lady first.*

"As soon as we get to town," I began, "Mara will park around the corner from Suzie's Restaurant on the main drag. It's one I've never frequented, and the odds are good I won't be recognized when Mara and I go in to order sandwiches and soft drinks for all of us."

"Food's a good idea," Mr. Smith said. "It'll be a long haul 'til eight bells." Everyone agreed, and Mara even tooted the horn a couple of times.

"After we get the food," I continued, "I'll drop the three of you off near your starting points. Once we're in our assigned places, we can eat whenever we wish—but keep alert. These guys don't appear to be fooling around. I should arrive at the house by six o'clock or earlier, just to be on the safe side."

"What if they have the same idea, and set up early as well?" Eleanor asked.

"Good question, but it's a chance we'll have to take. However, I don't figure they'll be there two hours ahead of time."

"You hope," my partner scoffed.

I ignored the crack, and went on with my game plan. "We're all going to arrive at our destinations within a few minutes of each other. When I get to the house, I'll park in front of the garage, leave the car keys in the ignition, and walk up to the front door. I'll use my own key to the house and go inside.

"While I'm doing that, the three of you will move from where I dropped you off into your home positions. If the bad guys are already inside the house, I'll make a loud enough racket that'll tip you off. Most likely, they'll shut me up, but not kill me. My bet is they'll transport me to a killing ground, where my enemy, who's hired these bozos, can take great pleasure in finishing the job. If I'm captured and they leave the house with me, Mr. Smith will slip into the car and follow them at a discrete distance."

"How will I do that in time?" Smith asked.

"Simple. Your spot is inside the garage. I need you to cover the right flank of the house. The old coal shute window is an easy access. If someone tries to get into the house from there, while I'm in the house, kill him."

"That'll make a lot of noise," Eleanor said.

"No problem," Mara interjected. "It's the night before Halloween. It'll sound like kids fooling around with some of their fireworks."

"Fair enough," Eleanor agreed. "So, where's my home position?"

"You'll be in the gazebo, covering any intruders that plan an attack by cutting through the yard from the side streets."

Eleanor paused for a moment. "How do they get over those big ol' privet hedges?"

"They don't. There are small, squeeze-through places between the hedges facing the two side streets, and the one that runs along the backyard."

She nodded and looked toward the front seat where Mara was driving.

"Where do you think I should place you, Mara?" I asked.

Raising her voice a little over the thrum of the V8 engine, Mara suggested, "Either put me down the street someplace as a spotter, or stick me in the gazebo with Eleanor. It might be tough for her to keep an eye on both points of a possible attack."

"Good idea," Eleanor agreed, "particularly if they strike from both sides at the same time."

It was settled, then. As my beatnik friend Mullen would say, "That's the plan from the Man, Stan!"

By 6:05 p.m., all of us were in place. The car was within a few feet of the garage. The garage door was open, and Mr. Smith was snuggled inside close to the vehicle. Sitting comfortably on a couple of garden chair cushions, he wolfed down his ham and cheese sandwich, his rifle nestled in his lap. He had a clear view of the side of the house, especially the basement window.

I had given Eleanor a key to the gazebo, and both women were ensconced inside.

Before going into the house, I'd taken a tour of the property. I had second thoughts about putting Eleanor and Mara together, instead of having one of them stationed as our spotter down the street at a local bus stop. However, the more I thought about it, the less I became enchanted with switching our plans. What we should have had, I realized, were walkie-talkies. But it was too late for that now.

After my excursion around the grounds, I entered the house, drew out my Colt M1911 and performed a slow circuit of the familiar rooms. Starting with the living room, I headed down the hallway, checked out the kitchen, the dining and family rooms. Everything seemed to be in order. Then I headed up the stairs, surveyed the den, washroom, bedrooms and closets. Again, everything in order, everything in its proper place—except for my mother. Next, I executed a thorough examination of the basement, followed by a search of the downstairs' closet for any unwanted guests who might be lurking inside its depths.

Finally, satisfied with my investigation, I sat in the living room, gun by my side, and waited for the sound of a key being inserted into the front door lock.

Time dragged, and I started to wish I'd brought along the latest book I was reading to alleviate my growing boredom. As you might guess, I favor reading mysteries—from Poe and Christie, to Chandler and John Dickson Carr, even Mickey Spillane's popular Mike Hammer mysteries on occasion. Sometimes, I venture into science fiction, particularly tales with a dystopian future theme. I was presently immersed in Walter Miller's *A Canticle for Leibowitz*, which I think someday could be considered a classic.

However, I hadn't schlepped it along with me, and thinking about the monks in Miller's postapocalyptic novel wasn't relieving my boredom. Finally, I pocketed my gun, climbed upstairs to the den, and rummaged around mother's bookcase.

Before long, I'd settled on the gothic mystery *My Cousin Rachel*, by Daphne Du Maurier. I'd read a few of her books already and liked them. However, I'd never read this one—only seen the movie with Olivia de Havilland and Richard Burton. So, after making a quick bathroom pit stop, I returned to the living room, book in hand, and settled in for an enjoyable read. Even the first sentence was an attention grabber. However, as captivating as the first few chapters were, I started to doze off.

The planning, the long drive, the small, niggling details—all had combined to take their toll on me. Before too long, I was sound asleep.

Until the phone rang. Once, twice, and I was awake. Checking my watch, I saw that it was almost 8:20. I had been out of it for over an hour and a quarter.

I tossed the Du Maurier book, rushed into the hall, and answered my mother's phone.

"Good evening, Mr. Gentry," a male voice said, his tone suave, cultured, dignified. And I could immediately picture the man behind the voice. Tall, middle-aged, handsome—with a large, glittering smile.

I'd bet my Jaguar that the man was wearing a black homburg hat.

Monday, October 31, 1960

Halloween

Last night, we stayed at my mother's house. Zuni Smith slept in Mother's old room; Eleanor slept in my old room, now Mother's den; and Mara took up residence in the guest room. I stayed on the living room chesterfield, and tossed and turned for what seemed like hours. Homburg Man's news hadn't been promising.

Sometime before dawn, I nodded off and was plagued by bizarre dreams, obviously related to our situation.

In one of them, the four of us, all armed, were spread out in the stands of Yankee Stadium. On the pitcher's mound, a woman who looked very much like my mother, Maggie, was tied to a tall stake. She was wearing a familiar navy suit, and a matching scarf that was wrapped around her mouth. She looked as if she'd been prepped for burning.

In the dream, I slowly meandered down the steps to my left, as if I was trudging through melted toffee. At the same moment, the other members of my party did the same from their places in the stands.

As the toffee thickened, it seemed to take me forever to arrive at the barrier between the stands and the field. But when I did, I discovered that we weren't alone.

Suddenly, out of the dugout appeared a phalanx of armed men. Each of them carried a rifle at the *port* position, and marched in unison like a precision squad.

As they approached the stake, they broke off and formed a semi-circle around my mother's trussed-up body. Then, coming to a snappy halt, they maneuvered their rifles into a *present arms* position. It seemed very impressive.

Then I looked around, and found that I was all by myself; somehow, Eleanor, Mara, and Zuni Smith had disappeared. When I glanced back at the rifle squad, they no longer appeared impressive. Instead, they were wearing grotesque Halloween masks—ghosts, werewolves, vampires, aliens from outer space, humanoid monsters. There were enough gruesome creatures to please the most ardent horror fanatic.

Then, as I was reviewing this collection of monstrosities, an unexpected movement from the pitcher's mound caught my eye. My mother was no longer wearing the scarf around her mouth; her eyes were no longer closed. In fact, the woman at the stake was no longer my mother.

This creature's eyes were ablaze with fire, and its mouth was unnaturally cavernous, a gaping hole that encompassed more than half of its face. As I was adjusting my mind to this spectacle, the creature suddenly emitted a bone-chilling shriek that sounded worse than any set of fingernails tearing across the surface of a blackboard.

Immediately I shrank from the screeching, but before this impossible-to-endure noise had faded away, the hole expanded, growing larger and larger, wider and wider, until it almost swallowed the face entirely. And inside that enormous maw, a ragged set of fangs dripped with pieces of some kind of flesh and a liquid that could only be fresh blood. Then the creature opened its mouth even more and … spoke.

With outstretched arms that were no longer bound, she hissed, "Come to me, darling. Come to your hungry mother, my beloved Cass."

This time, I was awake for good.

Later that morning, the other three tumbled out of bed nearer to ten o'clock than to nine. I rustled up a breakfast of bacon and eggs, toast, and freshly brewed coffee. After eating our fill in near silence, we retreated to the living room, and rehashed last night's discussion about the disappointing news.

Homburg Man had politely informed me that there'd been a change of plans. Instead of trading my mother for me at the house, they'd moved the swap to another venue.

This time, the transfer would take place about 10 miles out of town. The rendezvous would occur at a baseball park that the town council had lobbied for a number of years earlier. Mara explained that they had expected it to be a huge financial success, not only for baseball, but also for other popular events, such as car racing, fall fairs, soccer, and even cricket.

"It's almost like a mini baseball stadium," Mara said. "Think of Yankee Stadium in the Bronx. Then picture a structure that's 80% smaller."

Smith shook his head. "That's crazy!"

"The local council didn't think so," Mara responded. "They believed such a palace would bring in people and events from far and wide. They figured if you made it big and beautiful, and very professional-looking, folks would come from miles around and fill their 10,000 seats every time. They even gave it a fancy-schmancy name—Oxford Place."

"That sounds impressive enough," Eleanor muttered, "but what happened to it?"

Mara shrugged and shook her head. "Unfortunately, Oxford Place was a bomb. Although the fall fair was a financial success every year, the racetrack never materialized, and no parents wanted to drive their kids that far out to play peewee ball, when there were a half a dozen parks with diamonds in the town already. Even the Intercounty

Baseball League team can only bring in 700 or 800 paid attendees a game. Maybe a thousand or so when they make the playoffs. But even that is a stretch."

"What happened to their big plans for soccer and cricket?" I asked.

"Same story as the peewee league kids. There were soccer fields in several of the local parks, already, as well as one at the high school. As for cricket, nobody was interested. The closest the town ever came to cricket was lawn bowling, and that only needed one field in the whole community.

"What the town council had overlooked was that Riverton is a solid *hockey town*. Of the city's 25,000 or so people, I would guess that well over 70% skate or have skated in their lifetime. I'd also bet that most of the folks in town cheer for either the Toronto Maple Leafs or the Montreal Canadiens. And in my time there as a cop, Riverton Arena Gardens was always packed to the rafters. And it didn't matter if the local team was in the playoffs or not."

"Look," I interjected. "All this about overzealous politicians breaking the bank and building a white elephant is very interesting. However, sometime tonight, while all the ghosties and goblins are having fun in town, we have to get our asses out to the boonies and save my mother!"

"And there are some pretty attractive asses sitting here," Zuni Smith observed.

Eleanor and Mara snorted with laughter, and I believe Mara even blushed a little. The tension had been broken, thanks to Mr. Smith, and we set about planning our strategy.

"Mara," I started, "tell us more about this dream palace. Describe it for us. In detail, if you don't mind."

And she proceeded to do so.

Early that afternoon, we drove out to the stadium to prepare for a difficult encounter with Homburg Man and his hoods. According to his instructions, the exchange would be made an hour after dark. He gave the usual proviso about appearing solo, but I didn't really believe he was naive enough to think I'd come alone.

Once again, I figured arriving early might give us the upper hand. If they anticipated that move, we were prepared—we'd arrive even earlier than we had at my mother's house. We needed to get into place in unfamiliar surroundings and to be ready to put our plans into action.

Shortly after two in the afternoon, we were on our way, driving into a day that was bright and autumnally beautiful. The temperature was hovering around the low 70s. With this kind of weather, we were beginning to embrace the adventure.

About a mile out of town, we stopped at a roadside diner, ordered up some takeout barbecue chicken burgers and sodas, and hit the road for our encounter with the unknown.

After leaving the diner, Mara continued to drive, while the rest of us went over this morning's planning session.

Mara's information about the stadium had been very detailed, very precise.

"Oxford Place is located in an old farmer's field," she began, "and it looks very much like an upside-down bowl, with two tiers of seating. It's horseshoe-shaped, with the legs of the shoe extending toward the outfield."

"How far back does the field go?" Eleanor asked. "Is it wide-open? Partly forested? Is there a tree line close by?"

"Beyond the outfield is a large number of open acres," Mara answered. "The town council had planned for the racetrack to go there, as well as the cricket and soccer pitches. In the end, the only person whose dreams came true was the farmer who'd sold them the land. He became rich overnight."

Zuni Smith turned and looked at me. "There's no way that your Homburg Man and his mugs have any intention of driving up to the stadium and making their play out in the open."

"That's right," I agreed. "Instead, they'll want someplace enclosed, somewhere they can determine if I *am* alone—as well as vulnerable."

"There are two perfect places for us to position ourselves," Mara said. "On the ends of each leg of the horseshoe are refreshment stations. They're stocked and serviced by sales staff from *inside* the stadium. The customers line up *outside* and make their purchases through a large, wooden opening that can be closed and locked up when not in use."

She continued, "Other vendors, with strapped-on trays, were supposed to be selling product in the stands. You know—*Getcha peanuts, popcorn, Cracker Jack!* However, this seldom happened. The crowds were too small, and the teams couldn't afford the extra salaries."

"The refreshment booths seem like pretty good places," Eleanor declared, "but how about the dressing rooms?"

"Also a possibility," Mara agreed. "Not quite as good as the booths, but they have their advantages. They're located just inside the left arm of the horseshoe, just beyond each team's dugouts. Also, both have their own shower and washroom facilities, and both of them are a stone's throw from the offices and central lobby in the hump of the horseshoe."

"That's a good thing," I offered. "If the two dressing rooms and offices are that close to one another, the area could be patrolled by only *one* of us."

"Perfect," Zuni Smith remarked. "That would leave the fourth person to act as sniper."

"What do you mean?" Mara asked.

"Simple. What if they don't want to negotiate the trade in some enclosed place? What if they want to swap *out in the open?*"

"It's possible," Eleanor agreed. "However, a showdown in the open could lead to some pretty hairy stuff."

"Like what?" Mara demanded.

"Like grabbing Cass and keep Mrs. Gentry for further blackmail."

"It could also lead to a firefight," Mr. Smith offered. "A sniper could cool down a bad situation with only one killshot."

Mara scoffed, "It could also lead to the Gunfight at the Oxford Corral!"

Smith ignored the comment and asked her where the scoreboard was located.

"Straightaway center field. About 150 yards out. They tried to keep it away from right and left infield locations."

"Good. That's within my Winchester's range. I'll just climb up into the scoreboard keeper's box and sight the 30.30 through his opening. If things get dicey, *pop goes the weasel.* Or two."

Nobody had anything to add, so we broke up the meeting in mother's living room and prepared for the trip to Oxford Place.

As I finished mentally reviewing Mara's information, she was maneuvering the car into an old, abandoned farmer's lane. Slowing to a crawl, she nudged the Regent through a gathering of fallen leaves, and soon found a suitable opening between two oak trees. She barely had enough room to park between them, but it was sufficient for her needs.

"We'll leave the car here," she said, and started to pack up. "I don't want the punks to find it parked around the stadium, which would lead to some undesirable complications."

Each of us checked our weapons, grabbed our food, and started to hoof it to the stadium. Mara, our guide, was already half a dozen yards ahead of us.

After trudging down a dirt road for 10 minutes, we arrived at Oxford Place. On our descent, we surveyed the surrounding landscape. The stadium faced straight out toward a grassy field that was just beginning to prepare for winter. The property was impressive, in spite of its disappointing legacy.

As Mara had indicated, the stadium was horseshoe-shaped, with the hump of the shoe facing the entrance to the park, and the legs of the shoe pointing directly toward the outfield. The access road we were walking on lay between the back of the nearest leg, and a large, empty parking lot was situated to the left of the roadway.

The entrance to the building was around by the center of the horseshoe's hump and presumably opened into the legs and levels of the stadium, as well as to the ticket booths, lobby, washrooms, and tuck shop.

Between the legs of the horseshoes lay the pitcher's mound, home plate, all three bases and base paths, and beyond that the outfield. The scoreboard was well out of normal hitting range, although an eagle-eyed observer would be able to pick out some very noticeable dents.

The designers of Oxford Place's location had made good choices, as the direction of the setting sun was toward the right infield fence. If they'd located the scoreboard in that area, the fans would have had a difficult time reading the board, and the scoreboard itself would have had a lot more indentations than it had at the moment.

When we reached the stadium, Mara took us to the front entrance, and then cast a knowing glance at Eleanor. My partner, having been co-opted to perform the ritual of *open sesame*, happily withdrew what she needed from her traveling kit, and proceeded to perform her magic.

Once inside, Mara checked her watch, and quickly set about introducing us to the offices and various amenities in the main hump of the horseshoe. Then she gave us a quick tour of the two dressing rooms, showers, toilets, and players' lounge.

Once the tour was over, we gathered in the players' lounge—just inside the left leg of the horseshoe, and close to the lobby and parking lot— to decide who was going to cover each of the possible areas for the exchange.

"Eleanor, you get first choice," our hostess said.

"I'll opt for the refreshment booth," Eleanor replied.

"Which one?"

She picked the one on this side of the horseshoe, and I took the other one across the field.

"Fair enough," Mara said, as she withdrew her .38 Special from her shoulder holster. "How about you, Zuni?" She flipped open the barrel to check that all six bullets were in place. "Are you still thinking about hanging around the scoreboard?"

Mr. Smith gave her a thumbs-up and patted the stock of his Winchester.

She gave him an OK sign, and then told us she'd patrol the office area and the dressing rooms.

"Just remember," she concluded, "we're here to save Mrs. Gentry. But if the train goes off the rails, shoot to kill those sons of bitches!"

Near nightfall, everyone was in their prearranged spots. Zuni Smith was up in the scorekeeper's gondola, Eleanor was hiding under the display counter of the left leg of the horseshoe, I was in the same spot in the right leg, and Mara was covering the dressing rooms and players' lounge. All of us were quietly biding our time, waiting in silence with our own private thoughts.

Personally, I would've preferred to be closer to the main area, and my concern for my mother was mounting as time passed. For her sake, I didn't want any shooting, and I certainly didn't have any qualms about being exchanged for her safety. Nevertheless, my heart was heavy with the thought of anything happening to her, and I stewed away in solitary silence.

As the hours dragged on, my levels of anxiety and anger mounted in direct proportion to the slow movement of the setting sun. Through cracks in the boarded-up window opening, I could discern the gradual darkening of the day, as my watch face lit up in accord with the failing light outside.

For a moment, I pictured the streets of Riverton, with scores of trick-or-treaters—dressed up as ghosts, werewolves, vampires, aliens from outer space, humanoid monsters—roaming about, their bags stuffed with treats.

I woke with a start, realizing I'd drifted off to sleep in the dark, and that I'd revisited my dream from last night.

Then I heard the sounds of several vehicles on their way down the roadway to the park.

For the next 10 or 15 minutes, all was still. The vehicles had been parked, and no sounds interrupted the stillness of the night. More time slipped by, and then, without warning, things started to pop.

Suddenly, the entire park lit up, bathed in the bright stadium lights. I paused, and then slowly withdrew from my hidey-hole, clutching my Colt semiautomatic.

Then a voice, amplified by a megaphone, blared, "Cass Gentry! We know you're here, my friend. After a brief search, we found your car stowed away up the road in the woods."

I thought, *That voice could only belong to Homburg Man.*

"Come along, Cass," the voice urged. "We know you didn't come alone, as per our instructions, you naughty boy. We looked inside the car, and discovered the vehicle's registered to Miss Mara Lombardi of Hamilton, Ontario."

Homburg Man paused.

"We also know that Miss Lombardi accompanied you here, and we know *that* because we have her tied up in the players' lounge. Now, be a good fellow and come out to the pitcher's mound, before I'm forced to send some nasty fellows around to *dig* you out."

I moved over to the door and locked it, expecting that the goons were already on their way to start *digging*.

As I waited by the door, Homburg Man rattled on about having Mara hauled out to join him on the mound, where his boys would perform some very nasty rituals on her.

I didn't have long to wait. I heard one of the gunsels coming down the inside corridor to my location. Apparently, he got an ego boost from the sound of his own footsteps—he clicked along with a pair of cleats on the heels of his shoes.

Within moments, he was at the door and trying the handle. Finding it locked, he began to throw his weight against the door. Once, twice…I unlocked the door. When he bashed into the heavy barrier for the fourth time, I swung the door open.

He spilled into the refreshment booth, and his momentum propelled him across the room, where he smacked into the locked wooden window face-first at full force.

A gun flew out of his hand, and he caromed back into the middle of the room. There, he turned around, blood streaming from his nose, and blinked at me stupidly.

"Hi there, Grandma," I said pleasantly. "I'm the Big Bad Wolf."

He nodded dumbly, tried to catch the streaming blood with both hands, and started looking around the room—for his missing rod, I presumed. Or maybe it was something else—his teeth, his nose, his absent brains.

Regardless, I put him out of his misery with a sharp whack across the back of his head with my own weapon, and eased him to the floor. Then, I proceeded to tie him up—hands with his shoelaces, feet with his belt.

Finally, making sure he was turned on his side so he wouldn't choke on his own blood, I picked up his piece, left the room, and made my way up the western corridor. Soon I was around the roundabout to the left side of the horseshoe.

Meanwhile, Eleanor, having heard Homburg Man's diatribe over the megaphone, decided to lend a hand. She left the refreshment booth she'd been stationed in, and quickly moved up the corridor nearest her at about the same time as I was booting it up mine.

It must have been about that time that she bumped into another one of the thugs on his way to check out the left-leg refreshment stand.

"Who the hell are you?" he demanded.

"I'm your Fairy Godmother," she replied, "and I'm going to put you to sleep."

"Like hell you are," he snarled, and took a step toward her. That was as far as he got.

She booted him right between his legs, and as he gasped and bent over in agony, she kneed him in the face. Like a pinball, he bounced off the corridor wall, and was immediately met with a *Dragon's Fang* straight-arm in the throat. He sagged to the floor, and threw up all over his shoes. She smacked him across the head with her Colt Special, and moved on.

Somewhere near the players' lounge, we met. With our weapons drawn, we silently moved toward the lounge, where we expected to see my mother under an armed guard of at least two of the hoods. Turns out, we were wrong.

Instead of two armed guards, there was only one. Instead of Maggie Gentry, the prisoner was Mara, who sat with her hands tied behind her back.

I made a *shushing* sign to the punk who was on guard duty, but he had to be a hero. Instead of keeping his mouth shut, he made a play for his gun. Not fast enough. I fired a bullet into his face, while Eleanor put a couple in his chest.

At that point, I left my partner with Mara, fled the lounge, and found the closest dressing room. Just as I slipped inside, the megaphone came back to life.

"Is that you making all the noise, Cass?" Homburg Man said. "I wouldn't do anything rash, my friend. We have your mother out here, and she doesn't seem very happy with her two escorts."

As I opened the dressing room door to the dugout, I saw Homburg Man near the pitcher's mound. Off to his left, 10 or 15 yards away near home plate, stood my mother, accompanied by two armed thugs.

A dozen or so yards behind them, between home plate and first base, stood another two characters. One of them was dressed like the other creeps, while the second player was quite completely different— he was immaculately decked out in a three-piece gray suit. Whoever he was, he gave the scene a surreal air.

Although the hood was armed, the man in gray didn't appear to be carrying—but he was bizarrely different from the rest of the crew. He was wearing a red Halloween mask with horns—unmistakably the Devil.

"Come on out, Cass," invited Homburg Man without using his bull-horn. He'd glimpsed me standing in the doorway to the dugout. "We're all friends here. Aren't we, Mrs. Gentry?"

I stepped outside, still holding my Colt semiauto.

"Don't be bashful, Cass. We're all one big, happy family. Just put down your gun, and come on over here for the exchange."

Then he addressed the jerk on Maggie's right side, and his tone was a lot more frigid. "Jennings, if Sonny Boy tries any heroics, I want you to put a bullet into Mrs. Gentry's brain. Understand?"

Jennings hesitated a moment.

Homburg Man addressed the other gunsel, "If Jennings can't perform that task, you do the job, Connors."

Jennings and Connors started to raise their weapons at the same time, but the first hood now appeared to be more eager. Jennings' handgun was up and almost touching Maggie's head, but that's as far as it got. There was the crack of a rifle shot from center field, and Jennings' head exploded in a spray of blood and bone.

Emerging from behind the scoreboard, Zuni Smith climbed down from the gondola with his Winchester rifle in hand. Within seconds, he was booting it across the playing field to join the fray.

"That wasn't very sporting," Homburg Man said, as he dropped his megaphone and pulled out a revolver.

My mother's other guard, Connors, spun her around to face the outfield, while he attempted to hide behind her with his rod at the back of her head.

At the same time, Devil Man, in the gray outfit, snatched a hand-gun from out of a holster rig hidden beneath his jacket, while the thug beside him was pretending to be Roy Rogers, with a six-shooter in each hand.

At that point, all attention turned to me, but I was no longer alone. Beside me stood Eleanor and Mara, guns at the ready. We quickly moved forward and fanned out onto the open grass in front of the dug-outs—Eleanor to her right, near where Maggie was being held; Mara to her left, in a direct line to second base; and me between the two, nearly opposite the man on the mound.

"It needn't end like this," Homburg Man yelled. "In a shoot-out, nobody wins."

"All I want is my mother. Give her up, and we'll be on our way. No harm, no foul."

Nobody moved, no one spoke. Meanwhile, Zuni Smith pounded his way toward us from the outfield.

As I turned in Smith's direction, he stopped above second base and dropped to a kneeling position. Up went his rifle, and within seconds, he'd squeezed off a pair of shots. Nobody dropped, but Maggie visibly flinched.

"Stop shooting!" my gutsy mother cried. "You almost hit *me.*"

Smith's head dropped to his chest, and I heard him mutter, "I'm getting too old for this crap."

As I started to say, "Just get your wind back," Homburg Man swung around and fired off a couple of rounds in Smith's direction. One of them hit its target, and I could see the Winchester fly out of my friend's hands as he dropped to the ground.

Mara, who was closest to him, made a mad dash toward Zuni. At the same time, Roy Rogers and Devil Man ran in front of the pitcher's mound to join up with my mother and Connors.

Almost simultaneously, Eleanor and I fired our weapons.

Eleanor, who was closest to Maggie, fired twice at Connors. Both her bullets hit home, and Connors' chest appeared to blow apart. My partner hadn't taken any chances with her .38 Special; she'd loaded it with heavyweight 158 grain ammo.

Meanwhile, I set my sights on Homburg Man, the apparent ringleader. Sooner or later, I'd have to get rid of him, but I also had to find out who'd hired him for this Halloween extravaganza. For a brief moment, I considered the creep in the Devil's mask to be a strong contender. However, I remembered the old adage, *Better the devil you know than the devil you don't know.* So, I stuck with Homburg Man.

At the same moment that Eleanor fired, I let loose with a shot at Homburg Man before he had a chance to fire at me. My bullet winged him just above his left kneecap, and he dropped to the pitcher's mound in agony. I swore out loud—I was aiming for his upper thigh. However, on second thought, it worked just as well. Mr. Suave and Cool wasn't going anywhere soon.

Following my shot, I ran out to the pitcher's mound and immediately located the guy's piece. While he was rolling around, I checked out the situation behind second base. Mara signaled me that Zuni Smith was okay, and pointed to the upper part of her left arm. I nodded back at her, and shifted my focus to Maggie.

She was now in the clutches of Roy Rogers and the mystery man behind the mask. Roy had one gun trained on Maggie, while he'd holstered the other in favor of a strong grip on my mother's shoulder. Devil Man was standing on Maggie's other side, his own gun in hand.

Eleanor was still on the grass in front of the dugout, but her gun was trained on the threesome. Roy and Devil Man in turn had their weapons aimed at her.

As my mother's captors started to shift toward the left leg of the stadium, Eleanor moved to her right in an attempt to cut them off.

This maneuver prompted the gunslinger to stick his six-shooter under Maggie's chin, while snarling something at her that I couldn't make out. At the same time, they kept moving in an obvious attempt to escape by the lounge door.

"Go around the back of the stadium!" I yelled to Mara. "They're heading for the cars!" She gave me another okay sign in the air, and sprinted for the leg end of the building and the long run around to the parking lot.

As Mara took off, I turned in time to see Devil Man make a break for the lounge door on his own. That action and my yelling to Mara had distracted Eleanor, and by the time she turned back to take a shot at him, he was already inside the lounge. Her two shots only hit the outside door. Devil Man was well on his way to the front doors, and Eleanor's six-shooter was empty.

In turn, the gunslinger fired at Eleanor, barely missing her as the bullet thwacked into the end of the dugout. At the same time, I attempted to draw Roy's attention away from her. I fired off a couple of shots that deliberately went wide of his shoulder. Eleanor hardly noticed as she took off into the lounge, her empty gun firmly in her grasp.

Still holding onto Maggie, it was decision time for Roy. Either he could keep heading to the car lot using Maggie as a shield, or he could try to improve his chances by killing me and helping his leader, who was writhing on the mound.

In the end, Maggie made the decision for him. While he used up valuable seconds wondering what to do, she wound up and kicked him in the ankle. He performed an impromptu jig, and Maggie broke away for the dugout. I waited for the *dancing* to end.

When his hopping ended, Roy and I were staring at each other, like a pair of cowboys at the end of an old Western flick. However, this was reality, and I didn't give him a chance to make his move. I fired off a quick shot that drove him back a few steps. A look of surprise and pain crossed his face before he looked down at the hole in his chest to find blood oozing onto his shirt. Then his body slumped over and pitched to the ground. Even though I was a dozen yards away, I could tell he was dead.

Turning, I saw that my mother had stopped inside the dugout, but I ran into the lounge to find Eleanor. As I rushed through the front lobby door, I saw a dark car speeding out of the parking lot and tearing up the dusty driveway. I heard two shots fired from the far right of the building, but the car continued to accelerate.

The shooter must have been Mara, because I saw Eleanor walking back toward me. She was carrying her empty gun in one hand and the Devil mask in the other. Strange thing, though—as I watched her approach, she had the most unusual look on her face. I'd never seen her like that before. As she silently passed me, a chill slid down my spine, and I suddenly felt cold—very cold.

Monday, October 31, 1960

Later that night

Eleanor having Devil's Man's mask in her hand when she returned from the parking lot meant she'd had a good look at the guy. Shortly after, when I asked her about him, she just said, "I'll tell you later." Easy conclusion—she'd recognized him.

Back at the stadium, there were seven killers—four of them dead, two out of commission inside the stadium, and one wounded on the pitcher's mound.

My team and I had better statistics. Of the five of us, including my mother, one was wounded, three were in pretty good shape, and one was not talking.

As Mara headed back to get her car and drive it down to the ball field, I asked Homburg Man for the keys to their other car. He said they were in the ignition. I dispatched Eleanor to the lot to bring it down, and asked my mother to return to the dressing rooms for a first aid kit.

I comforted Zuni Smith, who was still upset with himself, but was no worse for the wear. I left him for the moment and went over to the pitcher's mound.

Homburg Man turned out to be a realist. We spoke for about 10 minutes, and we pretty well agreed on everything. The surviving members of his crew were to drive back to New York as soon as possible. The four dead guys had to be dumped where they would not be found for a long, long time.

"The solution is relatively simple," I explained. "The town of River-ton is situated on the banks of the Blyth River. The river is quite deep and very fast-moving in the spring, as well as this time of the year. All you need are enough weights and some sturdy strapping. All of that you'll find inside the stadium."

The man's eyes seemed to light up—especially when I told him we'd give him a hand with the operation. I knew of several places along the river that would be perfect for what he needed.

"Deep, dark and fast-moving," I said, "Just make sure you get enough weights to keep the bodies down where they belong."

As I left Homburg Man, Eleanor was parking their other car beside the three bodies on the field—Jennings, Connors and Roy. When she got out of the car, I waved her over to the lounge door and reminded her of the dead guy who had been guarding Mara.

Almost at the same time, Maggie was coming out of the lounge, a medical kit in hand. I told her to patch up Zuni Smith, and hold off on helping the guy on the mound until I returned.

She said, "Why can't I fix him up?"

I shook my head, gave her a sweet smile, and told her Eleanor and I would be right back.

We hustled down the tunnel that led to the refreshment booth where Eleanor had been stationed, but it still took a while to get there—a long, silent while.

I refused to ask about Devil Man again, figuring she'd be still processing the situation. Halfway down the tunnel, she spoke. "I'm still processing it."

Smiling at our synchronicity, I told her it was okay, then continued to wonder who the guy might be. Business associate of her father's? Former gang member of one of her father's competitors? Friend of the family? Former lover?

Before we reached the end of the corridor, we found the hood. Eleanor had done a real job on him. He was lying on the floor, nose broken, covered in vomit from his shoes to his face. There was also some blood, and a large lump on the back of his head, where she'd obviously put the finishing touches on him. It was a miracle he was still alive.

I said, "You're lucky he's still breathing."

"So what?" she said. "It was either him or me."

She had a point there, so I dropped the subject and concentrated on waking up Sleeping Beauty. After a little while, and with a lot of persuasion, the guy came around, but he was hurting. Big-time.

Eventually, we got him standing, and gradually walked him down the hall toward the dressing rooms and lounge. I was a few feet behind, holding my Colt, while Eleanor trailed three or four yards behind me, armed with an empty gun. I got the impression the guy approved of that parade order.

When we arrived, Mara had returned with the Regent, which was now parked beside third base. She was helping Zuni Smith into the back seat, while Maggie, who presumably had finished with him, was now tending to Homburg Man's wounded leg. I squeezed out a little *what-the-hell* grin, and shook my head.

At that point, Eleanor and I escorted our captive over to the gangsters' second car. It was a black, four-door Lincoln Continental Mark V—large enough to accommodate six adults, with a bit of room to spare. I shoved the punk into the front seat, while Eleanor sat behind him with her gun trained on the back of his head. How was he to know it wasn't loaded?

With fake seriousness, I told her to shoot him through the back of the car seat if he tried anything hinky. Then, I hustled back inside and beetled down the other way around the stadium tunnels. When I got to the end, to where I'd put one of the hoods out of commission, I drew my Colt—I was taking no chances—and kicked open the door of the refreshment booth.

After I cut the thug's feet loose, we started on the long trail back to the Lincoln. He still seemed to be in a daze.

I said, "Step on it, palooka, or I'll put a cap in your ass."

"All right, already!" he mumbled, and picked up the pace. However, I noticed he had a distinct limp, and I was beginning to think he might be suffering from a head injury after smashing into the booth's boarded-up window.

By the time we emerged from the building, Mr. Smith had traded places with Eleanor and was guarding the mug from the back seat of the Lincoln. Smith had another hand that could squeeze a trigger.

Around the back of the black monster, the trunk lid was open, and Mara, Eleanor, and my mother were stuffing bodies inside. The last stiff was a little uncooperative, but in the end, they were able to wrap everything up.

My limping guy was hustled into the front seat of the Lincoln to join his partner in crime. Zuni Smith guarded them from the back seat of the car, while the rest of us shut everything down.

Within 20 minutes, the Regent's trunk was loaded with weights, ropes, and heavy-duty strapping. The stadium lights were all shut off, and the building was locked up again, with the exception of one escape door.

The Lincoln Continental was poised to be in the lead. Eleanor's guy from the fight in the tunnel was driving. Homburg Man had switched places with my guy from the refreshment booth, and was sitting in the front. I was in the back, giving directions.

Next to me, my gunsel from the refreshment booth was sleeping. He'd been sleeping since we'd arrived back at the cars. Strangely enough, I was starting to worry about him.

In Mara's Regent sat the rest of the good guys. Mara was driving, and was going to follow the Lincoln. Zuni Smith, who seemed to be in better spirits, was sitting in the front with her. In the back seat were Eleanor and my mother. Maggie was having a little nap, while Eleanor probably was thinking about the identity of Devil Man.

Finally, around 10:40 p.m., two sets of headlights cut through the darkness, and two cars plowed up the driveway of a deserted Oxford Place.

As John Wayne would shout in those old western cavalry movies, *Forward, ho!*

The Blyth is a river that runs through much of Southern Ontario. Sometimes it's picturesque and meandering, sometimes dark and tempestuous—especially in the spring and late autumn.

When I was a kid, a buddy and I used to ride our CCM bikes from town to a secret spot on the Blyth where there were no houses or farms for miles around. There, we'd light firecrackers and stick them under an old soup can. The resulting *kaboom* and rocket launch of the can were pretty exciting for a couple of 10-year-olds.

So were the fast-moving waters of the Blyth around the Halloween season; then, it was considered deep and dangerous. Our parents insisted we never go near the river when it was in full flight.

But, what the heck! We were 10-year-olds, up to no good with firecrackers, tin cans, and all. Nobody would find out.

Now, a couple of decades later, I was no longer 10 years old, but I was definitely up to no good.

Tonight, the river was deep and swift-flowing, and there were still no houses or farms around for miles from the spot I'd picked to dump the bodies. I knew this because last year, when I was home visiting Maggie, we'd taken a drive down the old river road. All the farmland was owned by generations of Mennonites, and their properties were large and spaced well apart.

By 11:15 p.m., we were parked off one of the old side roads, and hauling bodies and weights down to the river's edge.

While Zuni Smith kept an eye on Homburg Man and the two hoods in their car, Maggie, Eleanor, Mara, and I were busy with the body disposal. Frankly, I think Maggie was having the time of her life; most of her work was simply supervising.

Shortly after midnight, the dirty deed was done. Zuni Smith got out of the Continental and joined the women. Everyone was milling around the cars while I spoke with Homburg Man.

"Where were you planning on crossing the border?" I asked.

"We thought Niagara Falls. Why? Would Fort Erie be better?"

"I would *not* advise the three of you to cross in the same car," I said. "It's late, and by the time you get to either border, you may appear suspicious to the border patrol."

"So, I just tell them we were visiting friends in St. Catharines. Playing poker with the boys."

"Doesn't work for me," I said. "This isn't Prohibition."

"What works for you?" he said.

"Break up. One of your guys drives across the border, but I'd suggest that you and the other one go by train. That way you don't have to drive with your bum leg. Drive to Union Station in Toronto first. You and your guy book separately, each getting a ticket back home to Grand Central or Penn Station. Your other man drives on, crossing the border."

Homburg Man was silent, mulling over the pros and cons of my suggestions. Then, very slowly, he opened his suit jacket with his left hand, looked at me as if asking for permission, and took out a small leather wallet with his right. A few seconds later, I was holding a card engraved with the name *Granger*.

"Is this your business card?" I asked. "Where does it say *Killers Incorporated?*"

He squeezed out a lopsided smile and pocketed the little wallet. "You've been a worthy adversary," he said, "and I want you to know that's my personal phone number on the card. If there is anything I can do for you—anything—just give me a call. It will be done without question."

"Actually, there is, Mr. Granger," I said. "Tell me the name of the man who wore the Devil mask."

"I can't tell you, Cass," he said. "It would mean my death."

"Why?"

"Because he's connected. He's mobbed up to the eyeballs. And I was told that your death was supposed to look like a Mob hit—not a job by freelance shooters."

"What the hell is that supposed to mean?" I asked.

He didn't answer.

Ten minutes later, we were on our way. Mara drove, with Zuni Smith in his usual front seat, and Maggie, Eleanor and I in the back. My partner was still pretty quiet, and likely thinking about the guy whose mask was on her knee.

I was thinking about Mr. Granger's response to my question---he was zipped up tighter than King Tut's tomb before Professor Carter arrived in Egypt.

We considered going back to Maggie's house tonight, but in the end we decided it might be better if we went to a motel instead. Just outside of Riverton, we found an all-nighter, and rented three rooms—one for my mother, one for Eleanor and Mara, and a third for Mr. Smith and me. I paid the bill, and slipped the night clerk a ten-spot to make us some sandwiches and four cups of coffee. Maggie was off caffeine, but the rest of us would have killed for some.

Fifteen minutes later, the food and coffee arrived, and all of us dug into the sandwiches. Twenty minutes after that, we were all tucked in, and I turned off the lights in our room. Five minutes later, there was a knock on my door.

I ambled to the door in my underwear, and immediately was invited outside by a good-looking blonde.

To be honest, though, she was a tired, good-looking blonde, and she had smudges of worry under her eyes. The first thing she said was, "Let's go for a little walk."

"Like this?" I whispered. "It's November!"

She smiled, and said she'd wait while I threw some clothes on.

A few minutes later, we were skulking around the back of the motel like a couple of teenagers on a secret rendezvous. We walked around the building in a counter clockwise direction. She said nothing. Then we walked around the building in a clockwise direction. More silence.

Finally, I stopped, turned to face her, and said, "Are we finished here? Or do you want another spin around the block?"

"Typical male," she said. "You don't understand."

"Of course, I *don't understand*," I said. "I haven't understood anything since you came down from the parking lot with that bloody mask in your hand."

She nodded, then caught me completely by surprise. "Do you love me?" she asked.

"Of course, I do!" I said without hesitation. It was the first time the subject of *love* had ever come up since we started working together.

"I love you, too, Cass. But are you sure? Really sure?"

"I love you very much, Eleanor. Almost from the first time I saw you—the time when my mother, Hemingway and I were visiting your father on your estate."

"Then you'll definitely understand why I've been acting a little strange."

"Damn right. It's pretty obvious, isn't it? You recognized the guy."

She managed a small, sardonic smile. "You can *definitely* say that again."

"So, who is he, darling?" I managed. My heart was pounding like a bass drum on the Fourth of July. "An associate of your father's? An old boyfriend? A relative?"

"Oh, sonny boy, you can say that last one again."

My heart kept up the beat. My face felt more than a little flushed.

Eleanor took a deep breath. "It's Joey," she said. "My brother, Joey Palladino."

While Zuni Smith happily snored away, I lay awake for hours, staring at the ceiling, then tossing and turning, then staring at the ceiling some more. I'd been prepared for almost anything, but not for Eleanor's brother, Joey.

He was supposed to be with relatives in Sicily. He was supposed to be *readjusted* after making some wrong *business* decisions. When your father is head of an organized crime's *famiglia*, you don't make wrong *business* decisions. Frankly, if he wasn't his father's son, he'd be dead by now.

The bad blood between Joey and me started 15 months ago, back in the summer of '59, when he showed up at one of my poker nights. The brother of that evening's host owed Joey a big favor, and had invited him along. I'm not exaggerating when I say Joey was a complete jackass from the very first moment he arrived. Within two minutes, his rudeness was on display, and he made it a special point to make fun of some of the guys, including me. By the time he left in a huff, because he was losing, everyone breathed a sight of relief.

Unfortunately, I took the extra step by following him out the building and proceeded to give him a lesson in party etiquette. That was the beginning.

Days later, when he tried to have me whacked, I gave him lesson number two, and that was followed by lesson number three, administered by his father because of some bad *business* decisions he'd made.

That was when the little *escremento* was exiled to Sicily for a lot of postgraduate education. It appeared that Joey hadn't stuck around for commencement ceremonies.

For more details about my connection with Joey, and how I met and fell in love with Eleanor, I refer you to two of my case files: The Death Merchants, *and* The Man With Hemingway's Face.

Tuesday, November 1, 1960

The morning after we'd dumped the dead hoods in the Blyth River, we slept in late. By the time we checked out of the motel, grabbed a late breakfast, and hit the road, it was pushing two o'clock.

After dropping my mother off at her home, we retraced our travels —driving down Highway 8, negotiating Clappison's Cut, continuing on through Dundas, then merging into Hamilton's west end. Mara lived in the Westdale district, and she suggested we drop off our borrowed weapons at her home on Dromore Crescent.

While Mara collected the hardware, Eleanor asked to use the phone to get in touch with her father. He needed to be apprised of Joey's sudden return, and what had transpired at Oxford Place. It would be a long conversation.

While Eleanor was on the phone, Zuni Smith hung around the house and entertained himself in the Lombardi's library. At the same time, Mara gave me a guided tour of the neighborhood, filled with elegant homes, manicured lawns, and clean walkways that led to a pleasant little park at the north end of Dromore. I enjoyed the walk, and even though it was a bit chilly outside, the tour left me feeling refreshed.

On our way back, I expressed my thanks to Mara for all her support. I told her that she was a true professional, and that I'd be honored to work with her anytime in the future. She reciprocated the sentiment, and we gave each other a collegial hug.

When we returned to the house, there was news. Eleanor's father was furious. *Don* Palladino was so upset with Joey, he vowed to have him tracked down by Rocco Narducci.

Now, this was a big deal. Rocco is no ordinary foot soldier— he's Frank Palladino's *capo,* his right-hand man, and Rocco had been ordered to bring Joey back home where he'd be given *a final lesson in obedience.*

Knowing both Rocco and Frank like I do, I asked Eleanor what the hell *that* was supposed to mean. She only shrugged her shoulders.

Both of us knew it wouldn't take Rocco long to complete his assignment; the man is very good at his work.

On this occasion, he was extremely good.

Saturday, November 5, 1960

Four afternoons later, I was sitting in *Don* Frank Palladino's den, in one of the most elegant homes in New Jersey's Teaneck Township. I always marveled at its grandeur, as well as at the security surrounding the five-acre property.

The first time I drove up to the main gates, I was confronted by men with Winchester autoload shotguns. At that moment, I didn't know if I was being invited to a party or an execution. However, when they saw that Rocco was sitting in the Jag with me, everything became *copacetic*. They greeted him as *Mr. Narducci*, and speedily opened the gates. A lot of water had flowed under the bridge since then.

On this occasion, I had no problem with the guardians of the gates. On behalf of her father, Eleanor had invited me to join her, and after a brief examination of my wheels and its trunk, they passed me on through. So did the guards at the front entrance of the Neo-Tudor mansion. One of them took me into the foyer, which seemed as big as a tennis court, and then ushered me into Frank Palladino's private office.

Having been there before, I made myself at home and sat down on one of the bloodred leather chairs that, with its mate and a three-seater couch, made up a conversation area. I was facing one of the mahogany paneled walls, with an old Howard Miller clock that told me it was 4:10 p.m.

But the wall mainly displayed the stuffed heads of animals—among them a kudu, a leopard, and a water buffalo—that once roamed the fields and woods of various continents. I was never a fan of big-game hunting—unless the game was roaming around on two feet, and I was being well paid for the job.

The room itself was not only Frank's office—with a desk and all the accompanying paraphernalia—but also his getaway den, library and study. The library portion took up an entire wall, and, from previous visits, I'd learned, surprisingly, that the lord of the manor was a very eclectic reader. No fool, he.

I was about to get up and wander over there to pass the time, when a secret panel suddenly opened under one of the animal heads, and *the man* himself appeared with his lovely daughter. He immediately walked toward me, his hand extended.

"Cass, my boy, good to see you!" He smiled, his white, even teeth gleaming in that patented grin familiar to tabloid readers. At the same time, he was applying an iron grip to my hand.

I reciprocated with a little bit of muscle of my own, and we traded pleasantries. Eleanor and I exchanged polite hugs, and the three of us sat—Frank taking over the middle of the couch, Eleanor and I moving to each of the matching chairs.

"So, I hear that the two of you had some excitement last week." Frank was not a man who shilly-shallied. Just like in his business dealings, he got straight to the heart of the matter.

"Yes, Frank," I said with a straight face, "but it all turned out well in the end. No small thanks to Eleanor."

He ignored the compliment, and asked, "How is your mother? Did Maggie suffer any ill effects?"

"Actually, she seemed pretty good when we left her at home. I think she rather enjoyed herself once the cavalry arrived."

"She's a pretty fine woman," the *Don* said. "I admire her a lot."

Eleanor and I exchanged furtive glances. Both of us believed that there had been some history between the two of them, *back when*. We didn't know any of the details, but I had noted it in my *Hemingway's Face* case file.

Palladino just nodded with a nostalgic smile, and muttered something under his breath. Then, he shook his head, and his voice turned serious.

"You're here, today, Cass, because I've made a decision what to do with my son, Joey—the little *stronzo*."

All of a sudden, he got up, walked over to the desk, and picked up one of the two phones that sat there. After a few seconds, he ordered the person on the other end, "Bring him in!"

We waited in silence, Eleanor and I sitting our chairs, and Frank perched on the edge of his mammoth desk.

Even at home, Frank—who I estimated to be in his mid-60s—was the epitome of his tabloid nickname—The Suave Don. Today, he was wearing pearl gray slacks, a spotless white button-down shirt, open at the collar, and a pair of matching leather slip-ons of the finest Italian craftsmanship. The entire ensemble complemented his full head of hair —snow-white in color, parted down the middle, and with both sides combed back in elegant waves. I'd guess that the entire ensemble would have cost him close to six or seven C-notes.

While awaiting the arrival of Joey and his escort, Frank looked at us with a saucy gleam in his eye. "So, my dears," he started, with a dramatic pause. "When are you two going to get married?"

Eleanor looked over at me. I looked over at her. Both of us started to answer at the same time. Both of us stopped, gesturing for the other to go first. Apparently, each of us was trying to think of a suitable answer---but only one of us had a gleam in the eye.

Frank started to laugh, but before either of us could respond, the secret door opened, and Joey Palladino entered with a sour frown on his face. Right behind him was the towering form of Rocco Narducci. Frank stopped laughing.

There was a long moment of silence among the three gangsters.

Finally, Joey spoke up with attempted bravado. "Can I sit?" he said in a sulky voice.

"Say again!" retorted his father.

"*May* I sit?" he amended.

"NO, DAMN IT!" Frank bellowed, as he slipped off the desk and took several menacing steps toward his son. "You are not here for a social visit, *bastardo!*"

Joey's face turned ashen. He stepped back so quickly that he bumped into Rocco.

Frank Palladino continued, "You are here for only two reasons. One is to apologize to Mr. Gentry, and the other is to receive your punishment."

Joey's voice was shaky, but there was no mistaking his message. "There's no friggin' way I'm going to apologize to *him!*"

"You sure as hell better, mister, or your punishment will be even worse than I've planned."

"Why, Dad? Why would you stick up for him and not for me?"

"*Because he's my friend,*" roared his *padrone*. "And you tried to have him killed."

The young man hung his head. "What about me?" he muttered. "Aren't I your friend?"

"No," Frank said. "You're my son, and I love you, Joey. There was even a time when I hoped you'd become my underboss."

Joey looked up at his father, struggling to keep from crying.

"But not now," Frank continued, his voice firm once more. "You've made too many mistakes. That's why I sent you back to Sicily, hoping a little time, a little appreciation for the old ways, would smarten you up."

"But, Dad—" A solid nudge from Rocco put an end to Joey's interruption.

Frank went on, "Instead, you sneak back home, get a gang together, and terrorize Gentry's business friends."

The *Don* took a breath, and it was clear he was becoming more agitated. Frown lines pinched together between his eyes, and his face was flushed. "Then you had the audacity to kidnap his mother. *His mother! For bait!*"

Joey started to say something, but Frank was in full flight. "*Fongool! Chiudi la bocca, bastardo!*"

Don Palladino took a deep breath, and gradually composed himself. Then, in a calm voice, he said, "Don't you realize if you were *not* my son, I would've had you *killed* by now? I would've had Rocco take you out back and into the woods."

Joey hung his head, and a teardrop fell. "*Mi dispiace, Padre,*" he said in a low voice. "I really am sorry, Dad."

Frank waited several seconds, then prompted, "And?"

"And…I apologize…Mr. Gentry."

"Do you swear by the Sicilian Oath?"

Joey paused a moment before speaking. "I swear. By the Sicilian Oath."

Frank let a few more seconds slide by, then suddenly extended open arms to his son. Joey almost leapt into his father's arms, and they stood there, motionless, clasping each other in a tight embrace.

Finally, the hug dissolved. Frank patted Joey's cheek, and told his son he could leave, grab a little fresh air in the backyard. Joey hesitated before the wide glass patio doors behind the desk, and Frank gave him the go-ahead, followed by another fatherly pat on the check. Joey slipped out, under the watchful eye of an armed guard patrolling the backyard.

Then, Rocco went up to Frank and whispered in his ear.

As Rocco stepped back, Frank said, "I know he lied. Like a kid, he had his fingers crossed."

"What do you want me to do, Frank?"

"Take him out back. To the trees. Give him a *Numero Tre.*"

Without a word, the towering *capo* made his exit.

Slowly, almost reluctantly, Frank Palladino walked over to his desk, and then beyond. He stood silently looking out the expanse of glass, his back to the room.

Neither Eleanor nor I moved, but we exchanged looks. I mouthed the words *number three.* She nodded, and held up three fingers of her right hand.

The old Howard Miller clock ticked on until the near silence in the room was finally broken.

Outside, beyond the tree line, there was a gunshot.

Thursday, November 10, 1960

The week had flown by faster than a Boeing 707. Both Eleanor and I were cleaning up personal matters, and I was working on a new case that involved a scam artist in the television industry.

Eleanor had filled me in on Joey's fate, and I wasn't too broken up. It appeared that Frank's *Numero Tre* was his personal code for a debilitating wound that was not fatal. However, it would prevent Joey from ever using his gun hand again. And it was the punk's last warning. Frank had had enough; next time, the shot would be in the heart.

Tonight, Eleanor and I had arranged to meet for dinner at *Casa Romano*, our special place. The little Italian restaurant on Queen Anne Road, out in West Englewood, was where we'd had our first date.

Signore Marcello, the owner, was serving. He was entertaining us with tales about his son. The young man's name was Alessandro, and the father was very proud of him. When it came time for ordering, Eleanor took over, speaking in perfect Italian, even though our host was pretty fluent in English.

Eleanor ordered *cappelletti con carne* and *veal scallopini*. She told him to hold the onions on the veal because we were on a hot date. *Signore* Marcello bowed, and left with a smile on his face. Eleanor and I grinned, because it was what we'd ordered on our first date. It was always the same dish.

While Eleanor left for the ladies' room, our host returned with some warm *calabrese bread*, winked at me, and left. On the speaker system, Dean Martin was softly crooning "Memories Are Made of This."

I quickly took a little something out of my jacket pocket. I'd been saving it for a number of months, but tonight, I placed it on Eleanor's end of the table.

It was a small square box. The color was Tiffany Blue.

Just the perfect size for an engagement ring.

To be continued...

ABOUT THE AUTHOR

Thom has published five plays, including his most performed work "Dark Rituals" and the thrillers "Club Dead" and "Ravens Cliff". Others include a stage version of the Anthony Hope classic "The Prisoner of Zenda" (co-authored with Elizabeth Ferns), and his popular family fantasy "Return to Wonderland". Book publications include "The Death Merchants", "The Man With Hemingway's Face", "Promises and Other Tales of White Lies", the illustrated Halloween collection "13 Tales from the Dark", and "The Christmas House, 12 Tales of Holiday Magic".

A former teacher, Thom has a PhD in Educational Systems Development and is a recipient of the Canada 125 Award.